"Wheezer and the Painted Frog is at once joyous and heartbreaking. You will ache for the suffering, be outraged by the wrongs fascinated by the way of life, identify with Sasa and above all you will love Wheezer. You will look for his spirit in every dog you meet! Good luck and all best wishes   Anne" **Anne Perry, author of Acceptable Loss**

...this book brought me back to the love of my childhood and youth, and I must say that reading Wheezer's story, the Cherokee people story, Sasa's story, captivated me as much as the best novels by Zane Grey and Louis L'Amour managed to do so many years ago.

I definitely recommend reading this book. You'll feel the richer for it. **--Annarita Guarnieri, author of How to Be Owned By A Cat**

From the time Europeans landed in North America, the People were forced out of the land they had known for generations. By the nineteenth century, the United States had pushed them into the remote and undeveloped area known as Indian Territory and promised them food and protection that never came. Plagued by the loss of their ability to farm and hunt, the lack of food and shelter, the disease brought by the White Man, every tribe suffered losses so great only the memories of the survivors could document the dead. This story, taking place among the Cherokee after the Trail of Tears, is a story for all the People.

—

Wheezer and the Painted Frog (Special Edition)

Written by
Kitty Sutton

Published by
Inknbeans Press

To Jim Sutton,
For your unfailing love and support.
And to Charlene Young
For the inspiration and time
you give to me.
And last, but not least
to Wheezer
for letting me in to your world.
WADO

Table of Contents

Chapter 1

The dog had been running from sheer panic, without any clue about where he was, nor did he take the time to stop and look around himself. He had been so frightened by the "big boom", a sound he had never heard before, that he had run blindly into the forest. As he ran deeper into this unknown place, everything became foreign to him, even the smell of the land. As he frantically ran, he took no notice of the splotches of blood that sprang from his paws as each hit the moldy ground, strewn with sharp rocks; his mostly white fur, coupled with small brown patches, began collecting thick knots of burrs and small crawling things on his otherwise clean coat. His heart thumped as it pumped, combining with his desperate panting, filling his ears, blocking out all other sounds.

The all-consuming rush of fear forced his muscles onward, working flat-out. His lungs burned painfully now and his breath began growing shorter, shallower. His blood red tongue lolled sideways, hanging to cool in the wind, while white, foamy flecks of spittle kept flying in all directions from its surface, draining him of much needed moisture. His ears, eyes and nose tried scanning ahead, sideways, behind... but mostly behind. Was the terrible thing following him? He wouldn't be able to run much longer! His gait was already getting erratic, but the wild surge that had sent him flying in bounds over boulders and branches, crashing and smashing through bushes as though there were none there, was still prodding him. In a storm of twigs cracking and snapping, vines tearing, branches whipping at his passage, he pushed farther into the unknown forest. His stride was no longer a gallop...running now, body elongated, low, close to the ground next to the leafy mat, as foxes would run when he hunted them...trotting now, staggering ever so slightly...he knew he must turn and fight or drop and hide. The blood pumping in his ears was not so loud any more, pain throbbed in the torn flesh of his paws and his burning muscles and lungs demanded that he cease his mad dash.

As quickly as it had begun, his mad run now stopped. He stood trembling in the twilight of this unfamiliar forest, looking in every direction for any movement that might indicate danger to him.

He looked slowly behind, halting, puzzled. He cautiously trod toward the setting sun which he could barely see through the thick trees. His heart still raced for the panic in him was still close to the surface, and his skin flicked and rippled in waves from head to tail as he proceeded, trying to get his bearings.

He topped a ridge and stopped cold in his tracks, panting in his thirst. He stared at the panoramic scene before him: an endless forest lay as far as his keen dog eyes could see, undulating with high ridges and deep hollows almost black and bottomless. He turned in a circle, not knowing what direction to step. Finally, his thirst won out and satisfying it became his only goal.

In the fading light, he noticed well-worn trails extending across the ridge he perched on and down the slope. Guided by instinct alone he moved forward and down, heading down the trail while taking care to listen to the forest noises. A soft breeze buffeted the leaves around him, warm and perfumed with all the forest scents. Sensing he was losing his light, he quickened his pace. As he followed the path, other trails joined it as if all were pointing the way. When darkness was almost complete, he came to a small mountain spring with cold sparkling water trickling over the rocks.

No other animals were at the spring yet, so he slaked his monumental thirst. He gazed at the moonlight reflecting off the small stream; he calmed and breathed deeply. Feeling vulnerable, he moved off into the forest a little way, circled several times upon some fern plants, then lay down. He could keep his eyes open no longer then and sleep overtook him.

Sasa, a girl of the Cherokee, sat next to a dry, creek bed. She could feel the thick dust with drying traces of long shed tears coating her rounded cheeks under large black-brown eyes. She had no family now.

Her parents and extended family of aunts, uncles, cousins and all the rest had made the "Long Walk" from their traditional Cherokee lands, now many moons away, to the east. As they walked a few more miles, each day, she had watched her family grow weak and sick, and now she thought it had almost been a blessing for some families when their elders and children were slaughtered by white settlers before the soldiers forced them to the west. Then, she had thought that her immediate family had escaped succumbing to sickness, starvation and death on the trail. But after the soldiers ended their long travail, they left them alone with many new problems: all the People needed homes, food and medicine.

Her red calico skirt and blouse were exceedingly worn and stained from endless days of walking. No amount of washing would ever remove the dirt from sleeping on the ground every night, nor the blood from her cuts and scrapes. She still wore the moccasins her mother had made her and that she had resoled several times with old hides that had been given to her. They were almost un-wearable, now, and even though she had repaired them, most of the beads her mother had sewn on them were gone now. Her raven hair was cropped short just under her ears. With each death in her family, she cut a little more off. Her mother would have hated the cutting of her hair.

"My little Swan, my little Sasa," she always said, "how beautiful you are with your long black hair. Be sure to comb it every day with the carved shell comb your father made you. "But there was no one left to worry if she combed it or not.

In some ways, this northeast corner of Indian Territory seemed similar to the forested slopes of her traditional home in the East, but it was much drier and the land was flatter to the west of her new camp. There were green forests to the east, but the west offered only endless vistas of rock and prairie. In a very few places there were well watered streams and land that could be farmed, but it was not nearly as rich as the land they had left. Her homeland of verdant green had been very different from Indian Territory. It was possible her people could make it here, with hard work and determination. Unfortunately, they had been made to march with only the clothes on their backs, and lacked weapons to make meat with until the government sent supplies for them. The soldiers departed, and the People were left to live or die as they might. But the winter had taken its toll and her mother was the first one to die in the new land. Even after they found ways to gather the wild unfamiliar roots, fish the streams, or snare small game the People continued to die.

The survivors began to call the forced march that brought them to this new land, *Nunahi duna Dlo Hilu-i,* "The Trail Where They Cried", but it was worse than the name implied. Daily walking through the camp of survivors, Sasa heard stories about that Long Walk... tales of death, each as bad as the next, that chilled her to the core. She had been a witness to many of those stories; others were new and frightening. Some said the dead were lucky because the living were still suffering, while the dead were not. She had heard of beatings, rapes, and robbery by white settlers on the trail. She had experienced walking in snow and ice with no shoes and no blankets, and seen the effects of cholera, small pox and many other deadly diseases they knew no name for. It was printed in the white man's newspapers that the blankets, given to some of the Cherokees waiting at different forts before The Long Walk, were brought from the small-pox hospitals without disinfecting them.

The tribe had been rounded up, allowing them nothing from their homes, and packed into stockades with no shelter, where fires were not allowed, and sanitary arrangements were nonexistent. They waited for months through the rest of the summer, then in winter were cruelly marched one thousand one hundred miles from Georgia through Tennessee, Kentucky, Missouri and down through Arkansas into Indian Territory. Sasa had also heard unbearably sad accounts, such as the one about a boat carrying over eight hundred Cherokee that had overturned in the Mississippi River and caused at least four hundred people to drown.

Sasa did not question the stories because she had experienced firsthand the cruelties of the trip. She and her family had traveled with Chief Ross and his family as they marched with the rest of the tribe. Usti Yansa had walked bravely with the refugees as well, but his blanket had been taken from him by a roadside gang of hecklers. Mrs. Ross, whom they called Quatie, saw him and noticed his lips were blue as he shivered violently.

"Look John, Little Buffalo will not make it much longer if he does not get warm," Quatie said as she shivered. "How many more babies and young have to die on this cursed march?"

Quatie already had a cold, but she took one look at Usti Yansa and gave him her only blanket. Her cold turned into pneumonia, and she died a few days from Indian Territory. It was ironic to Sasa, that Quatie gave her life to help Sasa's little brother live, just to have him die later on for no reason at all.

Her family had the same problems as the others did, for they had no tools with which to bury the dead. Her tribe believed that the dead should be buried the day after death to complete the cycle of life set out by the Creator, but it was winter; the ground was too frozen to dig. Everywhere the sight of stiff bodies that would rot when the weather warmed up was enveloped in the sound of a numb silence, for without their old and young ones who had died on the trail, the living felt dead already.

That time seemed only yesterday, but it was plain that many moons had passed. They had arrived in winter and now it was very early summer. When all the survivors had arrived, it was evident that there were no longer many old ones to ask for advice about how to live in this new land. There were few elders and extremely few young. Just yesterday, Sasa's little brother had died. Sasa had cried for hours because her little brother was only five and did not have a death song yet. Sasa herself was only thirteen. For a Cherokee, she was considered on the edge of womanhood and expected to take care of herself.

Mr. Edwards, the new Indian Agent, showed up on Cherokee lands a few weeks after all of the Cherokee arrived. His corpulent body would sway as he walked through the camps of the last to arrive. He occupied a log building that, she learned, was his lodge as well as the agency office. Sasa had seen little of his family; if there was a family, they chose not speak to the People, but stayed in their lodge. He brought food, but too late for some. Even after the food arrived, many sickened and died. That was when her father, so sad over all that had happened, refused to eat what Mr. Edwards offered. Within ten suns, her father closed his eyes and did not open them again.

6

For the last few moons, it had been up to Sasa to take care of her little brother Usti Yansa, or Little Buffalo in "the English", as her mother used to say. She worked hard to find food for him, but he never seemed to gain any weight. He had been a robust, healthy boy even after their first arrival, but something had changed. He began to weaken and complain of headaches, then he had the running of the bowels and his stomach hurt him while his fingernails started to turn odd colors as if he had pounded his fingers with a rock. Finally, he took to his bed, having vomited many times. Sometimes he would thrash about like a devil had him and afterwards he would sleep for long periods.

"Wado, Sasa," were his last words to her, which meant, "Thank You, Swan," as the English used to say. Usti Yansa gradually stopped talking and then one morning he just did not wake up. There was no other family member to mourn for him, so she had to do it. She had no idea how many of her clan relatives survived, and they were scattered over several miles of land. She did all she remembered, but with no other members of her family to assist her, she was unsure if it was enough.

She carried the boy out beyond the camp, his body not weighing much, and she walked for a long time. She wondered where she might bury her brother, and hoped she would recognize the right place when she saw it. Then, as she walked around a coulée, she saw in the far off distance a patch of Mimosa saplings, dripping with their pink, feathery flowers. Under the saplings stood a large rock shaped like a young buffalo calf. Her eyes had filled with moisture as she looked down at her brother, knowing she had found his place. She carried him there and laid him down under the Mimosa beside the buffalo rock while she searched around for a stout stick or thin rock to dig with. She was astonished to find the white bones of a long dead buffalo lying a short way from the buffalo rock.

7

She knelt and said a prayer to the Creator, thanking him for his help, then took the pelvic bone to use like a shovel. This spot was a green place, and the earth turned easily. Usti Yansa was unusually small, so she did not have to dig terribly deep. She laid him curled in a ball, placed fragrant sage in with him and slowly covered him while she sang the one and only death song she knew, her own.

His wet, black nose glistened in the sunlight, but he was so tired the sunrise did not wake him. The noises of the forest, the birds or the drinkers at the spring did not wake him either. What woke him was the sound of a far off call of a human, calling his name, "Jack", frantic with worry. He jumped up at the sound, but it faded with the sleep that drifted from his mind. Still tired, he circled again and lay down.

He heaved a huge sigh, laid his head on his crossed paws, his deep, dark brown eyes shifting about, watching for danger. He tried to remember how he got lost. He had been extremely happy in his home. It was in a place with many humans, and he remembered that he lived in a large white house with real tall white sticks, taller than a human. Jackson, his human, used to have to put a white sloppy liquid on them. There were humans of light and dark skin there, but his human was the leader, head of the pack. Everyone, including him, had to obey what Jackson said. But that was not hard because his human always rewarded him. And he made whatever they did together fun.

There was lots of room to run and sometimes Jackson would take him on a hunt. The master always laughed when he told him that he named him after himself. Jackson called him Jack. Jack Russell, he sometimes would say. Jack's job was to follow the pack of bigger dogs until their prey, usually a fox, would run down into a hole. Then it was Jack's turn to do what he was born to do. He would follow the fox, dig and crawl until he was nose-to-nose with it. Then he would kill it and wait until Jackson reached down, grabbing hold of Jack's short tail to pull him out, fox and all.

But what had happened to make him run away? It was hard to think of events in the past. What was it? Then his mind recreated the "big boom". Yes, that was it. He shivered at the thought. First there had been fire and humans running wildly over the lawn, carrying buckets of water. Jack thought it was a game and ran with Jackson, trying to grab the pail of water from his hands.

"No, Jack, get away! You men get to that storage barn. Hurry, the gun powder is stored in there. If the fire gets to it, we'll be blown to kingdom come. Now get on with ya all. Jack, get back," Jackson said while running along to the side of the house.

As Jack watched, he saw the fire race a fast line across the lawn, as if it were running of its own will. Jack chased it along. He could feel the heat on his nose, and began to bark at it. He could see where it was running. Jackson had said it was bad and that it shouldn't get near the storage barn. But there it was, greedily licking at the boards around the bottom of the barn.

Jack started turning in circles, looking this way and that, barking as loud as he could manage.

"It's here, it's here. Come get the bad thing. Jackson, come get it," Jack tried to say.

But, Jackson was paying no mind to him at the moment. Jack ran up to Jackson, bit his pant leg and pulled as he barked his warning. Jackson just kicked at him. Jack tried again and then again. Finally, Jackson turned to yell at Jack, but Jack ran toward the storage barn, barking and yelping as if someone were pulling his leg off.

"Jack, this is no time to...Oh My God! Boys, get the water over here. The storage barn is about to blow. Jack, Jack, get away from there, boy...." Jackson's last words screamed in his ears.

At that moment, Jack had heard an odd hissing noise, and a huge explosion of noise had cut his barking off, then hot timbers erupted from the barn. It had all been so loud and frightening that Jack had run into the woods and had kept on running. The sound seemed to continue in his head as he ran, dodging trees and jumping over rocks, deeper and deeper into the wild.

Sasa sat under the Mimosa saplings, watching the brilliant fuchsia and pink feathery flowers flutter to the ground. She had been coming there every day for a week now, trying to understand the upheaval in her life. Something was tugging in the back of her mind, and it had to do with Usti Yansa. She might think his name, but now could not say it because it is forbidden to speak the name of the dead. Now, with the first day of mourning time over, the nagging feeling that her brother had been trying to tell her something in those last few weeks kept intruding into her thoughts. He had told her that he had some big medicine that was going to help them and she should not worry. He was not a child that talked a lot anyway, but the way he grew silent each day, the way he ate but did not gain any weight, was still bothering her. She could not explain why. One of the last things that Usti Yansa had told her made no sense to her.

"I don't know why it is not working," he had said. "Maybe I am not doing it right or enough times." But he refused to explain what he meant.

It seemed to be after their father died that things started going wrong. Mr. Edwards had brought food for all, but there were problems with it just the same. First of all, it was not the food they had been used to eating in their homeland. She remembered the day she had gone to get her first allotment. She had just finished building a traditional wigwam, a dome frame of saplings, tied together with wild grape vines. In the olden times, they would have built communal living spaces made of logs notched to fit together, divided inside so that several families could live in one. If they had to be out in a hunting camp, they would make a wigwam and cover the frame over with tanned deer, elk or buffalo hides, leaving a hole at the top for smoke to escape. Sasa had no hides, and no cloth, so she used dried brush, tied together in bunches and tied to the frame. Because she used dry grass to cover the frame, she could not have a fire inside. Just one spark could burn the whole wigwam down. She built her fires outside the front flap, several feet away. However, for many years, the Cherokee had been living in log cabins, just like the white settlers, with furniture and dishes, pot and pans. This old, old way was much harder to do.

She left her little brother and her father inside on a bed of dry grass and leaves. She still had the blankets and some clothes that her parents had worn on the 'Long Walk' and now used them to make beds for all of them. At this time, her father was still alive, but he lay on the grass bed with sad eyes and did not talk. It was left to Sasa to go and get what was promised to them. The food given to her that day included oatmeal. She did not know how to cook it with no pots to cook it in. Her father would not get up from his bed and would not tell her what to do, so Sasa and Usti Yansa grabbed handfuls of oats and ate them dry.

"I am still hungry, Sasa. Is this all we are supposed to eat?" her little brother asked.

"No, we are supposed to have many things, but it might take time to get them. Mr. Edwards is supposed to give me meat in an airtight," Sasa answered.

"Sister, what is an airtight?" he asked.

"I am not sure. Mr. Edwards says that is where we will get our meat, fruit and vegetables. I have not seen them, but the headmen say they look like metal cups with lids that don't come off," Sasa explained.

"If the lids do not come off, how are we to get to the food, Sasa? I am hungry," Usti Yansa asked, concern in his eyes.

"I will have to ask," Sasa told him.

And ask she did, but the answers to her questions were not truly satisfying.

"Mr. Edwards, my brother and I cannot eat this food. We have nothing to cook with. Our headmen say you are to bring meat to us. Can I have this meat? My brother is hungry," she asked one day when she saw Mr. Edwards coming out of his agency office.

"Well, hello there, little squaw. Now ain't you lookin well. I guess I don't rightly know what your a talkin about. You got your allotment, didn't ya?" Mr. Edwards replied.

"Yes we did, but there was no meat in it. We got oatmeal, flour, some coffee, a box of powder they said was corn meal, with bugs in it, but nothing else. My brother is sick. We need this meat that our headmen say was promised," Sasa said as she tried to look into Mr. Edwards' eyes.

Mr. Edwards turned slightly, so that she could not look directly at him, and instead of turning his head to talk to her he spoke to her while squinting from the corners of his eyes.

"Well, I reckon I'll have to check into that, little squaw. Now, you go on to your Mam and Pap, and I'll see what we can do fur ya," he said while looking out to the far horizon, and before she could say anything more he was gone.

Sasa had asked him several more times over the few weeks after her father died, but Mr. Edwards answers were just as frustrating as before. Meanwhile, Usti Yansa grew sick and lifeless, his skin turned a sallow gray, and his lips faded to chalk.

Sitting where she had buried her brother, she remembered these things. There was a deeper meaning hidden within those memories, but she seemed to be missing some pieces to the puzzle. She would wait and maybe the Creator would reveal it to her.

Now it was only herself that she collected the allotment for. Even that was strange, because the size of the allotment did not change. The canisters of oatmeal, bags of flour and the bug filled corn meal were piling up in her wigwam. However, she did find a use for the coffee. She noticed that after the coffee was brewed by some of the mothers close to her in camp, they would throw out the used up grounds. Sasa noticed that earth worms liked the grounds very much, so she would scoop them up and run down to a nearby creek to catch a fish or two using a trap made of grape vines, and the worms for bait. Even the small fish were better than nothing to eat. She gave all her coffee to the mothers. Sadly, she thought, no matter how many fish she caught and cooked over the fire with a stick, and fed to Usti Yansa, he never stopped his decline. Oh, he ate as much as she provided, and the food kept her fairly healthy. That was one of the things that nagged at her, not letting her mind rest: why did the food not keep him alive?

Chapter **2**

Jackson Halley sat back against the white board steps of his large western Arkansas mansion, thinking about his family.

The Halley family, originally owners of financial institutions and banks in London, England, had then prospered in the Eastern part of this new country. After coming to the colonies and setting up lending houses in each of the original thirteen states, the Halleys had seen their fortune grow quickly. For many decades, the name of their firm, Halley's, had been synonymous with starting a business venture. In many cases, it was the only option for those with little capital and no record with The Second Bank of the United States, a national bank that was chartered to be the bank the government used to handle all its business.

Jackson grew up in the midst of some of the wealthiest colonists, who were now, happily, all citizens of America. Since his father had groomed him for the day he would take the helm of the family's financial ship, Jackson had enjoyed the benefits of the best education money could buy, even bringing the best tutors back across the sea from England. As a young man, the world of finance had excited him, making him eager to be the next in line to inherit his family's business.

Since the 1820s, however, life had taken a hard turn for the family business and the situation was even worse now, in 1839, with the company struggling to recapture its former wealth. Jackson's father had invested heavily in several business starts involving the Cherokee Nation, loaning various individuals funds to develop the land that the Cherokees held in common, but what had looked so lucrative, before the forced march that removed all the Cherokees from their rightful land, was turning out to actually be holdings of dust. The land Halley's had invested so much of their resources and planning into, now belonged to the land lottery of Georgia and even now they were quickly doling it out tract by tract.

This development was forcing Halley's to scale back business interests and number of employees so that they might recover from this catastrophe. Knowing that his continued employment in his family's business would not bring them profit enough to justify his salary, and wanting to help his father keep the business solvent, in 1838 Jackson had sold his shares back to his father, who left the running of the home office in Boston to a partner, and was now running the newest office in St. Louis, Missouri. His father would maintain control of the Board of Trustees and nurse the company back to health.

Jackson felt demoralized by the treatment of the Cherokee; many had been his close friends. Since he had come from the same circles and society as the men who had planned this horrible nightmare, he was privy to their candid proposal to find a way to lay claim to a land that belonged to a sovereign nation. He could now recognize the gleam of greed in their eyes and an utter thirst to take from those who were unaware of the trap being set for them. It became unbearable for him to mix daily with these same ones who would blithely say that the Cherokee were far better off than before, having a huge tract of land to the west, and one day he became involved in a discussion at his father's financial club, The Patriots Club of Boston, that helped him make up his mind about what to do with his life.

"Ah, Jackson, my boy. How very capital to see you today! What a fine day it is, too, what with the land lottery ready to begin in a few months, as soon as they get the last of the Indians out," said Colonel Dumont Jeffries, a land owner from Georgia. A compatriot of Andrew Halley,

Jackson's father, he had homes, property, and membership in clubs in Georgia and Boston.

"You don't say, Colonel Jeffries. It is hard to imagine that you would get so much enjoyment from something that has caused so many so much harm and is nearly destroying my father's company in the process," Jackson acerbically replied.

"Not so, Jackson, not so. Nothing of the kind, suh. Just the other day I remarked to Elsie, my wife, how very fortunate it was for your father that he will come out of this with his company intact. Very happy, indeed I am. But really, Jackson, don't you think it was a risky investment in the first place? Heaven knows that land was meant for God-fearing people. And what did they do with that land anyway? Those Indians had no forward vision about them. Now, you see, they will be all set up out in the west with land aplenty, yes, land aplenty, I say," chuckled the Colonel.

Jackson's neck began to turn a bright shade of red; he opened his mouth as if to speak and then shut it, before finally finding his voice.

"Sir, your attitude is abominable, to say the least. The very idea that you would call those scruffy, hard-drinking gold seekers God-fearing is beyond me. Those so-called 'Indians' are a proud people. They lived on that land for thousands of years with no help from us. And you dare say they will benefit from their ousting, body and soul? No sir, noooo sir, I will not hear it. Are you aware of how many have already been lost just sitting in those stockades with neither accommodations or shelter, nor sanitary provisions, with all they owned lost to them? And then, they will be made to go on that damned forced march ordered by our esteemed President, across rough country, rivers and mountains, meeting along the way hostile white settlers who can't tell the difference between these civilized and Christianized Cherokee and the wild Indians on the western frontier?"

cried Jackson. "Not to mention the old who can't even walk, the women ready to give birth and the ones already too sick to know where they are?"

"Well, uh, uh, Jackson, my boy, don't get so upset, suh. I merely meant that now they will have seclusion and will be free to do as they please," answered Colonel Jeffries.

"I can't imagine how you have got hold of such fiddle-faddle for information, Sir. Or is it possible that you yourself have designs on the land to be vacated by that tribe? And as for the being free to do 'as they please', Sir, you are utterly mistaken. The removal you so happily declare to benefit them, will cost more lives, maybe even thousands, marching them through the dead of winter with nothing... nothing, I say... but the clothes on their backs. Lives thrown away so that your so-called *'God-fearing'* gold seekers can swarm upon their land and do as they themselves please," said Jackson sharply.

"Oh, now, suh, you must be mistaken. Well, yes, I have heard some such a thing, but I say, it has probably been blown all out of proportion. No, what I do believe is that they were probably more glad to go than not, seeing as how they were surrounded on all sides by white settlements. It is just a matter of oil and water, suh, just oil and water. Not meant to mix. Your father can now invest with total abandon, if he so chooses, and will stand to show more for it, I dare say. Why, now the wheels of industry will roll, my dear boy, they will roll," crowed the Colonel.

Jackson's father had been watching from across the room and since the conversation had risen in volume, he made his way over to his son's side.

"Jackson," Andrew said in a subdued tone, leaning toward Jackson's ear, "I think it would benefit us all if we went home, Son. There is nothing to be gained in rehashing this hurt. As you can see, Son, they do not feel it and

17

probably never will. Come, Son, I will call for the coach," his father said before heading toward the door.

Jackson took a long look at the Colonel and marshaled his temper.

"This thing that has been done to that noble race will never set right in the craw of the American people, Sir," he said before turning to go. "I assure you that long after we are gone, this action will be known as one of the blackest stains on our own white race. Not just on our President or the government of our new republic, but a stain on all the God-fearing whites of this land, who will never be able to rub it off. I myself can no longer live among people who could perpetuate such a dastardly scheme and be able to sleep at night. Good night, Sir. May the buyers of that land choke on it."

As he spoke, Jackson knew that he had made the right decision.

Even before the forced removal of the Cherokee, he had had a bad feeling about what would happen to his friends and their families. He had talked things over with Archibald Flint, a full-blooded Cherokee and his best friend, chasing ideas around and planning what they could do, together, about the situation. Jackson had taught Arch to read and write in English, and just by being around Jackson's family he had acquired some of the ways of the whites. Once Jackson explained his plan to him, Arch had been very enthusiastic, so they had settled on a course of action. At the same time, Andrew Halley headed for the frontier boom-town of St. Louis. There, he would head Halley's newest investment office to provide start-up money for the flood of businesses, wanting to be the first to provide whatever services they could.

Jackson would leave the East and find his own way, make a new start with the money he had saved and received from the sale of his shares. Arch would bring as many of his family as would agree to come, and go into a fifty-fifty partnership with Jackson, he figured that giving Arch and his family fifty percent of the business was small compensation for the future loss of their traditional home, but it was all he could offer. Jackson, his dog Jack, Arch and several of Arch's family members headed west before the forced removal.

They would need workers. Before they left, Arch roamed the Cherokee lands, talking with those families who did not have much in the way of wealth and would be the most hurt if removal came. As he approached a rickety log cabin, deep in the Georgia hills, hoping to convince one of the members of this branch of the Ward family to come west with him, Arch took a deep breath. The Wards were descendants of a large chiefly family which had given birth to several famous rulers of the Cherokee, many generations back, and he hoped to speak specifically to Sam Ward, the eldest son of the household.

"Ho, the house," Arch hollered.

"Who comes?" a high, scratchy voice answered.

"Arch Flint. I came to speak to Sam. Is he here?" Arch asked.

A rail thin, diminutive old woman came forward and stepped out on the stoop with her head cocked and fire in her eyes. She wore a faded colorless calico dress with no shoes on her feet.

"Ah, Grandmother Ward, I greet you. May I speak to Sam?" he asked again.

"Arch, I heard what you are going to do. I can't believe you would give up your traditional lands for a place you have never seen. You need to make a stand here. Make them whites stick to their treaties they signed. My mother, my father and all my ancestors' bones are all here on this land. We cannot leave them alone and let those whites grow cotton on top of them," she complained.

Arch understood how she felt. He himself had done a lot of thinking before he decided to go with Jackson.

"Grandmother, I have not seen what your eyes have seen. But my eyes have seen that the whites make these treaties only to break them when they want more of what we have. I have searched my heart and I have prayed to the Creator. I am at peace with this decision. These whites will stop at nothing to get this land. I would rather go far to the west to start over. Grandmother, they want this land and they will find a way to get it.

"Sam is young like me. If he goes, he can make a place for his family for when the whites take this land. I hope you will allow him to hear my message," pleaded Arch.

The old woman gazed intently at him and was silent for a long time.

"I seem to remember that this land was not always our land," she finally said. "My grandmothers told me that our people traveled far, coming from the north with its sheets of ice. They killed animals that no one today has seen. I know things change, but it is hard for the old ones like me to bend in the wind. I will tell Sam. He will make his own decision. I will not talk against those who want to go. That is all I have to say."

With that she closed the door. Once Sam got the message, he decided to come, along with several cousins with their wives and children. No others in the family would leave their land.

However, others came...not entire families, but enough to help run Jackson and Arch's new business, that of breeding mules and selling them to the U.S. Army. They would be paid a wage like any white man. Jackson also promised to help them with homesteads of their own by putting the land in his name first and then finding a legal way for him to transfer the ownership over to each family later. All the members in the Halley family were abolitionists and he refused to use slavery to acquire workers for his home or business.

Some families turned Arch away with bitter words, saying that removal would never happen and no one could force them from the Cherokee lands. Already, however, there had been a small exodus of Cherokee families who took the land that the U.S. Government offered if they would move to the Arkansas Territory, as it was then called. Now that Arkansas had gained statehood, the state boundary was redrawn and those Cherokee families who had started over earlier were forced to move again into the new Indian Territory.

Jackson and Arch bought land just east of the new state line, outside the new small town called Van Buren, Arkansas, named after the Secretary of State, Martin Van Buren , who had been under President Jackson. Now Martin Van Buren was President, giving the new town some much needed recognition. Nearby was the old Fort Smith that had been abandoned in 1824; In 1838, however, just a few months previously the U.S. Army had returned and relocated the fort to a location across the Arkansas River, where they were busy adding new buildings and barracks for the men stationed there. That had been a stroke of luck for the business partners. To have a fort so close to their breeding business was going to be an easy sell since the U.S. Army used a multitude of mules for pack animals and mounts. This location was turning out to be a boon, not to mention the fact that the Arkansas River and Lee Creek, flowing in two different directions, made for easy transportation, as well as shipment of the stock on the flat-bottomed steamboats that plied the river.

Everything was going fine until the storage barn blew up. The loss of the barn and its contents was not really too bad, but the loss of his dear friend Jack was something harder to swallow down. As Jackson sat on his porch steps, he pondered what he wanted to do. He had thought Jack would find his way back, however, neither he nor his dog had been that way into the woods and there would only be Jack's trail for the dog to follow back. Jack had run due west towards the new Arkansas-Indian Territorial state line. Beyond that line lay the new lands of the Cherokee and other Native Indian tribes. If Jack did not come back by tomorrow night, Jackson would ride in search for him. He loved that little guy and no smarter dog ever existed on earth, as far as he was concerned.

Chapter 3

Jack was exhausted after that first night and a day in the thick of the forest. It had rained, and that had removed all but a faint glimmer of his own scent, lingering from his mad dash into the forest. Did he want to follow that vague scent back the way he had come, however, knowing something was there that he did not understand and that had chased him so relentlessly? The instinct of self-preservation said, "no"...and that meant that he would have to choose another path. Day after long day he followed the clear game trails paralleled by a fairly large creek which expanded or contracted, curved one way and then back on itself, but generally headed where the sun set every afternoon.

Food had not been a problem, since being a Jack Russell had its advantages. He was quick to spot small game and just as quick to pounce on it, jerk his head back and forth with the critter in his jaws, and ultimately snap its neck; moreover, he had a good strong set of teeth so he had no problems wolfing the meal down. The creek provided all the water he could want, so, on he went, albeit more slowly than before, so that his paws could recover. Occasionally he would see an animal that he had no intention of eating, having sated his hunger already, and would bound off after it just for the fun of it.

He had been traveling for many days among the trees with their long vines of wild grapes and the Carolina Creeper clinging and covering the trunks. On that day, he noticed that the forest was starting to thin somewhat and picked up a scent that was obviously human, even if he was still alone with all the tall trees surrounding and lining the creek. It was that time of the day when the sun was directly overhead above the trees. Being thirsty, Jack picked his way over a small hillock and down to the creek's bank to lap up some of the cool clear water. Gingerly, he stepped into the shallow water and bent his head, barely noticing a black stick laying in the backwater, close to him; when you are a thirsty dog, a stick laying in the water makes little impression. After his first satisfying drink, he raised his head to find he was staring into the open, oddly white mouth of a snake baring its long, sharp-looking fangs, ready to attack him. He had already turned to bound up the bank in retreat when he felt the sting of its bite on his right hind leg.

As the large snake slithered into the forest, Jack loped off down the path, not knowing he had been hurt, but he didn't get very far before he felt dizzy and fuzzy mouthed. He limped a little toward the creek and wearily sat down, noticing his bleeding leg. Slowly he began to lick the wound, but as he continued to take care of the puncture holes he vaguely noticed that the trees and plants around him seemed to sway. Shaking, he rose and walked in a tight circle for a while, feeling very tired, as a high-pitched ringing began to torture his ears and he suddenly felt extremely nauseated. Before he could finish circling to lie down, he collapsed onto the muddy bank of Lee Creek and arrived at death's door.

"Girl, you can't keep going on like you been doing. Cooking pots are not going to fall from the sky and say, "Now you can make something to eat", any more than my man is going to come back from the dead," said Mary Walkingstick, a name she had given to herself so she would have an English name. Her husband had died in a skirmish when the soldiers had come to remove them from their land. She did not even get to bury him.

"But, Mother," said Sasa, "I do not know what to do. My real mother has gone back to the circle of life and you know that no one brought pots with them from the East."

She had been cooking fish on a fresh green willow stick for days now, and Mary was tired of watching her struggle to feed herself. She knew there were so many gaps in family circles, and that elders like her would have to help out.

"Daughter, did no one show you how to make your own cooking pots from clay?" asked Mary.

"I have watched my real mother do it, but the last time she made pots I was much younger and we were in our homeland. The ground is different here, so I don't know what the clay here looks like," complained Sasa.

Mary stood up with a weary grunt and disappeared into her lodge. When she came out she held in her hand a ball of red clay.

"This is the clay that you can find here," she said, handing it to Sasa, "and if you walk towards the rising sun for a while you will come to the creek the whites call Lee Creek. Look along the banks and you will see the red clay. When you go, take a shirt or some other piece of cloth with you, pile the clay on the cloth and bring back as much as you are able to carry. Then I will show you what to do next."

"Thank you, Mother," she said. "You are being very kind. I am alone and many of my friends and their families are gone. You have been the first to offer help."

"Daughter, it is hard right now to know who is friend or foe. The Old Settlers, the Cherokee who moved here two years ago, are mad at the new ones. They don't want to share the land or have Chief Ross as their chief and accept a new government. They are few and we are many, but we have already heard of violence and fighting. I watched you for a long time before I decided to help. Now go and get that clay. If you get back early enough we can have a pot baking in the coals by tonight," Mary replied.

The forest lay ahead, quiet and cool, and though Sasa had not yet ventured far into its emerald green depths, she knew that Lee Creek exited the forest, crossing into Indian Territory a bit farther to the north. Sasa was not happy about where she was instructed to go, because actually going into the forest alone, walking east to look for the snaking course of the creek, was somewhat frightening. As she walked she began to notice plants with which she was familiar, things that also grew in her homeland back east, and that sight comforted her.

She thought it would be good to learn to make pots, since it was one of the things that everyone needed here in the new land, and maybe she could trade what she made for the things she needed that were not provided by the allotment.

What good is an allotment if the things they give us are not useful? She thought. *I am not sure, but I think there should be much more coming to us. My family is supposed to have land to farm, but now I am alone. I cannot work a farm by myself. Any time we camp in a place for too long it begins to stink, and the place where I have my lodge now is not good. There is no cover from bad weather and all the lodges are too close together. My father used to say that we were to be moved on to land of our own. I think I will ask Mr. Edwards again about this. I think I will have to go to his office and stand at the door so he does not run away.*

That was how she thought of her encounters with Mr. Edwards. He always seemed to run away from her when she asked a question, but her father had told her that the tribe had to address its questions to the Indian Agent, not to the government.

She was deep in these thoughts when she realized that even if she had entered a darker part of the forest, she was not as frightened as she had thought she might be, for that place was even more like her home. She would come here often to collect some of the plants she saw, some good to eat and some good for medicine. She might even build a brush lodge here in the forest to spend there the hot days of summer.

She continued to walk, gazing up at the treetops, sucking in the moist silky air. The creek appeared just ahead, where the flow made an abrupt turn toward the northwest and disappeared from view. *Truly a fine place,* she thought, as she began to examine the bank, skirting trees and thickets, willow brush and ferns. At first, she saw no change in the color of the soil next to the creek and she thought there would be no clay to find, but just then she began to see faint spots of reddish tinted soil. The farther she walked the redder it got, and she finally decided she had found the right spot where she could dig up the clay she needed.

She knelt on one knee and spread her old shirt on the damp ground. Good, the recent rain would make it easier to dig with the sharpened hardwood stick...hardened in her camp fire...that she had brought along with her. She dug up several clumps of clay before exhausting the spot of ground she was digging in, then she made her way a little further down the bank. There she saw another patch of deep red, just enough to finish her load, but when she stepped down the bank to the new spot, she found a fern that blocked her path, preventing her from getting at the clay without standing in the water. She reached down to sweep the fern aside and was astonished to see the inert body of a mostly white dog with a very short tail.

"Ugh, a dead dog," she said, screwing her face up into a grimace, but as she began to move away, fearing the smell of rotting flesh, she suddenly stopped because she saw one of its paws give a little twitch. She was a little wary because she knew injured animals were likely to lash out and bite you and this one could have the mad sickness. However, there was no evidence of foam at the mouth, so she tentatively put her hand on the dog's head and then let her fingers slide down the length of the body, pausing momentarily to see if there would be a response. Then she did it again. She was raising her hand to stroke him a third time when he opened his eyes.

He did not seem to be able to move, except for his eyes...those deep brown eyes that seemed to say so much. Sasa could feel a hard pull on her heart and an unusual feeling within her gut. Her bundle of clay forgotten, she looked him over to see what might be the matter. Ah, a snake bite, but what kind of snake? She knew that there were herbs that could help, but she didn't know what they looked like; she thought for a moment, then she gently lifted the dog into her arms and hurried back the way she had come. This time she did not dawdle as she had done while getting there.

While she hurried, she tried to think of who might be able to help her with this dog. They had lost so many on the Long Walk, and some of those that could have helped were gone. She decided to take him to the medicine man. He was not of her clan and she had nothing to give him for his trouble, but perhaps he would help her anyway.

The dog lay in her arms, not making a sound. His eyes were still open, a pleading worry emanating from them, and his flesh felt hot against her arms. Silently she emerged from the forest, padding quickly to Mary's lodge first, but Mary was nowhere to be seen. Sasa was getting very tired from carrying him for such a long distance, but she knew she could not stop: something about this dog urged her on.

Finally, she arrived in front of a small shack, a very rough and mean looking lodge made of cedar poles. The man inside was called Di Damv Wi S Gi or Medicine Man, and even if he also had another name, Sasa did not know what it was. Now she was out of breath, her heart beating wildly. She scratched on the old piece of deer skin that was used as a door covering, and waited for any acknowledgment of her request. She was beginning to think that there was no one there, when the covering was suddenly thrown back, slapping the side of the shack with a whack.

"Who are you and what do you want?" said an old, old woman.

Sasa looked up at her and immediately caught her breath. The old woman was deeply wrinkled, with lines even creasing her eyelids; her head had bare places on its old pate, which showed many freckles on the skin, and from it patches of wispy gray hair flew in all directions. Sasa had seen old people before, but she had never seen one this ancient.

"Well, what do you want, girl?" the woman said, as she stood looking up at her, speechless. "Can't you see I am getting older by the minute, standing here?"

"I am sorry, Grandmother, I meant no disrespect. I have found a dog by the long creek and he needs a healer. My clan healer is no more, so I came to ask your Medicine Man if he can help him. This dog has a snake bite on his leg and he is dying," Sasa said, as quickly as she could.

"I will see. Bring the dog in," the old woman said.

The shack was very small, only one room, but it did have a fire burning and a hole in the roof to let smoke out. It was not as good as the hearth and chimney that were to be found in some of the lodges, so the draft of upward air was almost non-existent, and smoke hovered in the air in a blue, cloying haze. The shack also had an odd smell, like hay and other plants set to dry, but she could not identify all the smells. As she stood at the center of the room, still holding the dog, the woman approached a recumbent form on a pallet close to a small fire. Sasa thought it was odd to have a fire on a summer day.

The form stirred, rolled over and grunted. When the woman motioned him to get up, the man sat up, staring menacingly at her.

"What is it, Ada Hi Hi? Why do you wake me up, eh? To torment the life out of me, that's why. And what is this person doing here with a dead animal in my home?" the Medicine Man asked.

The old woman only motioned Sasa to approach and explain herself to the man, who was now looking at her with hard eyes and a cruel mouth.

"Grandfather, I found this dog by the creek. He has been snake-bit and I do not know how to help him. I am learning to make pots, so if I make a pot for you will you use your healing medicine on this dog?" she said with eyes bulging, believing this man could do anything.

"I am a Medicine Man, but not of your clan. I have no use for healing a stupid dog. I am healer to chiefs and great warriors. I was also the medicine man for some of the Cherokee soldiers who fought for the British when they wanted their towns back. I will not be bothered with a miserable dog. You should knock it in the head and throw it on the trash heap, or better yet, skin it and eat it. I do not care, but take it away from me," he said, then lay back down on his pallet and turned his back to her.

The old woman took Sasa by the arm and guided her outside, where she did something unexpected: she took the dog into her own arms. Sasa was frightened.

"No! Grandmother, please do not kill him. I do not know why, but I must help this dog," she said, with tears brimming in her dark eyes.

The woman looked at her with a wry smile on her lips.

"I am Poison Woman," she said, "keeper of the medicine herbs and poison for killing vermin and I am sister to Deer Caller, but I am the only one who can call him that. Everyone else must call him Medicine Man. What does that matter now, when he just sleeps his days away and does not try to help anyone? I don't know what the matter is with him. I will look at the dog and see if there is anything I can do."

Poison Woman took her time and looked over every inch of the dog. She looked at the bite on his thigh, then she looked inside his mouth, noticing that the skin was naturally black there. The dog had his eyes closed tight, but began to make a wheezing sound. Then he opened his eyes again and gazed at the old woman, who gazed back at him; Sasa felt she was watching them communicate.

"I will help you with this dog," she said. "We have an understanding, I will give him medicine and he will not bite me."

She ran her hands down the dog's coat, over its ears and under its muzzle.

"There is something different about this animal," she said then. "I can see in his eyes that he has the heart of a human. He will have big medicine. Wait a moment for me, while I get the herbs and things I need. We will have to go to your lodge, because Deer Caller will not let me do this thing in his lodge."

Sasa waited for Poison Woman, and when she came back out they walked to Sasa's lodge together. She wondered at what the old woman had said. Was this the feeling that she herself had felt when she had stroked the dog? None of it would matter if the dog died, so she kept pace with the old woman and led her to her poor place, the dog watching her with his knowing, unblinking eyes.

Chapter 4

The man sat at his desk in his office, watching the door. He hoped it wouldn't be a long night, but his client was late for their meeting. Why had he ever come to this god-forsaken place? Indian Territory was far from his idea of a place to get rich, especially from the vermin, the Cherokee living on these lands, but it had proved to be quite profit-able...it had, indeed, and still was, with no end in sight. The government had been so eager to get the Cherokees off that land back in Georgia, Tennessee and the Carolinas, that they were now turning a blind eye on what is now happening in Indian Territory. He had known all along that it would be so, and he had planned accordingly. This was even better than the slow wealth his family had achieved over the last century supplying arms to whoever could pay, including wild, warlike Indians on the Great Plains.

He did not even have to be here most of the time, since he had acquired a flunky to oversee the transactions each month... those stupid Indians had no idea and never would. They had no aptitude for business and only cared about their hokum-pokum...or "medicine", as they called it... their clans, their wars and pretending they could be like the whites. Now, his Georgian family with their present land holdings could breathe a breath of fresh air, and get on with populating all of that prime property, some of it containing the luscious gold recently discovered.

It had been a piece of cream pie when it came to influencing the top man of the republic. Old Andrew Jackson had made no attempt at upholding the ruling of the Supreme Court's decision that Georgia had no say-so in land long held by the Cherokee. Yes, suh, Old Hickory knew what side his bread was buttered on if he wanted to keep his hands on the Republic. But his own appearance in Washington City, at the

Balls and Teas where the President appeared, making sure to be at his elbow, whispering forebodings of dire consequences if Georgia failed to get hold of all that chunk of land, had proved to be the most effective tool. Oh, nothing out in the open, nothing anyone could point to or say they had overheard, and certainly nothing written on paper, but effective all the same. And now, with Martin Van Buren as the new President of the United States, his influence was no less diminished. It was a boon to him that he himself was a leader in Georgian society, as well as in Washington City, and at all public functions he conducted himself with the highest order of propriety, just like any other gentleman attending. Yes, he was a respected man of means.

He only wished he had not soiled his hands with eliminating an Indian. Even though he had no sympathy for Indians, he would rather not risk that anyone took notice of the demise of one little Cherokee boy, which was why he had found a way to take care of that little matter. It had been so easy to do, and he had been back in Georgia by the time the boy died. After taking care of some business matters, he had then gone on to St. Louis. Besides, by then the boy had been buried, and nothing was left to point to, no one really knew how the boy had died, nor ever would. The man smiled to himself just thinking of it.

So, it made him wonder why he needed to be here now for this unplanned meeting. He wanted no connections exposed here, even remotely, if he could help it, but, with so much money at stake he had to make sure there was no unfortunate happenstance that he would need to resolve. If something drastic was needed, he would take care of it and use diplomacy as a last resort.

The visitor softly knocked on the office door. A proper young lady entered, her sateen dark green skirt shimmering in the lamp's light.

"What do I owe this untimely visit to?" the man said, puffing on a strong smelling, expensive cigar.

A Venetian lace gloved hand emerged from a side fold of her full sateen maroon cloak, the pocket there evidenced by dark green trimming, and extended toward him a folded piece of white paper.

She felt uncomfortable under his rude stare. As any well-bred young lady knew, it was unmannerly to look a man in the eye, especially if he was a total stranger, but so was meeting him in the middle of the night in a strange cabin hidden deep in the woods, not to mention being alone with him without a chaperon.

"My father sent me to deliver a message. I don't know what it is about, but he wanted me to deliver it personally to you," the young woman replied, while handing him the note and straightening the bodice of her shirtwaist.

The man read the missive and seemed to pale somewhat, but he quickly recovered his aplomb.

The note had said:

"I can't find the frog. I have even been in their lodge to look, and it is not there. What do you want me to do?"

There was no signature.

The man looked up at the young lady through the cigar smoke swirling in the dim light of the one oil lamp in the room, and met the curious stare of her hazel eyes, noticing the touch of worry trembling about her mouth.

"Fine, fine, young lady. Message received, tell your father not to worry," he said, while writing on the note to be returned by her hand. He had a smile on his lips that did not reach his eyes. For some inexplicable reason, she was mortally afraid of him, even though she had never met him before. The smoke from his cigar was nauseating, and she could feel panic begin to creep up her spine. She concealed the note back in her pocket without opening it and left the room with dread following close behind. Walking briskly, she neared her cabin. Then, breaking her promise not to read the missive, she pulled it out as she walked with the bright moonlight over her shoulder, and paused long enough to read, first her father's message and then the reply.

It said:

"Quit looking, they can't possibly figure it out. Forget it!!"

Again, there was no signature.

Jackson was getting ready to search for Jack. He swept a hand through his sandy brown hair and deftly pulled the long strands back to tie them. It had been several days since the fire and Jack had not returned to the house yet. It was very distressing for him, not just because he had spent so much time training Jack and they had become very good friends, but, most of all, because, Jack was special in some way. He could not say what it was, but Jack seemed to under-stand everything being said and then use the information to do anything he could to help. He realized that Jack had just been trying to help out that day when the barn blew up. He had been so frantic putting the fire out he had not taken even a heartbeat to figure out what his dog was trying to tell him. If he had, he might have gotten to the barn sooner and Jack would not be missing now.

He could remember when Jack was just a puppy. He had been acquired from a mated pair just imported from England, bred by a Reverend John Russell, an investor with his father's firm. The pup was delivered to them all the way from Boston as a parting gift from his father. The Reverend Russell believed he had succeeded in breeding the perfect terrier to be used regularly in fox-hunting and claimed they were invaluable for killing vermin that burrowed under the soil. The accompanying letter from the Reverend said that he planned to name them 'Jack' Russell Terriers, since most people called him Jack, not John.

35

Jackson's property here in Arkansas had quickly been cleaned out of moles once Jack was put to work. But, that was not Jack's special gift. He guessed that if he had to pin it down to one thing, it would be Jack's ability to communicate. He seemed to find ways, not dog ways, but human ways, to make his thoughts known, and he seemed to know what Jackson was feeling. If he was sad or glum, Jack would creep up on his lap, somehow without him realizing it, and lay his head on Jackson's chest, his outside foot and paw snugly clinging across him like a hug. Jackson would all of a sudden notice that Jack was there. No one had taught Jack that; he just knew.

Jack could also smile. Not the open-mouthed, tongue hanging out panting canine kind of smile. Jack had taught himself to smile with his jaw closed, showing his front teeth, and he would use that smile when pleading for anyone to play ball or come with him for a nice run on the grounds.

Jackson caught himself welling up with emotion. He loved Jack and he knew Jack loved him. Because of that, he knew the dog would come back if he could. At least if he tracked him down and found he had died, he would be able to mourn his passing, and heal. But the way things were now, not knowing was killing him and it was preventing him from concentrating on his work, be it the rebuilding of the barn or the breeding of the mules. Arch had to pick up the slack and it wasn't fair of Jackson to not carry his own load. Arch had also become attached to Jack, however, and was urging him to go out and look for him.

So here he was, putting the packs on one mule and riding another. He would have taken one of his riding mounts, considering he was a fairly tall man, but mules were better in rougher country and he was heading straight into the forested area between Van Buren, Arkansas and the Indian Territory border. Arch was also packing two mules to go with him, for he wanted to take some things over to Indian

Territory where the last of the Cherokee, removed from their land in Georgia, had been left. Arch had never been there and wanted to see what kind of land the government thought was useless enough to give to the Cherokee. Naturally, he doubted the People had what they needed, so he figured this would be the first of many trips to help his people.

"All right Arch, I think I'm ready. I asked around at Fort Smith about the land we are heading into. They said that if we spot Jack's trail near Lee Creek we should just stay close to that. It is the main source of water going west and northwest and most critters, dogs included, would stay close to it. Plus, where water is, so is food, for us and for Jack," Jackson said, as he cinched his saddle.

"Jackson, what will we do if we don't find Jack in the forest? I need to take these things to the camps in Indian Territory," Arch asked.

"Well, the trek to the border is about five to ten miles as the crow flies, and there is a lot of up and down, ridges and deep hollows, which means it will be a longer trip, with the trail gone stone cold by now. I'm afraid to hold out much hope of finding him, so if you don't mind, and if we can't track him, I'll just come along with you and get my first look at how our friends are doing. That way I'll be able to write to my father and tell him of their fate. He has been mighty worried since last winter, besides being angry at the former President," replied Jackson.

Sam Ward, a not-so-tall Cherokee with muscular shoulders, hurried out of the house and came to a stop before Jackson, handing him a letter.

"This came for you a few minutes ago on this week's steamboat, Boss. I thought it might be important," he said, out of breath.

"*Wado,* Sam. We should be back within a week or two, but if not, just keep on with the usual routine. I don't think we have any dams that will be ready to breed for at least three months. Other than that, you know what to do. That's why I made you the foreman," said Jackson while taking the letter to look at it.

"Well, speaking of the devil. A letter from my father, and I see it was mailed from Georgia. He probably is there tending to the financial dealings on some of that land the government seized. Most likely he wants to keep me informed, even though I sold him back all my shares in the company," he said, as he put the letter in his saddle bag.

"I thought he was not going to have anything to do with that land, since he had lost all that investment money," replied Arch.

"That's true enough, but I imagine that he is being forced to help finance some of the grantees who want to start businesses on their plot of granted land. He has to take all the business he can get to put the company on solid footing again. Don't worry, let's get started. I can always read it when we camp."

They mounted and wended their way slowly into the forest spreading before them, riding in the general direction they had last seen Jack heading. One or the other of the two partners would take his turn tracking, looking for broken branches, some bent over grass or a mark in the damp earth. They did find some sign of passage but there was no way to tell what animal had made the mark, with the exception of the occasional paw print that they knew had to be Jack's. Those paw prints were few and far between and they rejoiced every time they came upon one.

In the late afternoon, they got tired and began to look for a good protected place to camp. Topping a ridge, they could see Lee Creek flowing below them and started down the slope. About halfway down, they came to a rocky overhang with plenty of room for them to make a fire and roll out their bedrolls. Several hickory trees with a bunch of grass growing underneath stood close by, offering a perfect place to picket their mules. They removed the pack loads from the beasts of burden and together they led them down the slope to water them in the creek. The water was running clear and cold here, which had to mean that there was a pretty good chance a large spring was contributing to swell the normally murky water of the creek. The water proved to be sweet and invigorating.

After refreshing themselves, Arch refilled their canteens while Jackson scooped up a potful to make a good camp stew. They had brought with them some deer jerky and also some pemmican, a mixture of shredded deer or buffalo meat, fat and any type of berries that could be found growing wild. All this was stuffed into an animal's intestine. Most of the time it was smoked, then stored, and would keep on the trail. Tonight, Arch would use some to put into the stew, plus any roots he could find growing along the banks of the creek. Right now, in early summer, there would be plenty of wild carrots, identifiable by their tall thin stalks and delicate clumps of white flowers at the tops.

After their meal, before the fire died down, Jackson stretched his six foot frame over his blankets, settling down to read his father's letter. In some ways, he missed seeing his father every day and working with him on new ventures. It was an exciting business, but now he was going to make it on his own out here in this frontier wilderness, and that thought gave him pleasure. He opened his father's letter and began to read.

Dear Jackson:

I am hoping that this correspondence finds you doing well and happy. I do miss you and your friend Arch, but hopefully you will have a chance to come and visit me here in St. Louis. It is not a very long trip by steam boat these days.

39

Jackson, there are some strange things happening here. Things I am hearing about on the sly, so to speak. I have been hearing that the BIA (Bureau Of Indian Affairs) in Washington City is getting concerned about some misplaced funds or errors in bookkeeping. Son, the only time politicians in Washington City get up in arms, is if it involves a sizable amount of money. A loss that they would have to report to the Congress.

There is nothing official so far. All that I have heard is hearsay and innuendo, but something is in the wind. I feel that I owe it to our friends in Indian Territory to look into this discreetly and find out what might be happening. If there is anything I know, it is how to add two and two. If it comes up three then you know someone has their hand in the cookie jar. Only this is a mighty big cookie jar with lots of hands in it. So getting to the bottom of it might take some time. I just thought you might want to know.

The land grants will proceed at a furious pace with nary a thought to the death and heart-ache all this has caused. It is as though they have turned a blind eye to the suffering of the Cherokee. Some of the land grants most sought after are the ones that have established homes, farms and businesses already there. All the possessions of the people they displaced become theirs, like spoils of war. It's heartrending to watch, not to mention the fact that it was our company's money that helped to develop the land that they are taking over. They have no conscience to speak of that I can tell. Be glad that you are there and not in Georgia.

Be sure to write back a note to your dear mother at home in Boston. I am sure she is lonely

*for the both of us. Don't tell her, but I plan to build
her a fine house here if it looks like I will be here for
any length of time...*

This was distressing news, Jackson thought. If his
father was worried, then it was probably something that
needed worrying about. He put the letter back in his bag. He
would get it out again a few more times and mull over all the
information. He hoped it was not true; it would be such a
huge fiasco if the United States seized all that land just to
have the funds allotted to the tribes subverted. He would
hold off making an opinion until he knew more.

Following the signs of Jack's frantic flight, a couple of
days later they came upon Lee Creek again. This creek was
one of the major waterways going in a north-northwesterly
direction, not really big enough for a steam boat to traverse,
but large enough for a good sized canoe. It made wide hairpin
curves as it cut through the trees. All manner of animals, birds
and reptiles lived in or near this waterway, so they had no
trouble finding a meal to cook over the campfire at night if
they did not want to use their supplies. Fortunately, the
ground had been moist when the dog came through, his
paws making a lasting impression in the dried mud, and even
if there had been some rainfall, luckily the trees had
prevented the rain from washing the forest floor away.

They marveled at the beauty surrounding them.
Everything was eye-catching, from the sheer cliffs and sandy
beaches to the waterfalls surrounded by boulders, and the
backwaters where water lilies and cattails were so furiously
blooming that you could barely see the water. A huge variety
of trees always overshadowed them as they traveled... oak,
several types of hickory, cedar, pine and some trees they
could not name were abundant. There were many types of
fruit bearing bushes and plants along the way as well,
blackberry and raspberry the most prolific, and wild grapes

were also abundant. They were traveling through the southern boundary of the vast Ozark Mountains which continued up into Missouri.

As they rode, they kept a cautious eye on their surroundings, for there was always a chance they might come across a hunting party of Indians, since there were several that might traverse this forested area. The Delawares were known to have had winter camps in the Ozark Mountains, but were not noted for coming down as far as what was now Arkansas. However, this part of the Ozarks was the traditional lands of the Osage. They were a noble race, tall and intelligent, and even though they were supposed to be resettled in the Osage lands in Kansas, Jackson would not be surprised if he met a party of them here. He considered them a handsome people and hoped he would not make any enemies of them, for they could be fierce in combat.

Arch was watchful too, keeping his voice low and limiting his conversation. With trees so large and old, it would be easy for a party to surprise them. For all of the last half century, the white government and white settlers had steadily pushed all the Arkansas tribes into Indian Territory or Kansas. That did not mean, though, that groups of one tribe or another would not make a foray across the Indian Territory borders. Arch was raised alongside white settlements and the Eastern Cherokees were considered to be "Tame Indians". Here in Arkansas it was a different matter entirely. Many local tribes had just recently been pushed out of well-established villages and the Long Walk was only one among many sad and lethal problems for all the natives. Deep resentment and anger were the byproducts of these resettlements. Indeed, he had some anger and resentment of his own to deal with. They continued making progress until Arch spotted something unusual.

"Jackson, look at this," he said. "An old shirt with a pile of clay on it, like someone was here, gathering clay, but just dropped it and ran away. We must be close to the Indian Territory border. I wonder what frightened them. And look here, there is an indentation in the soft mud of the bank where an animal lay down," he went on, as he motioned for his partner to come and look.

"Yes, I see it, and these few drops of brown, here... that has to be blood. It doesn't look anything like the clay surrounding it. Something lay here injured," Jackson surmised.

They could read the signs like reading a book. It was plain that an injured animal had been lying there and someone had abandoned their chore of gathering clay to take the animal away.

"Hey, Arch, look here by the water, dog tracks. Several of them that lead up to where that indentation is. Something happened here, something bad," Jackson said as he stood to ponder the scene.

He bent down, picked up the abandoned clay and shirt, rolled it up and tied it snugly onto his pack mule. He was not sure why, but he felt it might come in handy in some way.

They followed the creek only partway now, seeing plain footprints in the loam. Maybe this was the way they should follow, considering that they had not spotted any more paw tracks since finding the shirt and clay. Jackson had no real answers, but he would follow the tracks anyway.

Chapter 5

Sasa knelt beside Wheezer while preparing some broth for him. He had improved some since she had brought him into her lodge yesterday. Poison Woman had come by twice today to check on him, and each time Sasa had been told to not give up and to stay close to him. She had instructed Sasa on how to dribble the broth down one side of his mouth, letting the fluid go where it might; every once in a while, the dog would swallow and she knew that he was getting some. Sasa was puzzling over something the old woman had said on her last visit to Wheezer.

"I can't figure out how he ever came to be in that forest. You might see a wolf or coyote, maybe even a mangy cur there, but not a dog like this. This was someone's friend. See, his coat is good where the burrs didn't get on it, and his teeth look like he's always been well fed. That tail he's got ain't normal, either. I saw some other kinda' dogs back east with tails like that and I heard that the whites cut some dogs tails off when they are babies. No, Wheezer belonged to someone, but to whom?" Poison Woman had said, as she retreated to her lodge, shaking her head so that her wispy gray patches of hair waved at the clouds rolling by.

After that visit from Poison Woman, Sasa had sat down to look a little closer at Wheezer. There were some very unusual things about him that she was just now noticing. He was mostly white with only a couple of patches of brown on his body, but his head was a mix of brown, white and black, with a scattering of black ticking. His face was divided by a thin white blaze from his sloping forehead to his nose, then the white seemed to spill over to his right side, close to his muzzle. The other side was a mix of brown and black. His ears had a way of sitting up, but bent in half and flopped forward. He had a perfect nose, and, to her astonishment, now that she was looking closely, she could see that his whiskers were black on the side of his face that was dark and they were white on the side that was white. That seemed impossible... how could such a thing happen? While pondering this, she noticed that on the side that was white, near his nose, there was a small black spot the size of a pea and another a little smaller. Without even thinking, she leaned forward and kissed him right on those spots.

Then she started to giggle, realizing what she had just done.

"Oh Wheezer," she said, "what a joy your face is to look upon. That spot on your nose was just right for kissing, so I will call that your 'kissing spot', where I will kiss you each day."

Wheezer moved his eyes to look at her and blinked.

As Sasa continued to feed him she heard a rustle outside. Before she could get up to look, Mr. Edwards was on the threshold, bending over to look into the lodge.

"Well, well, now. Howdy, little squaw. Ain't seen you in a while...why, you used to come to the Agency plum reg'lar. What's ya got there? Oh, you found a dog, did ya? Well, he looks like he might not be too healthy, if you ask me. Maybe you oughta toss him into a cooking pot. I heard you people like to eat dog." Mr. Edwards said, a grin plastered on his ruddy face.

He was breathing heavily, probably from carrying all that weight. It was funny to see him trying to bend over and talk to her at the same time, but Sasa kept her smile to herself. Actually, she did not want to see him, just now. He never answered her questions with a definite answer anyway, so why bother talking to him?

"I have been very busy here at my lodge. Why do you visit me?" she said.

45

"Well now, Missy, I just come by to see how you're a-doin out here. And, well, I just wanted to ask you a itty-bitty question about your little brother."

Mr. Edwards looked uncomfortable, bent over like that with his greasy brown-gray hair hanging limp towards the dusty ground. It was a marvel that he didn't fall over with his bulge of a paunch hanging over, barely covered by his soiled white shirt straining at the buttons with its bulk. Sasa wondered what he might want with her...it was obvious that he did not really want to be so close to her lodge, since he made no effort to step inside. She thought for a short moment and decided to be bold. After all, there was no one to protect her but herself, and she was not afraid.

"My brother is dead, Mr. Edwards. What do you want to know?"

Wheezer began to stir on his pallet but only managed to move his head so he could see who was there. Then he started growling, a low, almost inaudible sound deep in his throat, while his lips curled to show one side of his powerful canines. Sasa gazed down at him in surprise, since that growl was the first sound he had made, other than wheezing. Then she looked back at Mr. Edwards with the dawning feeling that Wheezer did not like this man.

"Now, I didn't come to ruffle no feathers, little squaw. I just wanted to...sort of...see if he said anything, well anything about the Agency or me. We was kinda' friendly like and I miss the little warrior."

"You were friends with my brother?" she asked, incredulously. "I did not know that. If you were his friend, then why did you not come to see him when he was sick? Why did you not give us meat? No, Mr. Edwards, I do not think you were his friend, and this dog does not think you are my friend, either. Anything that my brother said was for me to hear. He had nothing to say to you, and now he never will. Please go away," she went on, barely able to contain her anger.

Mr. Edwards stood up with a frown on his face.

"Say, little squaw, how come you act so grown up? Don't you know you're a-talkin to the Indian Agent? Why, I could report you to the government. If you don't mind your manners, they might come and take you away. You ought to be nice to me, little squaw," he said, then stood for a few moments, looking straight at her with an intimidating stare.

Wheezer's growl became louder, and he started flailing his legs weakly, trying to get up.

"Mr. Edwards, my name is Sasa. Not 'little squaw'. Before he died, my father told me that an Indian Agent is only here to give the Cherokee the allotment. You are not a chief here and our chief said that we have our own government. What more can your white government do to me... they have already helped my family to die." She rose and stepped outside her lodge opening. "Do not come back here or I will call the headman in this camp. He will know what to do," Sasa demanded with gritted teeth and a firm chin, her arms crossed under her small breasts.

Mr. Edwards paced nervously a few steps, then he turned and walked away. Sasa thought it was very odd: what could a boy of only five summers have had to say about a man he barely knew, especially while he lay dying? It was something to think about. She had a feeling deep down that this was part of the puzzle, too, but there were still pieces missing. She also marveled at Wheezer. Maybe Poison Woman was right about him. She would continue to try and help him get well.

Sasa padded back to where Wheezer lay and knelt down beside him. He looked up at her with his all-knowing gaze.

She bent to whisper into his ear, and it flicked when her warm breath caressed it. "I am giving you a new name, a secret name that only you and I know. You are Black White Whiskers. I know you have been sent to me. My heart is glad."

Sasa scooted back from the dog's pallet and lay down on her own bed of newly pulled fragrant green grass. She retreated into herself to think about the fine times, before the Long Walk. Then, she had been the daughter of Sitting Bear Cub, so named for his gruff but playful manners, but also because he was mostly seen sitting and making traditional drums, flutes and such. She was proud of her family, and very proud of her mother, too. New Dove had been one of the tribe's finest artists, very skilled in the use of quills to decorate clothing and to make interesting designs on ceremonial dresses of the highest order.

"Now that I am alone, who will I be? How do I fit in the tribe?" she muttered to the silent lodge.

The dog lay on the pallet, twitching and wheezing with every intake and exhale he made. She noticed his nose was dripping so she gently wiped the mucus away. He slowly opened his fevered eyes.

"Yes, Wheezer is a good name. But you will become strong again, you'll get well and then you will not wheeze anymore," she told him. He closed his eyes and was peaceful.

Chapter 6

Wheezer lay on his pallet watching the girl go about her chores. He was beginning to feel a little better, but he still could not walk, and the girl, Sasa, was cleaning up after him when his bowels or bladder emptied. She had been very good to him, even kissed him. He still did not know where he was or how he got there, and the smells that came to him on the light breezes were totally unfamiliar. Sometimes, however, when he looked into the girl's deep brown-black eyes, he felt a sort of connection there, as if this person was supposed to be taking care of him. She would talk to him as she stroked his fur, but sometimes he could not understand her words and then other times she talked just like Jackson.

He soon figured out that she had given him a new name. That was okay. He could adapt to it, but he had never seen a place like this before, where some of the people lived outside or in grass-covered huts. As long as he had been living with Jackson, in fact, he had lived with him inside a big structure; there he used to have his own bed in Jackson's room, which was only one of many rooms in the house, but this girl only had one room and she slept on the ground with only a pile of grass for comfort. He also was having trouble getting used to the fact that this place had no door, only a flap of something hanging over a hole that people could walk through. It made him nervous because he could see people walk by, or stop to look at him. Today a man came to the hut and Wheezer could tell that he did not have good feelings for the girl, and that he could be dangerous, but he had no way to protect the girl. So, he had sent her a message instead, with his low growl, and then he had showed his teeth to the man to send him a message, too. Wheezer would be glad when he could get up again, so that he could protect this place better.

His feelings were all mixed up, for he wanted to find Jackson, but also knew that the girl needed him. He could sense that she was unhappy, even lonely. One time when she was changing the grass bedding under him, and her hand came close to his face, he licked it, giving her a kiss back for he wanted to show her that he appreciated her care. She answered him with a word he did not know...'wado'...which he supposed was her way of thanking him for that little bit of affection. Maybe tomorrow he would be able to walk around, but for tonight he would just let the girl feed him, clean him and stroke his fur

.

Anna Eloise Edwards paced the floor of her crude bedroom located at the back of her father's multi-room cabin, allotted to him by the branch of the War Department for all Indian affairs they had named The Bureau of Indian Affairs. She had heard vague rumors intimating it functioned as a shield for graft by the unscrupulous, and while she had no experience with such things, the accusations raised against the department by which her father had been commissioned still gave her unsettling thoughts.

Anna had lived for many years away from her father, having been sent off for refinement to a girls school in the East: Miss Dorothy Cadwell's Finishing School. Her mother had moved with her and taken apartments close by, so that she might not be without her mother's ministrations; more-over, Mrs. Edwards was wont to stay in the East anyway since that was where genteel society congregated. Now these last few months spent in this lonely place on the new Cherokee lands had brought Anna face to face with the fact that she and her father had grown very much apart, but in spite of this she was determined to give the matter a little more time.

When she was sent away, she had been an uncouth, inexperienced child. Now she was a polished young lady fit to enter into any well-bred society and she had blossomed into a tall young woman with creamy tallow colored hair, whose strong, firm and well-defined features framed clear hazel eyes. During her last year in school she had attended a number of balls and parties, where she had been courted by the most available bachelors and accepted as fit company by any young lady of the highest rank.

Her society peers were not fully aware of her father's character, as he was always away from home, so they took the gentility displayed by her fine mother and the reputation of her mother's family connections as a testament to her worthiness within their society circles. They took her into their confidences and trusted in her obviously refined de-meanor. At that point, she had decided that the relationship between her and her father needed to be reestablished.

Before coming to the Cherokee part of Indian Territory to be with her father, she had no idea that he would end up being a complete stranger to her; not only that, but she was sure he was involved in something unsavory., and she was at a loss about what to do. Since her mother was still in Boston, Anna was the only white woman in the area and her father asked her not to stray into the camp. A few nights ago, how-ever, he had woken her up in the dead of the night, request-ing that she take a note to a perfect stranger, a man who looked like an icon of society but was strange, none the less. Her father had made her promise not to open the note she carried to the stranger, and she obeyed him, but then she could not help but peek at the return note. It was that small peek that made her blood run cold. What on earth was her own father mixed up in and what was that matter of the frog he could not find? A frog?

She wished she had never asked to come to stay with him for a few months. Her mother, Clarissa Edwards, had married Anna's father when she was only seventeen. She said he had literally swept her off her feet. She had met him at a military ball, where he filled her dance card for all of the night's dances. At the time, he had been the young U.S. Army Lieutenant Samuel Franklin Edwards, stationed in Boston. Anna was an only child, who barely remembered her father being at home for any great length of time. She had been only twelve when she was sent to school. They had been living in St. Louis, that at the time was just a frontier town with an Army outpost, having moved there when Anna was a baby. Mother had said that his family was from Virginia, where they owned a small estate, and grew cotton.

While she paced and thought, more and more of those memories kept coming back to her, as well as questions that had always puzzled her...such as why Mother was almost never seen in public with him when she had been a child. Mother had moved with her to Boston when she went to school there, saying she wanted to be close to her daughter, but now Anna wondered what might really be going on between her parents. Deep down she knew, however. The uncouth and condescending manner of speech her father used when speaking to any mortal he deemed lower than himself, his uncleanliness and disheveled appearance, and the lecherous way he looked at the native or black servants he employed in the house, were by themselves elements enough to let her guess that her mother probably could no longer bear the embarrassment. If there had been any society here at all, Anna would have been horrified to introduce him.

She felt her life was coming unraveled. With a strong Methodist influence from her schooling, she believed in equality of all races, including the Indians, and what she could see here sickened her and broke her heart. She wanted to go forth and help some of these destitute families but had no resources to do so. She had never encountered such poverty and broken spirits. She abhorred the herding of all of these peoples onto lands not their own. The uprooting of an entire race of people was beyond her comprehension, but that was not the most urgent problem facing her now. She wanted to know what her father had done that required such secrecy. She knew her father did not put any stock in a woman's intelligence, so it was beyond him to worry about her knowing. He thought all women were stupid; that was plain from things he had said to her.

Anna was a good, hardworking Methodist woman with grace, intelligence, education and strong moral fiber. Attending balls and dances and being part of a fine, genteel society was fine, as far as it went, but now her moral standards were demanding that she did something--- anything--- to help these people. The answer to that was still eluding her just now, but she would not give up, and something was bound to turn up, sooner or later. Meanwhile she would covertly keep her eyes and ears open for any information she could glean to shed some light on what her father was hiding.

Chapter 7

Sasa woke to a bright and sunny early July day. This was the month of the Ripe Corn Moon, when they would have had the Green Corn Dance and the First Roasting of The Ears ceremony. There would be none of that this year, because there were no crops. She had thought about those things the night before.

Now she was lying on her pallet, listening to the morning noises before she ventured to open her eyes. As she slowly opened them she almost cried out at the sight of two bright brown eyes staring back at her and hovering over her face, upside down. Suddenly she felt a warm wet tongue swipe her cheek and she joyously bounded out of bed.

"Wheezer, you are up, you are well. I am so pleased. Poison Woman will be pleased, too," she cried, dancing around him and clapping her hands.

Wheezer wagged his tail, then sat on his bottom and suddenly closed his mouth and parted his lips to show his front teeth: a real smile, from a dog.

"Aiee, what is this, Wheezer? Who are you? No dog can smile; you cannot be a dog," she said as he jumped up and bounded for her.

She caught him in mid-jump and they tumbled backwards, laughing. As they wrestled on the floor of her lodge, Poison Woman scratched on the door cover, for as long as history is, it has never been deemed proper to step inside a lodge without scratching on the hide cover and waiting for an invitation to enter. Poison Woman could hear the commotion going on inside, and she had to fight the temptation to rush in, until she finally received her invitation, albeit a giggling one.

"Ah, what a sight. How can he be so well in just a few days? Look, he is so happy," the visitor said.

Turning from his playful romp with Sasa, Wheezer noticed Poison Woman and trotted up to her. This time he sat, then he held up his paw, carefully stretched his neck and said, "urrr wooo".

"What? I can't believe this," Poison Women squealed. "Sasa, that almost sounded like 'wado'. Am I going crazy? Look Sasa, he's asking me to shake his paw," she said, as she reverently knelt down to take Wheezer's paw in her hands.

Wheezer stepped closer and gave Poison Woman a very wet kiss on her wrinkled knobby brown chin, which had more than a few hairs on it.

"Oh, what a special dog. I have not been kissed in many years," laughed Poison Woman.

Wheezer wagged his tail as he started jumping around the lodge and nipping at Sasa's thin, stained, red calico skirt. After a time, he loped over to the pottery jug Sasa had borrowed from her neighbor to keep water in. He nudged the jug with his nose and looked back at Sasa. When she did not react, he used his claws to scratch at the jug, making a rasping sound which made the water slosh.

"He is asking for water," Sasa said, hurrying to give him some. "Poison Woman, what should I do? You said he has a human heart, and you were right, for he knows things no other dog knows. The camp will be afraid of him, but I can tell his heart is a good one. I think the Creator has sent him to me, so I don't want anyone to make him leave."

"I believe that you are right. The Creator has sent him. But I will tell the people in the camp that he is here to protect us. They will help with feeding him, then. Do not worry, Sasa, you have been given a great gift. Look, he goes back to his pallet. I believe he has had enough for one day. Feed him some of this meat that I saved for you and him. It will make you both strong. I was given a rabbit for the stew pot yesterday, and I kept some meat and the rabbit bones for you. I will be back tomorrow."

Poison Woman handed Sasa the bundle and walked out of the lodge. Wheezer watched her leave, then settled down for a sleep, exhaling a big sigh of satisfaction.

Sasa sat down beside him and opened the small bundle of meat and bones, setting aside a portion for Wheezer when he awoke. Settling back against the woven branches of the lodge wall, she slowly began to eat her portion, then she lay the tiny rabbit bones in her lap, moving them around with her finger while trying to figure out what she could use them for. She had very few tools to work with: a chipped piece of rock she used as an awl, a round cobble from the dry creek to use as a hammer stone, a piece of antler, its edge smoothed on sandstone to a fine edge, that she could use as a scraper, and a partially broken and discarded flint knife a neighbor threw away.

Many of the People were having to resort to the ancient ways in order to survive. Even if the tribe had been promised farm tools to farm, only a few Cherokee families had been given any. The Cherokee had been farming their land for centuries, and their wives had seen the good use for a home garden, but even if they had the tools, they still could not plant without seeds. Even so, Sasa was doing the best she could with what she had.

An idea began to form in her head. She took one of the thinnest bones and rubbed one end on a piece of sandstone until its point was very sharp, then she used her awl to scrape a hole at the top. Taking the flint knife, which had no point, but still had very sharp sides, she cut some thongs from her hide door cover, then she settled down to cut the bones into small tubes of various shapes, and put holes in them. At last she arranged the bone beads in a pleasing order and strung them on the thong. When she was done, she looked at the finished necklace; this would be for Wheezer, and it would show all who saw him that he

belonged here in the camp. With that done, she went outside to start the day's fire.

Mr. Samuel F. Edwards paced the floor, worried and
unable to quiet his forebodings. He knew what the note said,
but the neck on the chopping block was his own, not that
highfalutin, so-called *gentleman* from Georgia. Well, of
course he could always see to it that if he were ever found
out, he would howl out all he knew and reveal the plan, but
that bothered him, too. If he had thought of that, then so
had the *gentleman* and his cohorts. Oh yes, he was sure
there were many of them. All a-plottin and a-plannin their
deeds of money-grubbin. How in the world had he gotten
involved in all of this? If it hadn't been for all those gull-
durned gamblin debts the casinos back in Atlanta, Georgia
held against him, they would have never known he could be
bought. Being the owner of one of those casinos, the
gentleman had been quick to see the possibilities. His being
named an Indian Agent was supposed to be a step up, a
change in his fortunes, but...heck, it turned out to be just like
everythin else. His life had always been mired in mud and, it
seemed, would be forevermore, since he could not see a
way of getting out of this mess.
Now, Anna had shown up on his doorstep. What was
he supposed to do with her? For the life of him, he could not
figure out why she would want to see him. Her mother had
long since abandoned their marriage, years ago. Oh, Clarissa
had been such a looker, and he had thought he was makin
out like a bandit while being promoted to Lieutenant, but
then marryin into that well-to-do family had proved to be
one of the worst things he could have done. From that
moment on, he had known he could never measure up.
He had told Clarissa's parents that his family owned
an estate down in Virginia, and planted cotton. Well, they
did live in Virginia, but were only pig farmers on five acres of

rotten land. He had thought those blue-bloods would never know the difference, but after the wedding, they had some-how found out. Clarissa's father, using his influence with the U. S. Army, had quickly moved to have him assigned to the farthest reaches of the republic, on one campaign after another. Finally, he had resigned his commission, under a cloud of suspicion of dereliction of duty, and had been given this post. At first he had thought that havin access to all the allotments intended for all these filthy Cherokee, who should have died on the march, was the answer to his wildest dreams. How so many survived was beyond him, but he guessed he wouldn't have had a job if some of them had not shown up.

Now he was tormented by things that had gotten out of his control. The boy, for one, always lingered in the back of his mind: if he didn't find that gull-durned frog he had given him, he might be set for a hangin. Maybe not, since he was just an Indian, but still, he could not be sure, for if they put it all together, they would find out about the lootin of the allotments. He didn't much care to protect the *gentle-man*, who did not seem worried at all... but then, he could go on his merry way while Edwards sat here just waitin for the ax to fall. Something had to be done, he thought, and quick. He had even gone to see the boy's sister, at her rat trap of a lodge, but she had refused to talk to him. Did she know, or not? She kept on askin for the things in the allotments and it seemed pretty fishy that she would keep sayin stuff about it. Had the boy told her what he had seen that night behind the stable? He couldn't say, so what were his options? He could sit and wait, and let the chips fall where they may, or he could make a decision without the help of this high-and-mighty *gentleman*, and he could make sure of his continued situation. Yes, somethin to think about, ain't it?

Chapter 8

It was a beautiful summer morning, with warm breezes. Wheezer was feeling better today; he could tell that strength was coming back into his legs, thighs and neck. The girl, Sasa, had put a ring of bones around his neck this morning. He thought it meant that she would take care of him, but actually she was the one who needed being taken care of. He had not forgotten about Jackson. He missed him, but somehow, he knew Jackson would try to find him.

Then Sasa told him, in Jackson's speech, that they were going for a walk along a nearby creek, because she wanted to catch some fish for dinner. Wheezer thought he could scare up his own dinner and help Sasa, too, so out of the lodge they went, followed with curious eyes by the nearby residents as they went about their morning ablutions. Wheezer kept close to Sasa's heels since he did not know where he was and it would take time to learn the paths back to her lodge.

She had taken a long thin thong with a hook shaped bone on the end. Wheezer could smell the rabbit meat that she was going to use as bait. He had gone fishing with Jackson many times, so he knew the routine: she would eventually sit down on the bank of the creek and that would give him time to look for any critters nearby.

They arrived at the creek and walked down the bank a little way to find a good spot. Once Sasa was settled and had thrown her baited hook in the water, Wheezer sidled up to her, sat on his haunches as if he were sitting on a chair, with his tail out behind him as a balance, raised himself up on his hind legs and put both paws together, pumping them like he was swimming in air.

"What, Wheezer? What do you want?" Sasa laughed at the sight and at herself for asking such a question, as if he could answer her. "Oh, I think I know. Yes, go hunting, and if you find a rabbit, bring it to me for our dinner."

Wheezer understood the command and off he went at a fast trot, head stretched out forward and low to the ground, sniffing out his prey. Soon he was on the trail of a hidden nest of chipmunks. Finding the burrow, he swiftly started digging, scratching out large chunks of earth, leaves and debris camouflaging the nest. Not only do Jack Russells have stupendous noses for finding their prey, they also have very keen hearing. Wheezer could hear the squeaking and knew he was getting closer to the prize. Soon, he was laying a few feet away from the nest, devouring his meal. When he was done, he remembered Sasa's request and with hunger sated, he set off to find a rabbit. Rabbits were quicker and trickier; he would have to be careful and fast.

He found the scent of a rabbit and proceeded to creep close to its location, but just as he closed in on his prey, an unusually fast, long-eared, long-legged and large rabbit broke ground and scurried away. He had not reacted because of the odd looks of the creature. He would not miss the next time. He continued on a new trail and proceeded to get close on the scent.

In the meantime, Sasa sat on the bank of the creek in the morning sunshine. This was the most pleasant day she had experienced since she had arrived there. With Wheezer living with her, the dark days seemed to melt away. She had already caught several fish and had them lying on the ground behind her, pinned down with a stick run through each fish's mouth and embedded into the ground, so that they could not flip back into the creek. They were all small perches, but they would be tasty once roasted over the fire.

Being Cherokee, Sasa had been raised to pay attention to her surroundings and to their sounds, such as the chirping of the crickets and the songs of the birds. Suddenly, she became aware of an absolute silence; all sounds had stopped, and that usually meant that something other than an animal was stalking about. The feeling of bliss faded as she realized there were no birds singing or crickets chirping. Then, she heard behind her a sound of footsteps that could only belong to a human being and for a moment she froze in terror, not even daring to turn at all. Then she forced herself to react and picked up a rock that lay beside her; she could almost feel the stalker's breath down her neck when she finally turned, her hand already rising to throw the improvised missile. What she saw brought complete astonishment to her eyes and froze her arm in the air: a huge black man was coming toward her with a large Green River Knife in his hand, ready to plunge it into her back. The man barely had the time to move one more step toward her when a white blur streaked past her vision, lunging at the throat of the attacking stranger.

Wheezer had caught his rabbit, but as he was bringing back his kill to offer it to Sasa, he saw someone sneaking up on her from behind. He could smell the fear in the man and knew that he intended something bad. Dropping his rabbit, he catapulted himself toward the stranger, with vicious intent. The man had very dark skin, but Wheezer paid no attention to his appearance, because protecting Sasa was foremost on his mind. He flew through the air, hitting the man at shoulder height and sinking his teeth into his shoulder, then he hung on there with jaws of steel, jerking his head left and right in quick motions while the man danced in a circle, trying to get rid of him. The momentum of the swing finally dislodged Wheezer taking with him a large chunk of flesh from the man's shoulder.

Wheezer hit the ground and immediately sprang up for another try at this human prey, but as fast as he was, before he could get up again the man dropped his great knife and ran from the scene, leaving Sasa still sitting with the rock in her hand, held high above her head, in readiness for a great throw. Once she saw the outcome, Sasa let the rock drop, staring open-mouthed with disbelief.

"Wheezer! You are a warrior dog! You saved my life. That man was going to kill me and you saved me," she said, tears coming to her eyes.

Wheezer turned back a few steps, bent to retrieve Sasa's dinner and trotted back, walking up to her to lay the rabbit in her lap. Would wonders never cease? Wheezer was indeed a special dog. She would honor him tonight at their lodge. After dropping the rabbit in her lap, he then turned and retrieved the knife, holding it in his teeth by the handle and bringing it to her. Now, Sasa had a good knife which she could do many things with.

But, what of the attacking man? Why had he tried to hurt her? She had never seen him before; he was not one of the slaves the Cherokee had owned and that had walked the trail with them. The only black men Sasa did not know were the ones that worked for Mr. Edwards. Why would he want to hurt her? Was it because she had refused to invite Mr. Edwards into her lodge? Or because she would not tell him what Usti Yansa had told her before he died? Was this another part of the puzzle? For now, she and Wheezer would take their food back to the lodge and make their dinner. After dinner, she would flesh the rabbit's skin, stake it to dry, and soon she would have something warm for her feet.

Twilight darkened the sky when Jackson and Arch encountered the first lodges of the new Indian Territory. Arch was all smiles, hoping to see old friends and family members. The people in the lodges began to come out into the open, wondering who it might be that would come from that direction, the first travelers they had seen since they had arrived. As they wandered past the lodges single file with the pack mules tethered together following behind them, some shouts of joy erupted here and there as they were recognized. Arch stopped at a lodge whose occupant he knew, and the man pointed him west, directing him to go past a few more lodges, to where he would find some of his family.

As they approached the lodge to which they had been directed, a thin young man with a gaunt face and tattered clothes came out of a ramshackle lodge built of bent saplings and large sticks. Arch was so stunned he could not speak. Jackson recognized the man as Arch's brother, David Flint. Arch breathed a sigh of relief that his brother still lived. After an emotional greeting, David showed them where to picket their mules so that they would have grass and water, and he then invited them both into his lodge, even though it was obvious that he was living in very poor conditions. They unloaded the mules and left them to graze, placing their packs inside the small lodge where no fire burned as yet. Arch silently went outside the lodge to bring in sticks of wood from a pile he knew would be just outside the door flap, and proceeded to build a small fire in the middle of the lodge where a ring of stones lay cold and desolate.

There would be no talking until they could smoke the sacred pipe of peace and friendship as was the custom. Even though they had received a fairly good education from the missionaries, David and Arch--- both members of the Flint family, back in Georgia--- still held to many of the customs they were brought up to observe. David produced a small clay pipe from a parfleche hung on the wall at the back of the lodge, but then showed there was no tobacco for it. Traditionally, the Cherokee fashioned their pipes from aged river clay hardened in a hot fire, and used small river canes to make the stem. Jackson went to one of the packs, removed a twist of tobacco and gave it to David, who could then proceed with the welcoming ceremony. After raising the lighted pipe to the East, West, North and South, and then offering it to heaven and earth, he sat and drew from it once before he passed it to Jackson, who did the same. After the smoke, they could talk freely and learn what had happened to Arch's brother and the part of the family that had chosen to not go with him to breed mules in Arkansas. David, his brother had stayed with the tribe in Georgia because their elderly grandmother refused to leave and someone needed to look out for her. Her age was such she could not be left on her own.

David began to tell the story of the horrors he had experienced along the way.

"Arch, we had no idea what was going to happen. Chief Ridge had already gone to the west, one of the first families to go. Then a letter from Major General Scott came, promising the soldiers would be our friends and would treat us kindly. It said there would be food and provisions waiting for us all at the forts where we were going. But, nothing of the kind awaited us, only misery, and soon after, the deaths began. Arch, our grandmother died in the stockade, one of thirteen stockades constructed in Georgia not to mention the ones in North Carolina and Tennessee and Alabama. All told there was thirty-one stockades built for the purpose of the removal of the People. Some were built at strategic points to corral us like they do their cattle. All our lands, worldly goods, livestock and harvests were pillaged. Thousands of cattle, sheep, chickens and pigs were confiscated and there was absolutely nothing we could do. People were dragged from their fields, soldiers burst in on families eating dinner. I think some were able to escape into the mountains," David sobbed.

"What of our mother and father? Did you not go with them to the same stockade?" asked Arch.

"Yes, Arch, we did... but with all of the commotion we got separated from them. Later I learned that they died of pneumonia on a spit of land trying to cross the great Mississippi River. Since ice was choking the river, they had been stranded on the Illinois bank for at least a month with no lodges, food, blankets, shoes nor any comforts at all, trying to sleep on a bed of ice and snow. It seems to me they intended for us all to die. The soldiers stood by and just watched it happen. But some survived and now we must pick up the pieces," David went on, solemnly.

Arch bowed his head and began to sing a mourning song for his family, rocking back and forth with tears running down his face.

"What happened to the group caught on the ice?" Jackson asked quietly.

"The ones who were in that group said that, when the march was resumed, several of them died each day. They were pushed along by the soldiers, making them leave their dead loved ones lying beside the road. As far as I know, when I got here I was the only one of the family who survived the march. I thank the Creator that some of our family escaped by immigrating to Arkansas with you, Arch," David answered, placing his hand on Arch's shoulder.

Arch needed time to absorb all he had heard. Even if he still clung to many of the old ways, he rejoiced in a challenge. Now it looked as if what was left of his tribe was going to need as much help as he could give. He rose from where he sat and paced the dirt floor, thinking. Jackson was used to this behavior. Whenever there had been a seemingly insurmountable problem with starting their business out in the wilds of Arkansas, Arch had been the first to come up with choices, plans or just plain guts to do what needed to be done.

"Arch," he said, "it looks like your people have some immediate needs that we can help them with on this trip. We brought with us some tools. A long ax and a hatchet, a hammer, horse shoe nails, several Green River knives, canvas, pemmican, plus the means to hunt and possibly bring in some meat for the most needy."

They also carried extra clothing, soap, a few blankets and lucifers...those new small sticks with a sulfur mixture on the top that could be scratched and would instantly leap into flame. However, they were susceptible to dampness so they had also brought with them several flints and strikers. Arch had brought as much as his pack mule could carry, besides what Jackson had on his extra mule. They would need to make more trips, bring more mules.

In the meantime, Jackson had to see if he could find Jack. They had followed his tracks to this part of the camp, but lost the trail about a half mile from it. First, they would get some rest, however, for it was dark now and they needed what rest they could grab because they would be working their fingers to the bone beginning at the break of day.

"David, hasn't the Indian Agent given out food, clothing and tools? I didn't see any industry among the survivors when we walked in," said Jackson.

"That man is a slippery one. Even Chief Ross can't seem to get anything they promised us out of Mr. Samuel Edwards. For months, we have subsisted on whatever we could kill, and that was pretty hard without even knives to make bows and arrows with. Most of the time we just sit here, waiting for whatever else might hit us next," said David.

"But, David, my father looked over the list of provisions that were supposed to be here waiting for the People. Do you mean to tell me that the Agent is here, but without the provisions?" asked Jackson hotly.

"That is exactly what I am telling you. It has gotten so bad that our women are having to use the door flaps to re-sole our moccasins and some families don't even have that. We have flour, but nothing to eat with it. We have no livestock and no chickens for the eggs, so the flour is useless to us. We can't hunt so we have no fat to even fry flour and water bread. Anyway, most don't have anything to cook it in. I am grateful for the coffee, that keeps me going, but you can't live on coffee. We do have oats, and the women make a gruel with it every morning in the few pots we do have, then they pass it out among their nearest neighbors. But the corn meal they give us has bugs in it, and it doesn't even taste like corn meal once you mix it up with water. It leaves a white grit on your tongue and does not satisfy the belly," said David as he pointed to a sack of corn meal sitting to one side inside his lodge.

Jackson stepped quickly over and grabbed up the bag, pouring some of its contents in his hand and tasting it. A puzzled look came over his face as he worked it around in the palm of his hand, then a dawning understanding lit his eyes.

"David, this meal has been cut with chalk, besides all the bugs crawling around in it. If your people eat this for very long it will plug up their bellies and make them sick. My father will need to know all this. His company is financing some of the providers who supply the Indian Agents. You are supposed to have all sorts of things coming down from St. Louis. If the good supplies are not coming here, then where are they going? That's what I want to know," said Jackson, stepping over to his saddle bags and extracting a notepad and lead pencil.

"I am making a list of all you said. As soon as we are back to Van Buren, I will post a letter to my father, and leave it with the Commander at Fort Smith. It can go out with the post, weekly dispatched by steam boat. In the next few days, as we work here, I will keep good notes, and include as much information as I possibly can. In the meantime, David, go around to as many families as you can and collect the *corn meal*, before anyone gets sick and dies from eating it,"

Jackson said, then he rolled out his bedroll, sat and started making his notes before bedding down for the night. There would be a lot to do, first thing tomorrow.

Chapter 9

Sasa was a bit shaken by the unexpected attack, and equally surprised by Wheezer's response. She could think of no braver act by any animal or human. He had been fearless and brutal, a true Cherokee warrior. She could not imagine how it would feel like to have a chunk bitten out of her shoulder. The black man had fled, dripping blood as he went, but Wheezer had not followed him, choosing to remain on hand to protect her. What kind of spirit dog was he? She decided that she needed to mull over some of those questions. Maybe she could go to Poison Woman in the morning to see if she could help. She also wanted to tell both her and Medicine Man what had happened at the creek. Somebody was getting desperate, but she had no idea why.

The next dawn found her sitting just outside of Poison Woman's door, waiting for some sounds from inside to tell her someone was up and about on this fine sunny morning. The trees in the distance swayed in the hot breeze. Wheezer was sitting by her side and staring at the door... in fact, he never took his eyes off of it.

When Sasa finally heard sounds coming from within, she scratched on the door flap, waiting for someone to answer. Sasa expected Poison Woman to come to the threshold of the lodge, but it was Medicine Man who appeared instead. He took one look at the visitors, let the flap fall back down and huffed away without a word. Sasa scratched again, forcing him to come to the door once more.

"What do you want, Swan? I don't want to see you and I don't want to see that dog, either. I don't want to see anybody. I don't even want to see this camp or this land," he grumbled, then looked at the dog. "I can see he did not die. He is just a mangy cur, and stupid as well," he added.

Sasa could not let that pass. "You are wrong, Medicine Man. Wheezer is a spirit dog. I have seen it. Yesterday he saved my life. A man tried to kill me by the creek, but Wheezer jumped higher than a buck deer, he got hold of the man's shoulder and ripped out his flesh. The man ran away, but now Wheezer stays by my side no matter where I go."

Medicine Man was stunned." A spirit dog, you say? Are you sure he is not a witch?"

"No, he is not a witch, he is here to help the People, and you can talk to him, he will understand you. Poison Woman says he has a human heart. So far everything she said has proved to be true," Sasa explained.

"Bah! Poison Woman knows nothing. Why should I believe you? You are just a stupid girl. Go away with your stupid dog. That is all I have to say."

"He is not stupid, he is very smart," she answered.

Suddenly, Wheezer stood up and ran pell-mell into the lodge, darting under Medicine Man's legs. The man turned back into the lodge, yelling at the dog to get out, and let the door flap swing shut. A moment later the shouting stopped abruptly and Sasa decided to enter the lodge even though she had not been invited to do so. By the sounds she had heard she was afraid that the man had clubbed Wheezer. Upon entering, however, she found Medicine Man on his knees holding Wheezer's paw and shaking it. She blinked in astonishment.

"The dog ran in here, but when I turned around I saw my only blanket had caught fire. I t could have burned my whole lodge to the ground. He showed me the problem, so I am thanking him. Wheezer and I have made peace. You are right, Sasa, he is here to help us. If he could, we would have a smoke," he chuckled. "You may bring him here any, time. I will get to know this spirit dog named Wheezer."

The lodge door cover moved away again. Poison Woman stepped in. She looked at Wheezer, then at Medicine

Man, and back to the dog, aghast at what might be happening. Several things passed through her mind in the few seconds it took her to register the scene: her brother trying to kill the dog or trying to burn the dog's paw in the fire pit. None of those scenarios matched what her eyes were telling her, however.

Sasa spoke first.

"Wheezer saved the lodge from burning down. Your brother has invited us to come to visit any time we like," she said. Then she explained the previous day's events to Poison Woman, who found her story so fantastic that she had to sit down to take it all in.

"Who was the man? Why did he want to hurt you? I do not understand what is happening," she said, as she scratched her patchy scalp.

"This is a great puzzle and I must find what the answer is. I think the Creator sent Wheezer to help me do that. There are many things that have happened of late that do not make sense to me, but I will not stop looking for the answer. Wheezer will go where I go and he will protect me. Today I came to tell you these things, but also to ask you a question. Did you ever see my little brother being friendly with Mr. Edwards at any time?"

Poison Woman and Medicine Man looked at each other, both with concern in their eyes, and then they looked at Sasa. "I only know of one time that I saw them together," said Poison, Woman. "Mr. Edwards was giving the boy a toy. I did not see what kind of toy it was, but it was painted in bright colors. Your brother wrapped it in an old cloth and ran to your lodge. It puzzled me at the time because Mr. Edwards does not seem like a man to give gifts to little boys."

When Sasa was done with her visit, she was filled with new questions to add to the old ones. Wheezer trotted by her side with his head held high, his short little tail snapping back and forth in time with his gait, and his ears perked up with the tips falling forward. Sasa marveled at his beauty. She felt blessed. Wheezer made her believe that everything would work out. She could not explain why; it was just something that she felt deep down inside.

Sasa and Wheezer went back to their lodge. If Usti Yansa had a toy, why had she not seen it? She decided she would search every nook and cranny for this brightly colored toy. Wheezer looked up at her with searching eyes.

"You did not know my little brother. He is dead, but there is something bothering me about his death. The grandmother and grandfather say that they saw my brother accept a gift from that awful Mr. Edwards, so we are going to look for it now," she told him.

After that explanation, Wheezer walked beside her with a purpose, not questioning her again. When they both arrived at the lodge, ready to begin the search, however, Wheezer's ears perked up and he stood stock still, listening. Then he began running in circles, sniffing the ground and the air, as he went around lodges and poked his head inside. Sasa tried to catch up with him, thinking he had gone crazy. It was bad manners to look inside someone else's lodge, but no one came out to complain. His tail was wagging furiously as he skipped from here to there, and he voiced quiet yips and low moans as he went. Sasa kept him in sight, for whatever this was, it was important to Wheezer and that was enough for her.

This was Jackson's first experience of sleeping in a true Cherokee lodge, among many lodges of the people. When he awoke, he decided it was the best sleep he had had in a long while. He took a deep breath and smelled the pungent odor of many camp fires all around David's lodge. If every morning in a village was like this, he could see why the People had continued this way of life for so long.

Actually, it had been many years since the Cherokee experienced camping like this. Being in contact with the whites for so many decades had rubbed off new ways of living on the Cherokee. One of those was a change from these brush wigwams to log cabins. Indeed, all of Jackson's friends had lived in log cabins. However, when a people, any people, was stripped of everything, old traditions would reassert themselves, traditions that had been the difference between life and death for generations back. Now the People were getting a taste of how their old ones were brought up. It seemed natural, in a way, like having the skills to live this way embedded into a person's soul and brought out when most needed.

David had already risen and was tending the fire to heat some coffee in a clay pot.

"Good morning David," Jackson said. "What a sleep I had. I feel perfectly invigorated. I see Arch is also up and out. Probably going around and distributing the things he brought to help out."

"I am afraid it will take much more than a few loads on pack mules to really do much for us. You can't expect to take on the responsibility that should be of the Indian Agency. Last night I had a dream, Jackson. In the dream, my clan's spirit helper, the wolf, came to me and said that I needed to stop mourning the losses of my people. He said that I needed to find out why the People are not getting what the government promised to send. There is no time to lose. With no meat being prepared now, there will be no food for winter and we will all starve," said David matter-of-factually.

"I did not have a dream, but I also have been thinking about the problem. First, though, I think that I need to help some of the most destitute here. I will go around the lodges in this area and see what needs to be done. If someone is too old or too sick to build their own shelter, Arch and I will do it. We can go out with the mules and pull up grasses for beds, bring big loads of firewood and do some hunting, too. Then I plan on talking to that Mr. Edwards about the allotments. It is two weeks till the next delivery of your allotment and I will be here to see and witness it. My father financed many of the providers for supplying the Cherokee allotment program. If those goods are not reaching their intended destination, he will want to know why." said Jackson.

"I will be happy to help, also, I think that if I help you and the People see this, they will take heart and begin to help themselves, instead of sleeping the days away with no hope," replied David.

After a breakfast of oatmeal and some pemmican that Jackson had brought, they set out into the camp to see what could be done.

A little after mid-day, Jackson had just finished cutting sticks of firewood to lengths easier to manage for a family still sick after months of being there, when he felt his skin begin to goose-bump. The small hairs on the back of his neck began to lift, and his scalp felt as if small things were crawling in it. He looked around him, but no one else seemed to be alarmed in any way. But the feeling would not go away.

Jackson began to walk slowly around the camp, looking behind lodges and around wood piles. He had no idea what he was looking for, but he was compelled to keep looking. As he came out from behind a lodge, he was so startled by a quickly moving white blur that he almost stepped on it. They had almost collided when both dog and master recognized each other.

Wheezer took a leap straight up into Jackson's widespread arms, furiously licking his face and taking little nips at his cheek with the small teeth at the front of his muzzle. Likewise, Jackson was landing kisses whenever he could get a clear shot at the dog's face and head, laughing, ecstatic in their reunion.

Just as suddenly, a young Cherokee girl with short black hair almost ran into him, because she was looking the other way, searching for something. She brought herself up sharply and stood dumbfounded at the sight he and Jack offered, then her deep brown eyes gaped wide and her tawny skin paled noticeably.

"Hello," Jackson said, when he finally found his voice again. "I am Jackson. I am a friend of Arch Flint. My dog, Jack, got lost in the forest. We set out to find him and here he is."

Beginning to realize that she was going to lose her friend, Sasa held back the tears that were visible in her eyes.

"My name is Sasa. I found him, almost dead in the forest. He was bitten by a snake and was sick many days. He is a special dog. I named him Wheezer. He has come to help the People."

Noticing the tension in the air, Wheezer squirmed out of Jackson's arms to the ground, then instantly jumped into Sasa's arms, licking away the tears from her eyes.

"Well, I think maybe we should sit down and talk. Jack, eh...I mean, Wheezer seems to be telling you not to worry. Maybe he knows something I don't. Besides, I am very indebted to you for saving his life. You are right, he is a special dog, and I have missed him very much."

Wheezer jumped down from Sasa's arms, waiting patiently for them to talk, watching one, then the other and taking in everything that was said.

"He is also a warrior dog. Already he has saved my life when a man tried to sneak up behind me with a knife to kill me. Wheezer attacked him and took a large chunk from his shoulder. I have not seen the man again. He also saved Medicine Man and Poison Woman. Their lodge was going to burn down and he showed them in time to stop it. I do not want you to take him away. He has come to help us. I think you should let him choose. That is all I have to say," Sasa said as she turned to go, with her head drooping, tears running down her cheeks.

"Wait, wait," Jackson exclaimed, reaching out to take her hand. "Let us go someplace where we can talk about this. I want to know why a man was trying to kill you. If Jack...Wheezer has decided to help you; there must be a good reason. He is a very smart dog, almost a person, really. Is there a place we can go?" he asked.

"Well, I live alone; all my family are dead. My lodge is not very good; I have no tobacco to offer you, nor food. But you are welcome to come to my lodge."

She made eye contact with Jackson as if sizing him up, then dropped down on one knee and whispered to Wheezer.

"Don't worry, Wheezer, you are Spirit Whiskers and you will not leave until you have helped the People. I promise."

Wheezer licked her cheek in response.

With that, she stood up to lead Jackson to her lodge, with Wheezer trotting in the front, tail wagging, pleased as punch.

When they arrived at her lodge, Jackson noticed the utter poverty in which the girl lived. She possessed very little in the way of material things. It was evident, though, that she had a good character. She had saved Jack, or Wheezer, when most of the tribe would have seen him as meat. Then he remembered the shirt and the clay he found by Lee Creek.

"Sasa, I think I have something that is yours. I will be right back," he said as he hurried out of her lodge.

"What could you have of mine? We have only just met," she answered as he went past.

Jackson returned with the rolled up shirt and the heavy ball of red clay she had gathered in the forest. She looked up at him with tears shining in her eyes.

"I forgot about the clay as soon as I found Wheezer bleeding in the forest. I thank you for bringing it to me. I am made to believe, we are meant to come together. Maybe, you and Wheezer are here for a reason," she said, putting the bundle down at the back of the small lodge.

I have to be very careful here. She has come to love him, and it might crush her if I take him away, he thought. He would have to think long and hard about this, but first he needed to find out this girl's story. Something was not right here, and if there had been an attempt on Sasa's life, then he felt certain that something sinister was lurking here.

Since he was white, the son of an important man connected with the allotments, he could go places, do things, and ask questions that any of the People could not. Maybe, Wheezer getting lost was a good thing. Maybe, he really was here to help the People.

Chapter 10

The man sat in his usual comfy chair by the hearth, sipping an excellent Concord from the vineyards of New York. He was used to more luxurious surroundings, while this house in the backwater town of St. Louis was devoid of the usual amenities. Heaven forbid that he would have to be here for very long. This town had only begun to acquire the things that would attract a civilized society; even though they had just built a fine theater, St. Louis still was a frontier town and would probably always be just a wide spot in the road. There was one consolation to being here, however, and it was that there were very few people in St. Louis who knew him, which allowed him to walk the streets in anonymity, free to accomplish what he must, in order to hold his plan together. He never forgot he was here for a purpose, for he was forced to make plans to take care of a potential problem.

That was the hitch, though, the fact that he had left someone else in charge of dealing with the problem and now his plans were coming close to discovery. He had heard rumors of missing allotment funds, listened to the cry for an accounting, even joined in somewhat, but that was the last thing he wanted. One of the loudest was the financier Andrew Halley, who also belonged to his own club in Boston. The man wanted to shut him up for good. Fortunately, Mr. Halley had no clue to his connection to the allotments and was groping for answers. If his luck held, he would never find out. However, there was that one unknown thread that could unravel it all. There always was. He had no idea what that thread was, but just to be on the safe side he had opted for keeping quiet, allowing them to sniff around to no avail, and had bought a house in St. Louis to keep a calm eye on his nemesis.

Yes, he would keep quiet, unlike one of his lackeys, that bumbler Sam Edwards. Edwards was so goosey, he drew attention to himself. So far, he had not been a liability, but if that changed, then the man would take care of that as well. Just in the past six months, he had raked in one hundred thousand dollars, and that was his portion after paying all the go-betweens. He would put the money to good use back in Georgia. More land, more slaves and the trappings of the very rich made him a pillar of society there. Of course, it was unfortunate that he had personally had to get rid of that little boy, but the boy had witnessed something that the man could not allow to be repeated. That was a loose end taken care of. Edwards could not get that into his stupid head. He needed to just stop worrying over it and leave it alone.

Right now, his plan was to see what he could do about salving Andrew Halley's worries. He would find a way to surreptitiously meet him, at a restaurant or possibly at the St. Louis Court House, then strike up a conversation with him to feel him out on the subject. But if that did not work, then he would be forced to do something more permanent.

They say fate is fickle, but he thought it was down-right nasty. Everything he tried had blown up in his face. The Indian girl would not talk to him, so he had done the next best thing, but the man he sent had come back with a huge piece of flesh and muscle ripped out of his shoulder.

"Mr. Edwards, I's done did what you done told me to do. I's was quiet as a mouse I's was a-creepin up on her. Boss, she didn't move a-tall, an well, out from the forest come this huge beastes. I dunno, it could-a-been a bear, an it grabbed hold of my shoulder, an just was a-rippin and a-tearrin like there was no tomorra," said Billy.

"There just ain't nothin like that out there, Billy. I can see you've been hurt, but I think you're a-fibbin to me. Did

79

the dang girl see ya? I mean, did she get a good look at your face? Speak up, boy, don't just stand there openin and a-closin your mouth like some fly trap. Heck, you're as useless as tits on a boar hog," Mr. Edwards said as sweat poured off his oily face.

"I's don't think so, Boss. It all happens too quick like, suh. But I's showr don't want to go back there, no suhree."

"Well, go on back to the stables now, Billy. And don't yah let any of those Cherokees see yah, especially with that bandage on yah shoulder or I'll whip yah within an inch of your life now, yah hear?"

Now he was sitting at his desk, even more worried than before. He knew he should have let it be, but he just couldn't stand not knowing what that little boy had told his sister. He realized he would have to back off for a while. He'd stuck his neck out far enough for the time being. Maybe another opportunity would come along.

After all, he had no other reason to protect the man, other than to save himself. But, shouldn't he be doing more to protect him? He guessed it was possible for the man to leave him holding the bag. Well, if that happened, he would have no reason not to sing like a blasted bird.

Mr. Edwards took the keys out of his pocket and unlocked the side drawer of his desk. That was a drawer no one was allowed to look into, for he had things in it that might prove fatal for him and damaging to his family, and he had no desire to hurt his wife, Clarissa, or his daughter, Anna, even though they were more like strangers than family to him. However, he realized that any dislike his wife felt for him was probably justified, because he lied his way into their marriage. Soon, unless he was mistaken, Anna would hate him, too.

He could see she had a kind heart. Really, these were just stupid Indians that should have been wiped out by the Army long ago, but he had watched her on occasion, especially when she was observing the scum who came up to the agency begging for food, and he could see her heart go out to them. Without even a word, he knew she felt sorry for them, and the knowledge chafed at him.

This was his own daughter; something in him wanted her love and respect, which she would not give to him just because he said she must. His best chance would be to marry her off into some rich family. Ha! Impossible, out here in this god-forsaken Indian camp. Oh, why did she have to come here?

He took out of the drawer his Paterson Colt Percussion Revolver, the newest in Colt's line, one of the first pistols a person could shoot on the fly. It had a cylinder that held six rounds, plus six nipples for the percussion caps, and a shiny black seven and one-half inch barrel. Several boxes of .36 caliber rounds lay to the side, and the powder flask lay at the back of the drawer. Under the gun was a black silk-covered accounts book, containing a record of every cent he had fan-dangled, where it had gone, and who it had been given to, not to mention where it had come from. This was his security blanket, the one thing that the man in charge knew he had in his possession. That way, if he went down the river, then they all did, including the mastermind of the entire scheme. It was as simple as that. He gave the book a pat, putting it back, along with the Colt and rounds, and then he locked the drawer again.

He rose from his chair and walked over to the window that faced the majority of the lodges that sprung from the final delivery of Cherokees to Indian Territory. He watched them go about their daily chores, making do with whatever they could glean from the surrounding fields, forests and streams. There were so many who had died during the winter and could not have been buried in the hard frozen ground, and now that the spring thaw had come the rotting smell had been unbearable to endure. He'd had to ask the Army to come and dig trenches for mass graves. The day all those putrid corpses had been covered up, the Cherokee had set to wailing for more than three days. Apparently, they had not liked the notion of their dead being all piled on top of each other and covered up without ceremony or permission. Well, it didn't much matter who the dead ones were, anyway. This was just going to be a footnote in history, barely worth mentioning.

However, there was one question that was beginning to take form in his mind. Over the past few weeks he had begun to have the odd feeling of paddling upstream and losing ground. He couldn't really put his finger on the cause, but things were not working out how they should have. It had all started with the death of that little Cherokee boy. Edwards did not believe in ghosts, but there was something working against him and it was getting stronger. There was no direction in which he could attack, for he did not know what the force was. All he knew was that it disturbed him just the same, intruding into his dreams and coming up every day, some way or another. Could it be that Samuel Edwards was a doomed man?

Chapter 11

Jackson had spent a few days repairing lodges, hunting and handing the game over to the women to make jerky and pemmican out of the meat, as well as to flesh the hides to put to good use among the worst off and most needy. The chore seemed gargantuan in size. He knew he would not be able to do it all by himself, for there were too many to care for, but he simply had to try. In a few weeks, he would have to go back to his business in Van Buren, Arkansas, in order to keep things going there, but not before he figured out and assessed what was really happening here.

It was odd that Wheezer preferred to stay with Sasa in her lodge, rather than to come with Jackson to David's lodge. Jackson knew that the dog loved him very much, so there had to be a reason why he stuck to her, other than the fact that she had saved him. He had learned to respect the views of the Cherokee about things pertaining to nature and their surroundings. These things had meanings that white men could not comprehend. Sasa swore that Wheezer had a higher purpose here, and Jackson was beginning to believe it.

Sasa was a good little worker. Together with Wheezer, she was staying by Jackson's side, ready to act as an interpreter with the families that did not speak English, explaining what he was doing, and asking what their needs were. Jackson spoke basic Cherokee, however it would take up too much time to explain everything himself. Plus, she was one of their own, and they would feel much more comfortable with her words.

She helped in stacking kindling and firewood for the neediest lodges, starting camp fires and patching leaky brush wigwams. Jackson made sure she, as well as Wheezer, were fed, but sometimes the dog found his own meal when a disturbed rat would break cover and run, only to be caught in the jaws of the feisty terrier.

Arch was always at hand to help, either chopping heavy trees or dragging in kills that were too heavy for Jackson alone, and helping with more delicate communication than Sasa could manage; it was of great satisfaction for him to be able to do something good for his people, but at the same time, he was feeling a little guilty at not having risked his life on the Long Walk.

"Hey, Arch, I've got a buck deer ready to be dragged up here. It's back by that first bend of the creek, you know, by that stand of willows we had lunch at yesterday," Jackson said as he was dragging a doe he had shot, at the same time as the buck, to the waiting group of women who would butcher and prepare the meat for storage.

"Sure, Jackson, I will get to it when I get to it," said Arch glumly.

"Arch?" Jackson said as he pulled up beside him.

"Yup?"

"What's the matter? You sound perfectly down in the dumps. What's bothering you, brother?"

"Jackson, just let it be. I'll get over it; I just need to be alone with my thoughts." He paused a moment, then said, "I may go to the large double bend of Lee Creek, the one with the waterfall, for a swim and to cool off. If you want to join me there, I might be able to give you an answer by then. But now is not a good time. It will be good to talk later, anyway; I have some information I have gleaned from the People that might be of interest to you. OK?" Arch replied.

"Sure. Just let me know when you are ready and I will be there, Arch. I have some items of interest for you, as well." Jackson nodded as he prodded his mule to continue on with their chore.

Wheezer was glad in his heart. Now that his master, Jackson, was here, he might be able to help to protect Sasa. He had no way of knowing why someone had tried to hurt the girl, but he felt in his bones that more would be coming. The problem was getting Jackson to understand. How could he communicate to him that Sasa was in grave danger? Try as he might, it was not easy, when talking was beyond his ability. There was light at the end of the tunnel, however, because Jackson had already sensed that something was wrong. Wheezer did not understand all of the words, but he did understand the tones and inflections given to those words, and he knew Jackson was very concerned about something happening in this place.

His focus was mostly on Sasa. He was already sure of at least one enemy here and that was that Edwards person. Wheezer knew that he was dangerous...had felt it from the first moment he had laid eyes on him. No matter how much Edwards smiled, talked in soothing tones and professed his friendship, he knew the man was up to some bad deed. He could smell it. Why it had anything to do with Sasa, he could not fathom, for dogs are limited in the depth of their understanding.

However, he could use the assets he did have, to help, and those assets included that same keen sense of smell that allowed him to detect scents on the air that humans ignored. Since his ears did not lie down on his head but were perpetually perked up, very few noises went unnoticed. His sight was much better than any human's, not to mention other animals, and he had a mouth full of teeth any alligator would be proud of. Added to all that was a remarkable agility which allowed him to turn on one paw, virtually pirouetting to change direction, claws, that if allowed to grow, would combine with the strong muscles in his chest, would catapult him up a tree, and the wherewithal to stick to his prey no matter what. Yes, he was a formidable weapon. But there was one last thing that made him the best of helpers and that was his intelligence.

Reverend Russell claimed he had bred one of the smartest breeds of dogs that could be found anywhere and Wheezer was no exception to the rule. Wheezer often understood things of which Jackson had no idea. His brain was always working. He would cock his head when trying to figure something out, but once he had it, it was there for good.

Arch was already there when Jackson arrived. He was under the waterfall rinsing off his hair after rubbing and lathering it with that kind of soap weed known as the yucca plant. Jackson slid carefully in, not trusting what boulders might be on the bottom to knock him out if he jumped in.

The mid-summer twilight had a decidedly pink hue and the breeze was soft and silky. The light was fading fast, but the moon was already up on the opposite horizon. It was a quiet place, a place of trees lining the flowing Lee Creek, which joined with the Arkansas River at the same point where their mule breeding ranch stood. If they hadn't had the mules with them, they could have floated back home. In fact, it was not such a bad idea to float needed goods back to Indian Territory when the mules would not be needed any longer. Even the few rapids and waterfalls could be portaged around.

The scenery changed drastically where Lee Creek flowed over the Indian Territorial border. Even though the northeast corner was vastly greener than the rest of the territory, it still lacked the canopied forests, lush plant life and adequate rainfall the Arkansas side had. It was almost like flipping a switch. Heading towards Indian Territory, once you cleared the forest, it was like coming into a huge spacious theater of bright sun and dryer air, dust devils and tornadoes.

After a while of silent soaking, the pink hue vanished and the moon sparkled on the water. This was a perfect place to discuss important matters since the forest around them absorbed any sound, making their exchange private. Arch broke the ice.

"*O si yo,* Jackson." Cherokee for 'hello'.

"Hey, Arch, boy, isn't this fine? I think I had ten layers of dirt on me," said Jackson.

"I don't mind this, but I have become partial to a big tub of hot, steamy water with a large cool cup of herb tea," said Arch as he glanced over at Jackson, feeling hesitant to speak his mind.

"Well, it's a wonder anyone could stand the smell of me. It's a far cry from a good hot bath, though, but this has its own pleasures to recommend it," said Jackson, not knowing Arch was thinking the very same thing.

"You'd better get used to this for a while, until we can get back to the ranch. You know, I don't think we would be done by winter, even if we stayed here. There is just too much to do and not enough minutes in the day," said Arch.

"Yeah, I know; I've been trying to only take care of the most urgent needs. Only thing is, it's all urgent," replied Jackson.

Arch was quiet for a few moments while he gathered up what he wanted to spit out.

"Jackson, my friend, my people are going to have a really tough winter if something isn't done soon about the allotments. This is only one among many camps in the same situation. More will die if we don't find a way. And besides that, today I heard that there has been some violence within the Cherokee tribe. It seemed to involve the ones who moved here some years ago, you know, the ones they are calling 'The Old Settlers', and the new arrivals. They aren't agreeing on the structure of government, on the distribution

87

of the land and on whatever else you can throw in. It's not good for my people to be fighting between themselves.

"There is a faction that is very angry at 'The Treaty Party'... at those chiefs who signed the Treaty of New Echota which brought about the removal. You remember, it was Chief Ridge, Stand Watie, Elias Boudinot and several others. Chief John Ross, the rightful Head Chief and the other chiefs and headmen, along with the majority of the People, were against that treaty. The People blame those signers for the over four thousand deaths and their present state of poverty. Tempers are running high. You know, my people are not all that far removed from our primitive roots. I think something really bad is going to happen. That is what is eating me up inside. I don't think the Cherokee Nation can stand it. I am deeply afraid the Nation will be dissolved by the United States Government if an answer is not found," Arch replied.

"We will just have to try harder, then. The next allotments are scheduled in about a week. After that, we'll have to get back to our business. We've got some brood-mares that will come into heat. I need to be there. Sam won't be able to handle that part. He has only been with us for a few months," Jackson muttered.

"Yeah, that's the sad part, isn't it? My people did not dare to hope before we arrived. Now they have come back to life just to face tragedy again. It hurts my heart. I wish we could do more. Do you think we could come back in the fall to see them settled a little better?"

"Sure, Arch, we can, but that is really not the answer. These people should be getting help from the government, since that help has been promised. I know for a fact that my father holds the escrow accounts for the government. He has financed some of the business that needed working capital while they worked to put together the large orders of goods, and this could be a devastating blow to his firm if something unlawful is going on. So, we've got to find out where the breakdown is if we are to really help my father and your people," Jackson said as he looked over at Arch, a few strokes away from him in the creek.

"That brings us to the other thing I wanted to tell you. I heard from some of the families close to the agency office that they have seen a lot of visitors there over the last few weeks. And you're not going to like the next part. They also told me that they have seen a black man out by the stables with a bandage on his shoulder. He's so badly hurt that he can barely move his arm. I'm thinking that this man might be the one Sasa told us about. You know, the one that Jack...Wheezer attacked. That man is Edward's slave, one of several he has working for him. What do you think that means?" Arch asked, as he splashed water onto his broad copper shoulders.

"If it's true, it must mean that Edwards had something to do with it. But I don't know how. That is something we will have to determine while we are here, if we can. I must have some proof before I can say anything.

"What I wanted to tell you was something I heard today...that he has a grown daughter cooped up in that building and he won't let her out. She's not allowed to set foot in the camp nor talk to the Cherokees. They've seen her looking out at them like she is wishing she could talk to someone. You know, we've been here for a week and we haven't seen hide nor hair of Edwards. Maybe it's time I put on my visiting clothes, go over and introduce myself," Jackson said as he squeezed the water out of his long hair.

"Maybe so, Jackson, but be careful. I don't dare go; he won't look at me any different from the way he looks at the rest of my people, no better than a lowly worm. It wouldn't help you any in your investigation. You might want to take Wheezer with you, if you can convince him not to attack Edwards; he might come in handy, for you have no idea what you might come up against once you are inside."

"Well, that's something to think about. In the meantime, I have something I want you to do for me. It might be dangerous. Are you up for a little skullduggery?"

"I thought you'd never ask," Arch replied, as he pulled himself out of the water to dry off, then turned and added, "*Wado*."

Chapter 12

Anna felt sullen. She had been kept inside the house ever since her arrival over a month ago, and she was annoyed with her father for being so unreasonable. So far, she had not been able to find out anything concerning what her father was mixed up in, but she knew it was on his mind, whatever it was, for he was nervous and had taken to drinking a little more than she was used to seeing him doing. He was even bringing whiskey to the dinner table, now.

"Father, I so do want to go out of the house tomorrow. I want to meet some of these people, and see what I can do to help them. You may not know it, Father, but I volunteered to help the needy back in Boston. I was taught that it is our Christian duty to help when we see a need, and these people need help. I am excellent with a needle. I could be sewing clothes for some of the little ones and I..." pleaded Anna.

"Absolutely not, young lady," her father broke in. "It just ain't... uh... isn't proper for you to be a-wanderin around this here camp without a proper chaperon. I am too dang busy here at the agency, I just don't have the time to go on a pleasure walk with you, 'little sister'. If there was a gentleman here to take you, why, it would be all right, but I don't see that happening anytime soon. So, you might as well simmer down and stay out of my way. Anyway, I been a-thinkin' that maybe you'd be much better off if you was to go on back to Boston so you can do whatever voluntary works you want," Mr. Edwards blurted.

"Father, I can't believe you just said that to me. In my whole life I have spent less than a week at a time in your company. I am a grown woman, Father. Don't you think it is high time you got to know me? After all, I am your only offspring, your flesh and blood. I came out here to get to know you, but you don't want to even give me the time of

91

day. Is there something going on here that you have not been telling me? You have spent no time whatsoever with me since I came, and I am virtually a prisoner here," she complained, her cheeks taking on a rosy glow.

"Now see here, I don't have to tell you a dang thing about what I do. This here is official Indian Agency business. I am not gonna discuss any of it with you... why, you're just a woman! You need to learn to not put on fancy airs, Missy," Mr. Edwards exploded.

It was shaping up to being a fairly heated discussion when Mazy, the slave woman who cooked for them, came into the room to announce a visitor.

"Suh, theys a mans at the door, he say he wants to come for a visit. What should I tells him?" she said.

"Who in the devil would be coming at the dinner hour? Mazy, did you get the man's name?"

"Yes, suh, he say it is uh...Jackson Halley," she replied, unsure now if she was in trouble.

"Halley? Halley. That name rings a bell, but he couldn't possibly be Andrew Halley's son all the way from Boston. It is just too far-fetched," he said, more to himself than to anyone in the room, "Well, heck, I am done with dinner anyhow; take him on into the parlor, Mazy. Anna and I will be there directly," he pondered, and then, turning to Anna, "Now Missy, I expect you to mind your manners. If this is who I think it is, well, we just have to make sure he's fat and sassy when he leaves so he won't say anythin bad to his pap."

"Father, you paid for me to go to one of the finest finishing schools in the East. I think I can serve refreshments to anyone who might show up at this door," she said as she turned in a huff and walked to the parlor to greet their guest.

Anna had managed to enter the parlor, a very small sitting room set off to the right of the front door, seconds before her father, who had deigned to put on his dark gray cutaway coat for the guest. As always, Anna was properly attired to receive, as she was trained to do, regardless of where she might be. Today her dress was a simple fine white lightweight silk damask over pale blue taffeta, with large balloon sleeves and white crocheted lace at the collar and cuffs with pearl button accents down the front.

Together with her father, she stopped in front of the guest, who stood up to introduce himself.

"Hello, Mr. Edwards, my name is Jackson Halley, late of Van Buren, Arkansas, Sir."

"And this is Miss Anna Edwards, my daughter. Well," Mr. Edwards said, "I am pleased to meet you. Am I right in thinkin you are the son of Mr. Andrew Halley of Boston, the bank man?"

"Uh, yes, Sir, he is a financier, you are correct, Sir," Jackson nodded, while thinking that Edwards did not really seem to be a true gentlemen, as he had supposed, for his speech was uneducated. "I am here because my dog got lost in the forest. Happily, I was able to track him down here. I was very fortunate to find him being cared for by one of the fine Cherokee youngsters just arrived here, and I thought it was only proper to present myself to you, since I might stay at the camp for a few days longer, to visit with several families I am well acquainted with. My father has been doing business with the Cherokee people for years." As he spoke, he motioned to Wheezer, patiently sitting beside him but keeping intent eyes on Mr. Edwards. Wheezer's gaze never left Mr. Edwards' face, he did not utter a sound, then, finally satisfied it was safe, he turned to Anna and made a happy yip.

"Oh," she laughed, "How delightful. I adore animals, especially dogs. You say his name is Wheezer? A unique name for an unusual dog. He has intelligent eyes, I see, and he's looking straight at me. Most dogs will look everywhere other than in a person's eyes. How kind of you to bring him with you, Sir. If you don't mind changing to a chair, Mr. Halley, I shall sit on the settee so that Wheezer can sit with me," Anna said as she sat and patted the wooden seat. Wheezer jumped up onto it, then sat down again, putting his paw in Anna's lap.

Jackson beamed at her, noticing how pretty she was, with her light hair, white and blue dress and pale unblemished skin... she looked like an angel, and one with intelligence, too.

"I'm not fond of dogs myself, mangy creatures," said Edwards sourly. He never noticed how pretty his own daughter was and took no note now. His mind was on other things.

Wheezer growled and bared his teeth at him.

"But...but I will suffer the dog because it pleases Anna," Edwards said quickly, looking fearfully at Wheezer. "Now, how long do you expect to stay, Mr. Halley?"

"Only a week or two, Sir. I am helping out with some of the needs of my friends. Then I will have to go back to my business," answered Jackson.

He could not resist putting some pressure on Edwards. "I should still be here when it is time for the allotments to be given out," he went on. "I think my father might like a report on his investments. As you know, he is deeply concerned for the Cherokees, or what is left of that noble nation. How are they faring, Mr. Edwards?" he asked, hoping to draw Edwards out.

Mr. Edwards was startled, to say the least. He was not prepared to answer any questions about the allotments. This was surely the worst situation he could imagine being in.

"Uh...Well, I think they are a-doin well, for the most part. I ain't noticed any real problems. I'm sure that your services won't be needed so long, seein as how you need to get back, and all."

Anna gasped, then quickly covered her mouth with the tips of her fingers. Her father had just told a bold-faced lie.

"Oh, no problem, Mr. Edwards. I am happy to do it; I wanted a chance to walk through this camp, and possibly a few of the others spread around Indian Territory, to see of what help I might be. I am in no real hurry; my friend Wheezer has made some dandy friends here."

Wheezer made a low woof in his obvious acknowledgment of agreement.

Anna had a flashing thought, and even before giving it due consideration she voiced it straight out.

"Mr. Halley, since you are going to be here for a while, I wonder if I might prevail upon you to accompany me in a walk through the camp...say tomorrow? My father will only let me go if I am with a gentleman or lady of society, and I am sure Mr. Halley, you are the utmost in gentlemen. I can see no better opportunity than this."

Now it was Mr. Edwards' turn to gasp, only he made no attempt at concealing the rudeness of it.

"Now, my dear, we are askin too much of Mr. Halley. I am sure he has better things to do than walkin you around through a camp full of Indians." He could barely control his anger.

Jackson perked up, remembering the things said about Anna being held in the house. He quickly perceived her desire to be let out of the house.

"I see no problem at all," he answered. "I would be happy to accompany you. Would ten in the morning be suitable for you, Miss Edwards?"

Wheezer stood, wagging his tail. It was arranged and done before Mr. Edwards could say another word. He was not sure how it had happened, either. No matter: he had bigger fishes to fry

Chapter 13

Andrew Halley paced the floor of his office in St. Louis, Missouri. He had been hearing disturbing information from the grapevine that bothered him intensely. Now the letter from the Commander at Fort Smith confirmed it. What to do about it was the problem. He stopped at his second floor window. He could see the corner below where Market Street crossed 4th Street. He had always loved the view offered by this lofty perch, feeling a deep satisfaction at seeing the city grow, especially when he remembered that he had helped it grow by investing in many of its businesses. He took pride in the city, as well as pride in himself. He was a man of honor; unwilling to stoop to the money-grubbing practices used by many of the other financiers flooding into St. Louis.

This might be one of the hardest decisions he had ever had to make. He had just received a letter by steam boat packet, from the Fort Smith Commander. Some months ago, Andrew had asked the Commander to keep a protective eye on his son, whose business was just across the Arkansas, in the back country of Van Buren. He sat to reread the letter for the fifth time:

From:
Captain William Belknap
Commander
United States Army
Fort Smith, Arkansas

To:
Mr. Andrew Halley,
Halley's Financial
Market St. and 4th

St. Louis, Missouri

July 15, 1839

Dear Mr. Halley:

As requested, I am reporting on activities in the region that may affect your son and his business. I give the following report.

Approximately on June 26 th, Mr. Jackson Halley came to the fort to inquire of the whereabouts of the Cherokee lands of Indian Territory, and the route through the Arkansas woodlands due west of his mule ranch. He told us that his dog, Jack, had been lost in the forest, which necessitated his departure to find him. He also said that he and his business partner, Archibald Flint, would be taking a small mule train of supplies to the camps in order to provide added aid to the Cherokees newly arrived there.

To this date we have not heard back from Mr. Halley, and must assume that he is staying longer than planned. However, I feel it is my duty to mention a situation that Jackson might encounter while there. It has become known to us that the Cherokees are badly malnourished and that they are still dying in fairly large numbers. It is also reported that the provisions, which I am aware you are paying for out of the escrow set up by the War Department, are not reaching the intended destination. It is further now known that whatever provisions have been distributed among the Cherokees were badly flawed or inedible. Please make note, the Indian Agent for that part of Indian Territory is Mr. Samuel Edwards. Checking into Mr. Edwards' past credentials, I found that he left the Army under dubious circumstances. After further consideration of the facts, I have become concerned that Jackson may have walked into a dangerous situation.

I have no authority to take my troops into Indian Territory unless there is violence and can take action only if that violence is between white people. Any disturbances between the Indian population is strictly the responsibility of the tribal government of each Indian Nation. We, of course aid in relations between tribes, such as between the Cherokee and the Osage who have been enemies, and now endeavor to live side by side in Indian Territory. However, we must be careful not to make a tense situation worse. At the moment there is no proof of what is happening to the supplies and therefore we must be cautious.

We will continue to send you updated reports on both your son and the matter discussed.

Sincerely...

What was he to do about this terrible turn of affairs? If he did not find out what skullduggery was going on with the allotments, he could be ruined for good. Not to mention that his son Jackson could be in dire danger. He felt helpless, unnerved and betrayed. The best thing to do, he thought, would be to follow the chain that the orders for the allotments would follow. Each supplier took out a loan from Halley's to be able to keep the flow of goods going without draining their businesses dry. Halley's received payments from the U.S. War Department and was assigned the task of doling out the U.S. Government funds once the goods were delivered. Each supplier agreed to pay each portion of his cash flow loan every time payment to the suppliers from the government was completed. He knew there was no way of circumventing the flow of funds between the War Department and Halley's Financial escrow accounts, so he would have to start checking from his payment to the various businesses supplying the goods, to the shipment of those items and then finally the delivery and signature by the Indian Agent.

So much was at stake here, not just his son or his own business, but also the welfare of what was left of the Cherokee Nation. He knew that he was not the only financier who was backing up the businesses of delivering goods to Indian Territory. He also knew beyond a doubt, however, that this particular theft was happening in his part of the contract he and others had been awarded by the War Department. The problem could be wider spread than that, but he had no control over the other contracts, only his. Now he needed to follow the chain of command down to Edwards.

He pulled his black and gray checked claw-hammer coat from the waiting coat tree by the door, and put it on as he hurried down the stairs to an office set on the first floor, at the back of the building. This was the accounting department of his firm, the one place where he was most likely to find Mr. Horace Northrop, his chief accountant, head of the department. Horace kept all the records of who the contractors were that the War Department had assigned to supply their part of the allotments, as well as the payments made by the U.S. Government to buy what was agreed, according to the treaty with the Cherokees. This was where common sense told him he should start. He politely knocked on the office door before entering.

"Ah, Mr. Northrop, how are we today?" he said, in greeting.

"Mr. Halley, what a pleasure. Do come in; I was just looking over some receipts," Northrop answered, clearly surprised at seeing the owner in his office.

"Mr. Northrop, I am so sorry to interrupt your work, but I really do need a bit of information from you if you could spare me the time, sir," Halley went on, as he looked at his pocket watch.

"Why certainly, sir, whatever you need. I am at your service," Northrop replied.

"What I need, Mr. Northrop, is a list of all the names of the suppliers we selected to supply various items to the Cherokee in Indian Territory. I also need each supplier's address and the owner's name. Will that take a long time to produce, Mr. Northrop?"

"Actually, I have what you ask for here in my files. I even have a couple of duplicates," Northrop said immediately, reaching into his files to pull out the needed information. "Here we are. This is a list of our suppliers. At the right of their names are the cities they operate out of, but not necessarily where the goods are coming from. Then, in the next column is the list of the type and quantity of goods they are to supply. Lastly, you'll find the locations and dates they should present them to the various Indian Agents. We have received steady copies of invoices, along with their monthly payments on the first quarter of their loan withdrawal from our bank escrow. All seems to be current at this time, sir," replied Mr. Northrop.

Andrew took the list from Northrop's hand, scanning the names, dates and goods, as he stroked his chin, clicking his tongue against his upper teeth. Several of the suppliers were working out of other major cities in the East, but he found a few who were stationed in St. Louis, well within his reach to investigate. Out of three companies based within the city, the first was Jacob Sanderson. His company-- Sanderson's Drygoods and General Store-- supplies corn meal and oats. He decided to head over to Sanderson's store to see if he could have a quick word with Mr. Jacob Sanderson.

"Thank you, Mr. Northrop. I will get back to you if I need any further information. Also, as far as the companies on this list go, I want to hold off on giving them any more of their loan funds out of escrow until I personally sign off on it," he said as he looked down over his glasses at Mr. Northrop.

"But, sir, are you sure? I mean, really, they will be quite upset. What should I tell them?"

"Tell them that there is just a snag in the accounting process, or that Washington is late with their deposit to buy the goods, and we will get with them directly, but do not, under any circumstances, mention my checking into this list. Is that clear, Northrop?"

"Whatever you say, sir. Of course, I will rely on you. I just hope that I have not done anything that is causing you to make this, uh, investigation."

"No, no, no, Northrop. This has nothing to do with you, I am sure. However, you must keep this under your hat, so to speak. It is extremely important. Now, I will be out for today, and possibly tomorrow, as well. If any of these suppliers show up in your office and refuse your explanation, refer them to me. My assistant will take the messages," he said as he walked out of the door with the list in hand.

Chapter 14

Arch was unsure exactly how to proceed with Jackson's request, but he knew what he was expected to accomplish. He crept from the last of the lodges, going over barren ground trampled by a thousand feet, and headed for the side of the stables. It was just a few hours before dawn, so he had to work fast or risk exposure. The moon had already set, which was a blessing, but he was not sure of the precise location of the slave living quarters in the large agency compound. Reaching the stables, he put his back up against the dry boards, sucked in his breath, held it and listened for any nearby noises. Slowly he let his pent up breath flow out, making no sound whatsoever, then proceeded around the corner to the back of the building.

Silently slipping up behind Arch, another form crept. Every step Arch took, the shadowed form took, and every pause Arch made, the silent form made. The surreptitious follower made no move to close the distance between them, but continued on the same path Arch was taking.

Arch had a hunch the slave quarters for the single men would be located at the far back end of the stables, while slave families would probably be located nearer to the house, so that the women could be used as house servants. The stables building was fairly long, with few trees to hide behind, so if anyone were to come out of the back door there would be no way to avoid being seen. Steeling his resolve, Arch continued slinking silently toward the only door at the back of the building. He was so focused on the door, he never looked behind him, and he heard no noise to alert him of being followed.

His saliva caught in his throat, almost choking him, as he put his ear to the door, listening intently. He slowly turned the rusty knob, the sound of it seeming like a great screech in the night. Opening the door a crack, he again listened and heard the breathing of only one person, sound asleep. Finally inside, he left the door ajar, afraid of the sound it would make if he closed it behind him, and crept over to a bunk in the corner of the room. It was all too easy for the follower to slip into the room as well. An oil lamp, dimly burning from the next stall over, gave off an extremely eerie light, but it was just enough for Arch to see the sleeping form just ahead. He was relieved to find he had entered the correct room to find his quarry.

Silently he knelt next to Billy's sleeping form with the bandage glowing oddly in the pale light. Arch took out his knife and held it to Billy's throat before nudging him awake. When Billy opened his eyes, Arch clamped his sizable hand over the slave's mouth and whispered, "Don't utter a sound or you're a dead man." Billy nodded his understanding, then Arch removed his hand, but not the knife from Billy's throat.

"Who are you and what do you do here...whisper it!" asked Arch.

"I's Billy, da stables slave to Masta Edwards, suh."

"OK, Billy, now I want you to tell me truly the answer to this next question; a lie will not be good for your health."

"Yes, suh...yes, suh...whatever you says, suh."

"Now Billy, how did you get that bad wound on your shoulder?"

"A big beastes come an attacked me in yonder forest, suh."

"What were you doing out in the forest, Billy, and who told you to do it? Don't you dare lie to me."

"Oh, suh," Billy sobbed, "I knowd it was goin ta come back to haunt me, I knowd it."

"Out with it, Billy."

"OK, suh, OK. Masta Edwards toll me to folla dat gal an when she ain't lookin ta take a knife he give me an kilt her dead. But, suh, she OK, I's kinda' glad dat there beastes come an got me, cause I's didn't want ta do dat no how anyways. But, the Masta beat me ifn I don't do what he say."

"This is my last question Billy, so don't mess up now. Why did Mr. Edwards send you to kill the girl?"

"I's don't know, suh, I's swears, suh, I's don't. Masta just say go do it an I's tries ta, but dat banshee from the forest protected dat gal, an liked ta kilt me."

The follower finally made his move to come forward, slipping under Arch's arm that held the knife. Wheezer stood on his hind legs to get a better look at Billy. Billy's eyes locked with Wheezer's and the man froze with fear, sweat pouring from every pore, but Wheezer made no sound as he probed into Billy's soul.

"Eeeeeh," Billy squeaked as Arch finally noticed Wheezer's presence.

Arch smiled down on the dog, then pondered for a moment. Clearly, Billy had no knowledge of the reason he was made to attack Sasa, so before he left he would make sure of Billy's silence about this meeting.

"Billy, I am going to leave you now. Don't say any-thing about my coming here or I'll be sure to have this…uh… beastes here come and visit you again. You just pretend I was never here, OK?"

"Yes, suh, I's promises," Billy said, all aquiver.

Before Billy's last word had escaped his mouth, Arch and Wheezer were out of the door and gone. Billy didn't have the courage nor the desire to get up to see who the intruders were. He just rolled over, deciding it was just a bad dream after all.

Wheezer glided through the camp as if trotting on a cloud. No one noticed his passing, for all were asleep and would awaken only a couple of hours later when the sun would start peeking over the horizon far to the East. Wheezer, however, was not ready to call it a night. After

Arch patted him on the head, thanked him for his help and turned off the path towards his brother's lodge, he had continued, easily locating Sasa's lodge in the dark. Nudging the door cover aside with his long snout, he slipped inside, but instead of lying down on his pallet, he trotted over to Sasa's bed and began licking her face. Sasa batted the air above her as if a horse fly was pestering her, but Wheezer continued, determined to wake her up.

Finally, Sasa opened her eyes. Instead of being surprised, she reached over to pet Wheezer on the head, but he would have none of it and began snatching at Sasa's blanket, pulling it off and leaving it in the middle of the lodge before coming back to tug at her clothes.

"All right Wheezer, what is it? I am awake now, is someone hurt?" she asked the dog.

Wheezer moaned loudly in response.

"I don't understand, Wheezer. What do you want?" she looked around the lodge, not seeing anything amiss.

Wheezer paced around the room, pulling things out of their places with the firm grip of his teeth as he furtively checked behind each bundle, whining as he went. Sasa got up, following him around the lodge, trying to understand what he was looking for. Wheezer paused and pawed at a horn cup Sasa had stashed behind the food stores. He pulled it out and gripped it in his mouth tenderly, setting it at Sasa's feet; he knew that this was the only thing in the lodge that had a scent that was different from Sasa's, and yet, oddly similar. It was important to him.

"What's this? Why do you want a cup? I don't use this cup anymore; it belonged to my brother. It was the one thing that I did not bury with him. I needed something that was his," she said as she picked up the black bison horn cup.

She turned it over and over in her small hands. Wheezer wagged his tail, trying to infuse his thoughts into her while encouraging her to get the point of his search. She sat down in the same spot she had stood in, thinking about the times she had filled this cup with good broth or stew... but nothing had kept her brother alive, nothing. Wheezer sat in front of her, putting his paw on the cup while he looked deep into Sasa's dark eyes, pleading with her to understand. Then, as if dawn were coming up inside the lodge, she began to remember. She remembered asking Wheezer, many days before, to help her find her brother's toy, the one he was supposed to have gotten from Mr. Edwards.

"Wheezer, this cup has my brother's scent on it. Can you find anything else that was his? Is that what you want us to do?" she asked.

The dog stood, wagging his tail furiously, yipping several times, making sure she grasped his meaning.

"Yes. We can do this now. In fact, this is the best time to do it, since there is no one to interrupt us or get in our way. I will follow behind as you search. Find me anything else that has the same scent that is on this cup," she instructed, which was really unnecessary, since it was his idea in the first place.

He began inside the lodge to the left of the door, sniffing and moving inch by inch. Wheezer put his nose to the ground, swinging from side to side, sniffing, then snorting to clear his nose of the dirt. Sometimes he would stop to dig with his strong claws, but finding nothing of note, they continued around, until they came to the other side of the lodge door. Instead of stopping, Wheezer slipped out of the lodge, continuing at the same slow pace all around the outside until they reached a spot directly behind the lodge. There he stopped abruptly, taking long sniffs and breathing deeply, then he started to dig, this time with added vigor. Before long a small wrapped bundle appeared just under a few inches of loose soil. Once he had uncovered it, Sasa reached down to pluck the bundle out of the sandy soil. Handling the bundle with care, Sasa folded back the layers of what looked like a dirty rag. Sasa came to the nucleus of the dirty bundle. Gently picking up the object from its bed in the rags, Sasa held it up in the faint light of pre-dawn, gasping aloud as her mind immediately recognized the shape: she could not see the color of the object, but it was obviously the carving of a jumping frog with its legs stretched out behind him, and it was no longer than the length of her hand. Still on her knees, she clutched it to her breast as an electrified jolt ran through her body. Somehow, this frog was important.

Sasa laid the carved frog back on the dirty rag lying in the dirt, as Wheezer bent to take a sniff. What started as a low moan became a menacing growl as Wheezer peered at the frog. Sasa could see better now that the dawn was breaking. Wheezer's body was trembling as if he were freezing, the stiff hairs that ran down his back were standing straight up and his short stubby tail was vibrating. Sasa became frightened, not so much of Wheezer, but with him. She sensed down in her core that there was something about the carving that was dangerous, but what, she could not say. Quickly she re-wrapped it back into the rotten rag, then stroked Wheezer's fur to settle him down. Wheezer gazed up at her, torn between ripping the bundle from her hands to rebury it in the soil or sticking with Sasa every moment to protect her. Wheezer realized he had little choice, knowing Sasa needed this thing.

"OK, boy, let's go back inside. You have done well again, Black White Whiskers. We will have a better look at this thing when the sun is high. I will take it to Jackson, and maybe he will know what it is or why it was so important to my brother," she whispered to Wheezer.

Upon entering the lodge, Wheezer went to his pallet, but instead of sleeping, he kept a wary eye on the wrapped bundle as he waited for the day to begin. He would have another day in which to help his two favorite people in his world.

Chapter 15

Sasa had overslept, not awakening until well after sunrise, and now she felt groggy as she yawned, rubbing sand out of her eyes. Wheezer had not moved from where he had laid down in the wee hours at the beginning of dawn. His eyes shifted from side to side, a wrinkle forming at his brow between his eyes, showing his concern. As Sasa prepared something to eat, outside at the fire, she noticed that Wheezer did not follow her as he had always done before, and she looked over her shoulder at him, still lying wide eyed on his pallet. She finished preparing the venison stew, using strips of dried deer meat and wild onions. This morning, there would be no need for Wheezer to go out into the forest to find another rabbit. Jackson had distributed large chunks of the game he had shot to those most in need in the camp, Sasa and Wheezer included. She had made enough stew for them both.

She placed portions of stew in two wooden bowls Arch had brought to her to add to their limited eating utensils. Gently, she blew on Wheezer's portion before she handed it over to him. He got up, stretched, and began to eat, but continued to watch the bundle. By now, his morning routine would have included a trip to the edge of camp to relieve himself, but he made no move toward the door.

"What is wrong, Wheezer? Are you sick?" said Sasa.

Wheezer just stared up at her, and then back at the bundle on the floor. The motion made it obvious to Sasa that Wheezer was anxious about the bundle they had found behind the lodge.

"Finish eating, then we will go to find Jackson," she murmured, stroking the soft fur at the top of his head. "I know you are worried, but I don't understand why. Maybe Jackson will understand what you are worried about."

After breakfast, she wiped out their bowls with a piece of deer skin, put the pot of leftover stew to the back of the lodge and covered it with an old piece of her father's clothes. As she bent to retrieve the bundle, Wheezer began to moan and followed her out into the sunlight.

She went about looking for Jackson, or for any of his pack mules, to see where he might be working that day. She was brought up short suddenly when she spotted him coming out of the Agency's quarters with a young woman. Sasa had heard rumors about a woman being kept prisoner, but evidently she was prisoner no more. The woman was lithe and beautiful, with creamy white skin, pale eyes and hair the color of winter wheat. She wore a pale tan dress with a short-waisted jacket to match, and she carried a white lace parasol to shield her delicate skin from exposure to the harsh sun. Sasa had seen women in Georgia towns that dressed in a similar fashion, but they rarely came onto Cherokee lands. Now she was seeing this apparition as they walked among the destitute hovels and homeless people of her tribe.

Sasa was reluctant to approach Jackson as he walked with that fine lady, but the matter was serious, and she simply had to have Jackson's advice and help with what they had found. Wheezer stood beside her, not taking his eyes from the bundle. His tail did not wag, but stayed erect and stiff. Sasa decided to follow the two along as they went walking into the midst of the mass of dwellings.

"Is it not a nice day, Miss Edwards? I believe it will be quite hot by the afternoon. You will definitely need your parasol. You only need look at the skin on my face to know what the Indian Territory's bright sunlight can do," Jackson said, trying to make small talk. He felt he was a little out of practice, for it had been some months since his last having to address a lady.

"Oh, please call me Anna. No need to be so formal. I know I must look silly walking around with this parasol, but my skin is so pale! I suppose if I had more opportunities to get out, I might accustom myself to this sun. As it is, my father absolutely refuses to allow me out without a chaperon, and I think I am about to die of boredom," Anna replied, as she looked boldly at her escort.

"All right, Anna. Please call me Jackson," he nodded, wondering how he would be able to escort her and yet do the things needed to be done in the camp. "To tell you the truth, Anna, I would be very pleased to escort you on a daily basis, but I am afraid I may not be available. There is so much to do here, and we do not have enough time to do it in. Arch and I, oh, excuse me, I'm referring to Archibald Flint, my best friend and business partner, who is here with me. He has family in the camp. Anyway, Arch and I go out almost daily to hunt because the camp is desperate for meat. Then there are the ones who are too sick to make shelters. As much as we are able, before we go back to Arkansas, we will build shelters for them as well as repair others already existing. That means cutting down trees, organizing the preparing of the skins from our kills to be used on the lodges and trying to do it as quickly as possible."

"Did I hear you correctly, Jackson? Are there sick people here?"

Jackson was startled. How could she live so close to the camp and not know there were people dying left and right?

"Why, uh...yes, Anna. There are many who are severely sick in this camp as well as in other camps all through Indian Territory. There have been a large number of deaths, and I assume there will be more. I am not a doctor, but I believe most of their illnesses to be the result of malnutrition. These people should be getting more food than they are. They are defenseless against the elements, as well," he replied. He was cautious about giving out too much information. He had his suspicions about her father, but he had no idea if she had a part in any problems here. He sincerely hoped she did not, for he was hoping to get to know her better.

"Oh, my. I really had no idea, Jackson. I wish there was something I could do to contribute to your effort," she said without guile.

"I see your heart is in the right place, Anna. But I can't think of what you might be able to do. Most of it is dirty, smelly work. These lodges are sheltering people just waiting to die. It is cruel and heartbreaking to witness. I don't think a lady like you would be able to withstand the difficulties."

Anna drew herself up to her full height of five feet two inches, her jaw hardening as her eyes flashed like a flint striker.

"I assure you, Jackson, that I am completely capable of doing what needs to be done, here or anywhere else there are people who need care and succor. I volunteer on a regular basis back in Boston. I help the poor and the destitute, and that includes cleaning sick rooms, bathing patients and taking out slops, if I have to. I am no shrinking violet, sir. I may not be able to fell a tree or shoot a deer, but I am a very kind, caring individual with no little knowledge of how to take care of the sick. I would deem it an insult if you excluded me on the basis that I am a lady," Anna seethed.

"Please forgive my blunder, Anna. No insult intended," he apologized, running a hand through his sandy brown hair. "I had no idea of your background. I was only going on what I know of the ladies of society. They might feel good about taking some jars of vegetable broth around to the poor, but they normally would not stoop to the menial tasks needed here. Not to mention the fact that we are talking about helping in a camp of Cherokee Indians."

Anna relaxed a bit, and a faint smile touched her lips.

"Oh, goodness. You had no way of knowing. I should not have jumped at you so. It's just that my father has made such a concerted effort to keep me isolated that I think I'm about to crack under the strain. But I truly would like to be of help." Anna stopped to ponder for a moment, then she added, "Could you always call on me no later than ten in the morning? I have duties I must take care of as a help to my father, but he usually forgets I'm alive right after breakfast. I don't intend to discuss my intentions with him because I don't want to give him the chance to forbid me doing this, plus if I abide by his own rule of being escorted, he can't object without seeming a fool, and if I get back home in plenty of time to clean up and help with presenting his dinner, he may not even notice. For a while, at least. Are you willing to help me so that I can help you?" she asked, gazing up into his earnest blue eyes, as if searching for something hidden in them.

Jackson hesitated. If he allowed Anna to help in the camp, she might figure out that he was investigating her father's connection to the missing allotment goods, and while he had no wish to hurt her, he had no intention of letting anything stop him from finding out the answer to the mystery. He had no way to stop her, however. She had every right to walk wherever she pleased, in fact, more right than he, since she was the Agent's daughter. He held his hand to his brow as he gazed at the sun's position, trying to think of some way to find out what she really knew about all this. Finally, a few threads of thought surfaced. He turned back to Anna to make a first tentative step towards resolving the dilemma.

"I can't think of anything I would like better, Anna, but I get the feeling that you are at odds with your father. I don't mean to pry, but there are some things here that might be dangerous for you. Is there some other reason why your father might not want you to go into the camp?" he asked.

"You know, that's something that I've asked myself. He seems very unreasonable on the subject. You would think he would want to spend more time with me, but only yesterday, just before you arrived to visit us, he told me he wanted me to go back to Boston. He has spent little to no time with me and when he does, he is surly, secretive and suspicious of me. There are certain places in the house where I am not allowed to go, like his office. I can't think for the life of me what he thinks I could do to mess anything up. I don't mind telling you, that I'm not only bored, but lonely, too. I would truly consider it a privilege to help out here. At least I will have something to show for the time I have wasted, sitting in that house doing absolutely nothing," Anna said, with hope written on her face.

Now came the hard questions Jackson had to ask. He looked around them to make sure none of Edwards' workers were about. He could only see Sasa and Wheezer a few hundred feet behind. He took note of her presence, then turned back to Anna.

"I am sorry that I have to bring this subject up. You may have no idea what I'm talking about, but I have to ask anyway. Anna, something is going on in the camp that is disturbing. I am not sure to what extent your father might be mixed up in it, but so far it doesn't look good. Part of what I'm doing here is investigating what might be a very serious problem, especially for your father," he said, with concern written on his sunburned face.

Anna gasped, catching her breath, then she coughed violently while Jackson patted her back to help her regain her breathing. Once the spell passed, she turned her gaze towards the far off horizon, to the west. Her eyes became misty and her lips trembled slightly. Then she straightened her spine, leveled her shoulders and turned to Jackson with conviction glowing in her visage.

"Jackson, I have to tell you...I am worried too. I know my father is mixed up in something here, but it is so ominous I have been reluctant to think about what it might mean for him, me or the poor souls living here in Indian Territory," she said as she looked around, now noticing Sasa coming closer to where they stood talking. "I...I don't think we should talk about this now. If we can find a more private place later today, I will tell you all I know, which isn't much, but is enough to make my blood run cold."

It would be difficult for her to determine what to tell him. She just hoped he would have some answers for her. At the same time, Jackson was a truly handsome man, but also a good man. She could tell that instinctively. But where did her loyalties lie? Did her father deserve unfailing loyalty from his only progeny, or did a man, any man, have to earn the loyalty others gave to him? The only thing she knew for certain was that she would not be a party to anything illegal, and that was something she needed to make sure of. No matter what, she had to be true to herself.

Chapter 16

As Jackson was nodding to Anna in the affirmative, Sasa finally came forward. Wheezer barked his hello, but he didn't jump up to get his customary hugs and kisses from Jackson. There was no time for Jackson to wonder about it, but it struck an off key note that registered somewhere in his being. Sasa appeared concerned, while Wheezer held his attention on a bundle she carried carefully in her hands.

"*O si yo*, Sasa. I don't think you have met Mr. Edwards' daughter. Sasa, this is Miss Anna Edwards. Anna, this is Sasa, which means 'Swan' in Cherokee," said Jackson.

All of a sudden, Sasa felt very shy. She wanted to talk to Jackson about their important find, but should she speak of it in front of this stranger? Quickly, she regained her equilibrium. It was considered very rude not to be hospitable to a stranger introduced by a friend.

"I am pleased to know you, Miss Anna Edwards," she said, not knowing just how to use the stranger's name.

"Oh, just call me Anna. I am so happy to meet you, as well. And I already know Wheezer, a truly remarkable dog," Anna said.

The fact that Anna liked Wheezer and, it seemed, Wheezer liked Anna, made her feel a little less apprehensive. The news was too hard to hold back, so she plunged on.

"Thank you, Anna. Jackson, we have something important to tell you. Do you have time to come to my lodge?" she asked, coming to the decision that it would be better to talk of this where she could be candid with Jackson.

"Sure, Sasa. Would it be all right if Anna accompanied us?" said Jackson.

"I, well, I suppose it will be all right. Wheezer is not worried, so it is all right with me," Sasa said, as she turned to lead the way to her lodge.

Jackson offered his arm to Anna, who took it.

"I know you are a gentleman," she whispered to him, "but in the future, while I am working in the camp, you will not need to be so formal. You will not offend me if you don't offer your arm when I walk from one lodge to another. It's just not practical, Jackson."

Jackson nodded his assent as a pleasant wide grin spread from his mouth to his bright eyes. He was pleased that he would not have to babysit her every minute.

The four arrived at Sasa's lodge and entered it without hesitation. Sasa pulled the door cover down, but shifted it to one side to allow some light in. They gathered around the bundle and got down on their knees with Wheezer crowding in the circle, his eyes stern and focused on the bundle as if what it concealed would jump out of the rag it was wrapped in to attack them at any moment. Sasa laid the bundle on the dirt floor of the lodge where a beam of light struck the form, and began to unwrap the dirty rag as she explained what had occurred the night before. Jackson's face showed his curiosity, but also that he could not think of why this would be of such importance. Seeing his expression, Sasa decided it was better to give them a little background information.

"Jackson, I knew nothing of this thing when my brother died. Later, as I told you before, Mr. Edwards came here, asking strange questions. He wanted to know if my little brother had said anything about him before he died. I did not know they had ever met, but Mr. Edwards claimed he and my brother were good friends. Something kept tugging at me, so I asked Ada Hi Hi, Poison Woman, and her brother Di Damv Wi S Gi or Medicine Man, who now lets me call him by his before name, Deer Caller," she said, explaining the names for Anna's benefit. She then waited for Anna to nod, showing that she understood so far.

"It was Poison Woman and her brother who told me they had seen my brother receive something like a toy from Mr. Edwards. They thought it was strange, but did not interfere. They were both surprised when I asked if they had seen my brother and Mr. Edwards together. I found this thing out on the day Wheezer and I found you in the camp, Jackson," Sasa paused to take a breath, then Jackson interrupted.

"I don't understand, Sasa. What did Mr. Edwards say that made you concerned?" he asked.

"I am getting to that part, Jackson. Let me tell this in my own way, or I will forget some of it," she replied, a little disoriented at having to remember where she had left off. Jackson nodded his assent, while Anna smiled at Sasa to encourage her to continue.

"When Mr. Edwards came, I was taking care of Wheezer here in the lodge. My lodge opening was not covered when he came. He stood outside and did not ask to be invited into my lodge. Wheezer was lying close to the opening. Even while Mr. Edwards was saying he had been a friend of my brother, Wheezer was telling me that he was our enemy, so I did not answer any of his questions. When I asked him, if he had been a friend to my brother, then why he did not bring us meat to help my brother live, he went away and I could see he was very angry.

"Last night Wheezer woke me up a little before dawn. He began to search for something in the lodge and found my brother's cup. That reminded me of the day we first saw you, I asked Wheezer to help me find the toy my brother was seen with, but then forgot about it. So, last night, I asked Wheezer to smell the cup, since it had my brother's scent on it, and we began searching for the toy. Wheezer finally found this bundle buried behind the lodge, not very deep, wrapped in this old rag. Let me show it to you," Sasa finished.

Wheezer began to tremble, his eyes glued to the bundle, as Sasa began to unwrap it layer by layer. Finally, the sun rested on the form of the jumping frog, painted in varying shades of green and splashes of yellow.

"Now that is an unusual toy. It looks carved, like it was hand made by someone. Did you ever see Usti Yansa with this, Sasa?" Jackson said, as he gazed down on the frog on the ground.

"No, never. And he never told me he had a toy, never told me he knew Mr. Edwards. But Jackson, he did say something to me before he died. It was not about Mr. Edwards, though," replied Sasa.

Anna interrupted, "Usti Yansa? What does that mean?"

"That is Sasa's brother's name. It means Little Buffalo, Anna, but it is forbidden for Sasa to say his name out loud for at least a year. I didn't know his name until Arch's brother, David, told me about the deaths in Sasa's family. Go ahead, Sasa, what did your brother say?" Jackson asked.

"Well, this was before he quit talking completely. He said, *"I don't know why it is not working. Maybe I am not doing it right or enough times."* When I asked him what he meant, he would not tell me," Sasa answered, as she looked at Jackson to see if he had an explanation.

But Jackson was not looking at Sasa at that moment. He was noticing something odd about the frog carving. On the surface of the wood, on top of the painted sheen, was a white haziness he couldn't quite define. He reached down to gently lift the frog to examine it closer. Wheezer began to growl, his eyes trained on the frog, but Jackson took no note of his dog's reaction as he lifted the frog to his nose to see if it had a smell. At that moment, however, Wheezer exploded from his place in the circle; hurling himself in the air, he used his head to butt the frog from Jackson's hand, then he placed himself over the spot where the frog now rested and violently barked his warning to stay away.

Suddenly remembering how he had attacked the man who tried to kill her, Sasa immediately understood what Wheezer was trying to say.

"Jackson, Wheezer says that it is dangerous. There is something about the frog that is bad. He is trying to protect you, just as he protected me."

Jackson put his hand up to pat the air as he spoke soothingly to Wheezer.

"Shoosh, boy, I see. This is a bad thing. OK, OK, I won't put it up to my mouth. I will be careful. Here, I will put it back on the rag, is that better?" he said, as he calmly placed the frog back in front of them.

Jackson and Sasa remained calm, but Anna was frightened.

"Jackson, he could have bitten you. Is there some-thing wrong with him?"

"No Anna, Wheezer would never hurt me, or anyone who is my or, obviously, Sasa's friend. You see, I raised him from a pup in Arkansas. I named him Jack," Jackson reassured her, then continued to explain how Jack's name had changed to Wheezer when Sasa saved his life. "Sasa is right, he may have just saved my life in some way…a way only he knows," he added, as he touched Anna's hand.

That touch brought a pink glow to Anna's cheeks. Jackson turned his attention back to the frog. As he knelt in front of the bundle he slowly wet the tip of a finger with his tongue, reached down and touched the frog where the white haze almost blocked out the colors, then he raised his finger to his mouth to taste it. His sudden intake of breath startled all in the lodge while his eyes widened and realization dawned in them.

"Oh, my God, this is coated with rat poison," he said, as his voice rose. "Just holding this thing for any length of

121

time could kill someone. And look here on the surface. There are rows all along the length of the surface where the white haze has been rubbed off...see the color is bright only in those places. Sasa, I am not sure what these rubbed off places are, but if your brother had this frog in his hands for any time at all, then he was poisoned."

Sasa looked stricken as the wheels of logic rolled around in her brain.

"Jackson," she said, feeling wounded, "are there signs, you know, things to look for, if a person is poisoned? My brother was sick, with many symptoms, but what could have I looked for?"

Jackson thought for a moment, weighing his words carefully, "I am not a doctor, and I have never actually seen a person who had been poisoned, but I have heard their fingernails turn blue and that there are other signs, too. Sasa, if you are thinking you could have saved him, you're wrong: without a doctor here, it is very unlikely that you would have recognized the signs before it was too late, so please don't start blaming yourself up over this. This was a deliberate act."

In just a moment of time she relived all the days she nursed her brother, trying to make him well, when all along he was being systematically murdered. Among the Cherokee, there were only two things they deemed deserving the punishment of death. One was to marry inside your own clan and the other was murder.

Her eyes became slits, her lips pressed together so hard they turned pink, then white. She clenched her fists as she started to get up.

"Mr. Edwards. He is the one who gave this to my brother. He is guilty of murder and deserves death. I will avenge my brother," she said, starting for the door.

Jackson grabbed her arms, pulling her down and forcing her to come back to the circle.

"Sasa, you can't just go kill him. We have no real proof that he did this. In fact, all we really know is that he was seen giving the toy to your brother. We don't know if he put the poison on the frog, or if he even knew the poison had been put on it, but there are things we can do to find out," said Jackson.

Then it occurred to both Jackson and Sasa alike that Mr. Edwards was Anna's father. There was no way to know for sure how she was taking this news. Jackson turned to Anna, only then noticing the tears running down her face.

"How...how could he do such a thing, Jackson? Oh, God, he is a murderer...what shall I do, how can I go back and face him now that I know what he has done?" she cried, then hid her face into her hands and wept. Momentarily forgetting her seething rage, Sasa put her arm around Anna shoulders. As for Jackson, he was at a loss for what to do, for he did not want to intrude into her misery and yet he felt that there had to be a way to face this terrible tragedy for both Sasa and Anna.

A scratch sounded at the door flap of the lodge. When she pulled the cover aside, Sasa saw Arch standing in the sunlight, his stocky body tense and a grim smile on his face.

"*O si yo,* Sasa. Is Jackson here? I have news for him," he said, as Sasa motioned him to come into the dark lodge. He was puzzled when he saw the young woman inside, crying her eyes out.

When Anna quieted down, Jackson introduced Arch to her and then related what had brought them all together in Sasa's lodge. The look on Arch's face when he filled him in about the poison was incredulous. He gazed at Sasa, then nodded, as if to say justice will be done.

"Jackson, I have news about that errand you sent me on," he then said, motioning for Jackson to follow him outside if he wanted to speak in private.

"Arch, at this moment I think all of us here should hear what you have found out," Jackson replied.

Arch gritted his teeth, steeling himself to speak the news that he knew would hurt both Sasa and Anna.

"Last night, I talked to the man who attacked Sasa..." he began.

Sasa suppressed her desire to cry out, and remained as quiet as she could.

"Actually, Wheezer was a big help to me last night."

"Wheezer?" Sasa and Jackson both said at once.

"Yes, he followed me to the back of the stables. When I found the man with a bandage on his shoulder, he frightened the man so badly he was happy to tell me the truth," chuckled Arch.

Anna looked wide eyed now. "Are you talking about Billy, our stable hand? Father said a horse kicked him," she whispered.

With Sasa's help, Jackson quickly explained to Anna what happened in the woods, and Wheezer's timely rescue of Sasa.

Then Arch turned serious.

"I hate to tell you this, ma'am, but Billy told me that your father forced him to try to kill Sasa. Mr. Edwards gave Billy the knife out of the allotment stores, pointed out who she was, and threatened him with a beating within an inch of his life if he did not obey. Before you ask, Jackson, he had no idea why. He said he was glad that the, as he called it, "beastes" stopped him from killing her. I think Wheezer made his point very clear, and Billy would run away rather than do something like that again."

Anna was baffled; it was written plainly on her face.

"So, now there is evidence he put Billy up to the attack on Sasa? But, why? I can't see any connection. Why would he risk his entire career? There seem to be pieces to this puzzle that are missing," she said.

Sasa looked up sharply. She thought, *Yes, pieces to the puzzle. Anna may have some of the missing pieces without even knowing it. If she does, then she is also in danger, even if he is her own father.* She dragged her attention back to the conversation at hand. Anna was explaining something.

"Jackson," Anna began, as she put her hand over his and reached across the circle for Sasa's as well. "I was going to wait until we were in private, but in view of what I have just heard, I feel I must tell you all. I have been holding this secret for weeks and it's about to burn me from the inside out. Some weeks ago, my father woke me up in the middle of the night. He bade me to dress and take an important secret message to a man whom I had never seen before. He made me swear to not open his note. I assume he did not want me to read it. I have felt guilty for what I have done for a long time. I can only ask God's forgiveness,"

Jackson was intent on listening, but Arch broke the spell.

"It seems you must have read it. Anna; if your father is doing something illegal, you have no reason to feel guilty. He is the one doing wrong, and it is your duty to tell us what you know, for many of my people may die very soon when there is no food for winter. Please tell us, what did the note say?"

Anna bowed her head for a moment, as if in prayer. She eventually came to a decision, and prepared to speak.

"You are correct, Arch, I did read the note, but not until after I delivered it to the man I was sent to give it to. My instructions were to go to a lowly cabin, due south from here. It is a place well marked since it was the first building the Agency worked out of before this new compound, with the present stables and warehouses, were finished. The man sat in a small office, full of a pungent smelling smoke. I could barely see him in the dim light, but I was able to see that he wore fine clothing and gold jewelry that glinted in the haze. I was so afraid. I was alone, for my father had refused to allow anyone to accompany me, even though the cabin is quite a long walk in the dark."

Anna stole a moment to steady her nerves. A fleeting thought passed through her mind. She did not know these people very well; was she sure she was being loyal to the right people? However, as she weighed the alternatives in the balance, her sense of Godly morals asserted itself again, and she proceeded with her explanation.

"This man spoke with a southern drawl and he seemed very self-assured. Even when I gave him Father's note, his expression did not change, smiling at me with that Cheshire cat grin of his. It was the grin you would imagine your house cat has on its face just before it pounces on an unsuspecting mouse." Anna shuddered involuntarily.

Wheezer scooted forward, placing his paw on top of her hand in a gesture that made her smile. She felt that his gaze was one of sympathy, protectiveness and loyalty, and she felt comforted by it as she went on.

"On my way back from the cabin, I remember I looked all around, but I could see nothing in the blackness. I had heard the hoof beats of a horse fading away just after I left, so I supposed the man was already gone. The only available road ran from north to south, and since I was walking north he had to have gone south. I felt it was finally safe for me to take the note out and read it. That is what I am so ashamed of," she cried. "I am an honest woman, trust-worthy, law abiding and I am not a liar," she said as she took a handkerchief from her hidden pocket, placing it against her small, white nose.

"I could not seem to help myself. I had become so alarmed by the implications of a secret meeting in the dead of night between me and a man I didn't even know that I just had to look to see what was so important that my father would risk my reputation for it. I stopped and opened the note. I have committed it to memory. My father's message, in his handwriting, was, *"I can't find the frog. I have even been in their lodge to look, and it is not there. What do you want me to do?"* I was totally baffled. I..." Anna had to stop, for the sight of the look of shock and disbelief in Sasa's eyes had almost paralyzed her.

"You mean he was here? Here in my lodge? Looking through my things, my family's things? I don't understand; if he gave the frog to my brother, why would he want it back now?"

Jackson and Arch looked sharply at each other. They understood the implications only too well.

"Sasa," Jackson said gently, "If Mr. Edwards gave the frog to Usti Yansa, and he put the rat poison on it, then it stands to reason that after your brother died he would want the evidence back. Or, if this other man had something to do with this, they could be working together. That might explain why he came here asking you if your brother said anything before he died. From the note Anna read, he's been trying to find this frog," he went on, pointing at the painted frog lying on its bed of rags in front of them. "We just don't know all the facts."

Arch was equally counting the possibilities.

"We do know he wants to find the frog and that he put Billy up to killing you, but Jackson is right; there are so many other unanswered questions, such as, 'what did your brother know that got him killed?'"

"But he did not tell me. He only said the words I told you, and they were words not meant for me anyway. It was like he was saying them to himself. If this is all true, then my brother did not have to die and I would not be alone," Sasa whispered, her voice beginning to crack with the strain of holding back her rage.

"That was not all of the message, though," Anna cut in, raising a hand to forestall the others. "The man wrote a

127

message back to my father, and that was the message that really made me worry about what my father had gotten himself into, but I had no idea it might be murder. The message he sent back to my father was, '*Quit looking, they can't possibly figure it out. Forget it.*' But, who was trying to figure it out? What has he done that murder seems the lesser of evils?"

Seeing that everyone in the lodge was upset, Wheezer felt a natural inclination to help if he could. He was not sure of the reasons, or why some were sad while others angry, but he knew he now had to protect all of them; in his mind those three were bonded together, and that made it his responsibility to make sure they all came to no harm, including Anna. Even if they had only just met, from that brief connection of their gazes he knew they were kindred spirits... or that was what he would have said, had he been able to put it into English words. For him, it was more of a feeling than a thought, a profound connection.

Electricity sizzled in the gloom of the lodge, as all inexplicably held their breaths, then Wheezer moved closer to the center of the circle, put his muzzle under the frog and flipped it toward Jackson's lap. The reaction was instant.

"Of course!" Jackson exclaimed. "Wheezer has the answer. Our only clue is this frog. In fact, there is more than one clue in it. The questions are...who made it? Where would Edwards get such a thing? Where in the compound do they keep rat poison? And, who else may have seen Edwards give the toy to Sasa's brother? But, above all, why did Edwards need to kill Usti Yansa? As I see it," he went on, "we have more work cut out for us than we thought. We have to continue to help the People, but at the same time, we must try to talk with them, ask questions, draw them out. Arch, you can enlist David in this. Many of the survivors are resentful of what's been done to them, so we must be careful not to raise an insurrection here, but we can make it known that we are trying to fight for their allotments. They may give us information, things they know but aren't aware of knowing.

"Sasa, there are places you can go here where adults might be noticed and you would not. Go down to that cabin, you and Wheezer, and check it inside and out. Bring back anything that should not be there, anything that looks out-of-place. We need to know the identity of the man at the cabin.

"Anna, if you still are interested you can play a part as well, but remember that it may be dangerous. I don't want you taking any unusual risks," said Jackson.

"Oh, believe me, I want to find out as badly as you do, Jackson. Just tell me what you want me to do, and I will do my very best," said Anna.

"All right, I will continue to call for you in the mornings for your help in the camp. If your father finds out about your helping the sick, tell me and let me deal with him. I think I have the persuasive edge to convince him to leave you alone for the time being. Here is the most important thing you can do for us: since you have access to the house and the compound, and we don't, try to track down where they keep the rat poison. Ask the hands if it has been used of late, and by whom. Snoop around as much as you can without alarming your father. If you can talk to the slaves out of your father's hearing, they might have some ideas about that frog. Whatever you do, if your father gets wind of what you are really doing, don't stay in that house. Run, don't walk, out to the camp and find me or Arch. Since we don't really know how deep he has dug himself into this, your father may be just as dangerous to you, even though you're his own flesh and blood."

Chapter 17

As he walked down the narrow back street, Andrew Halley noticed the light beginning to fade. He could not tell if the dimming was from the closeness of the drab, mean buildings by the St. Louis waterfront, or if the sun was actually going to set. Either way, he hurried to find the address he sought. *This is an odd place for a dry goods store*, he thought, since the waterfront of St. Louis was notorious for harboring all kinds of unsavory individuals. Shipments of all kinds of goods, from nails to fabric, were first unloaded onto the docks by men of dubious histories, then stored in tumbledown warehouses, crawling with vermin, roaches and mold. The Mississippi River, by which St. Louis was founded, was the life blood of the city, and its oldest part, but almost anything could happen to an unwary pedestrian.

Men of all types were streaming to this frontier town, but some years before, in 1804, it was just a stopping place from which to launch a great expedition. Louis and Clark had embarked on their famous exploration they named, "The Corps of Discovery". The Mississippi River, which flows beside the town, gave the explorers easy access to the mouth of the Missouri River which empties into the Mississippi just north of the city. And it was the Missouri River which took them nearly across the continent. Since that time, the town had started bursting at its seams. The influx of settlers looking for their rainbow, the rough and ready nature of the mountain men coming in to sell their furs and buy new supplies, as well as to visit the taverns and bordellos, and the business investors coming for their slice of the pie, had all contributed to St. Louis' development into a profitable, but dangerous place.

Fifty three years old now, Andrew Halley had only been an eighteen year old, inexperienced boy, just starting out to carve his own niche in the making of America when Louis and Clark had left on the greatest exploration in the fledgling country's history. That trip to the Pacific Ocean and back had electrified the people and stirred in them the pioneering spirit that would later settle the wildest of places between the two oceanic shores. In 1839, that process was still in its infancy, but gaining momentum, and St. Louis figured heavily in it as the 'Gateway to the West', as it was being named.

Having served in the War of 1812 against the British, Andrew had seen his share of war and fighting. However, the battles he had fought, together with other Americans, had been no holds barred, blunt confrontations, nothing like the surreptitious attacks by greedy, lawless men in a frontier boom town. Nevertheless, he proceeded cautiously down Elm Street walking toward the Mississippi River waterfront. When he was almost to First Street he noticed a sign at the head of an alleyway, "Sanderson's Dry Goods Office", with an arrow pointing down the alley to his left. The buildings were suffocatingly close together, but in the dim half-light Andrew almost missed seeing the door to Sanderson's to his right.

As he approached, he noticed the door was slightly ajar. It did not occur to him as odd; it was, after all, the end of the business day. He paused outside the door to gather his thoughts as to how he would frame his questions. Above all, he did not want to antagonize this man, especially if he was involved in fraud. He knew if he scared any criminal badly enough, he might take to flight instead of providing the information he needed. At this point, he was not certain that Sanderson had anything to do with the missing allotments, but he still needed to be careful. Taking a deep breath, he opened the door.

It had been a terribly hot day, and being next to the slow moving current of the Mississippi River added to the sweltering heat a heavy moisture, making it hard to breath. As Andrew stepped inside, the moist, overheated air of the warehouse assailed him from all sides, almost like being in a sweat lodge...something which he had experienced by invitation one summer in Georgia at the invitation by one of Jackson's Cherokee friends. Before he could take another step into the room, however, he was aware of a pungent metallic odor which drifted upon the moisture-laden air, an odor he was well acquainted with, so much so he did not have to stop to identify it, for he knew the smell of blood.

Reaching behind him and under his jacket, he pulled a small Allen & Thurber pepper-box revolver from its holster as he scanned the dim room, lit only by one oil lamp in the corner, and advanced soundlessly. His eyes adjusted to the gloom and he could finally determine that there was no one in the room where he stood. Noticing another open door to the back of the room, he headed that way, passing into a much darker area of the hot warehouse. Just a few steps past the door, a dark inert form lay on the floor, in an ever widening black pool of what he knew was blood, dripping and seeping into the long thin spaces between the dusty dry boards. He bent down, touching the form's wrist; there was no pulse there and the skin was still warm.

A chill crept up his spine as he realized he must have arrived within minutes, even seconds of the murder. He had never actually met Sanderson, but somehow he felt certain this was the man he had come to see. His only thought now was to make his way back the few steps to the office, and then to the outer door to summon the law. He rose to head back toward the open inner office door, the dim light of the single lamp burning, now seeming fairly bright. Just as the thought of safely making it out of the warehouse passed his mind, a dark form moved from the ebony shadows to block his path.

"Ah, Mr. Andrew Halley. What a grand surprise this is, suh. I see you almost beat me here. I had not intended for you to catch me here," the man said in a half amused tone.

The man stepped closer to Andrew, and as his face caught the light from the office, Andrew gasped his astonishment of recognition.

"You? In St. Louis? It's just not possible. Why would you do this despicable thing?" he exclaimed.

"My dear suh, you underestimate me. I don't mind telling you now, I am a very rich man and will continue to be, especially since I have eliminated one of the weak links that would have led to my identity," the man chuckled. "And the allotments will continue to flow, a good portion of it, into my pockets. At the same time, I will be doing a service to my country, by eliminating the drag on the American people, that of trying to keep a no-good pack of Indians alive."

"You can't get away with it. I won't let you..." Andrew meant to finish his sentence.

Without warning and in one smooth movement, the man pulled a nondescript handgun from his pocket, a blast ringing, echoing against the warehouse walls, the shot hitting Andrew in the chest. The impact of the ball felt like a light tap, but then he felt himself falling on his back, as if in slow motion, and a moment later he was lying on the floor. He watched as the man stepped forward to hover over him as his thoughts were becoming fuzzy.

"I am sorry, Andrew. I would not have had to do this if you had kept your curiosity at a minimum, but now I will have to finish you off. Before I do, suh, I want to inform you, so you may not rest easy in your death, from here I plan to go on to Indian Territory directly, and once there I shall happily send your meddlesome son to join you. Oh, you didn't know? Never fear, suh, you won't be lonely," the man smiled down at Andrew, with a glint of evil in his eyes. "Oh, yes, I am aware of your son's whereabouts. You see, I

133

have...shall we say...Inside information. There is no end to the information a person can glean when being perfectly amiable. Yes...a person in your office was happy to tell me the whereabouts of that hot headed progeny of yours. Be assured, I mean what I say. Out in that wild territory there will be no one to impede my progress to that goal, suh.

As the man began to take aim, Andrew remembered his own handgun still in his hand, finger on the trigger. He had not the strength to lift it from the dusty floor, but managed to squeeze its trigger, firing it just the same. The ball caught the man's foot, his fine Castilian leather boot disintegrating at the toe like a burst tomato, knocking him down onto the floor. The man began screaming and thrashing from the pain of it, but when his cries subsided to a numb moan, the man could hear voices from not too far off, and the running of feet pounding on hard packed earth. He had to get out of the warehouse before he was found there with two bodies. Knowing the blood from his injured foot would leave a path leading to him, he ripped off his shirt, quickly wrapping it around his foot, and limped away into the darkness of the warehouse; a moment later a door at the opposite end opened, letting the pale twilight light pass through. Andrew watched as the door closed, then the man was gone as the light in Andrew's eyes began to fade. His last conscious thought was of his son Jackson, then darkness enveloped him.

Chapter 18

Wheezer and Sasa had been up since dawn, had eaten their breakfast and prepared for the short journey to the abandoned cabin Anna had described. Something was different this day from other days, for Sasa now had a mission. The pieces to the puzzle were coming together faster than she had ever thought possible. Now, she felt a grim deter-mination grab hold of her mind. She would follow the clues until the full picture became clear. For now, just knowing that her brother had been murdered put a steel rod into her will, and she vowed that the person responsible for his death would not continue to live once their identity was revealed.

She tied the Green River knife she acquired from the attack on her life around her waist with a braid of rawhide Jackson had given her. There had been enough rawhide left to make a sheath and loop to secure it to her side. From the first day they had met, Jackson had taken a few minutes of each day to show her how to throw the knife. She hoped she would not have to use it against another human being save for one, her brother's murderer, and at least now she could protect herself somewhat.

Wheezer, too, had a grim purpose, that of keeping Sasa safe. He could not understand the deeper meaning of the revelations from the day before, but he did understand that Jackson had instructed him to go with Sasa. That only meant one thing to him...that he was responsible for guarding her, a job he did well.

They walked down the dirt road, heading south from the agency office. Sasa could not see the cabin yet, for it was a good distance away and the road curved into a forested area. As they traveled, she was alert to all that surrounded her. Upon hearing a stirring in the brush, Wheezer pricked his ears but made no motion to chase the prey he knew was there. It took unusual will power for a Jack Russell not to heed the call of the chase, but he kept trotting resolutely beside Sasa, matching her steps, neither lagging behind nor getting ahead of her.

They made virtually no noise as they walked, and they made it to the cabin before mid-morning. It appeared to be a lonely structure, built of logs chinked with mud in the gaps between them. To her wonderment she saw windows made of glass, something that was considered an extravagant luxury this far west. Weeds were growing up around all sides of the cabin walls with a hornet's nest--- complete with hornets--- in the eave of the roof, on one side. The spot was an overgrown mess and it puzzled Sasa that anyone would build something amongst the closeness of the trees and brambles. It was truly a solitary place. She was suddenly glad that Wheezer was with her.

The door had no special lock or knob on it, only an iron bar that you pushed in. The door moved, complaining loudly as it was forced to open. Inside there were only three rooms. A room was on either side of the door, but no doors were in the openings. Beyond was a room that stretched the entire width of the cabin. If there had been a stove to warm it, there was none now, but the hole for the pipe was plain to see. In the middle sat a flat tabled desk, thickly covered with dust, and a straight backed chair. Behind the desk was another, larger window on the back wall. It amused her that there was nothing to see but weeds and vines from that grand window. An oil lamp sat at the corner of the desk, curiously with oil still in it and a new looking wick.

Wheezer proceeded to examine all the rooms, probing into every corner, scratching at cracks in the boards where mice had obviously been. He wagged his tail as he walked, but when he sniffed a scent, the tail would stop and vibrate a little, then return to its wag as he continued on his inspection. Finished with the first two rooms, he came into the room where Sasa stood looking out of the large window.

"Did you find anything, Wheezer?" she said.

He looked up with his tail pounding, then continued to make the circuit of the third room as Sasa turned her attention to the drawers in the dusty desk. She looked in every drawer but one. All were empty, save for a few mice droppings. The last drawer was locked. She pondered over what to do. There was so much at stake, but she worried what would happen if she were found out. Her desire to know what was in the drawer overcame her trepidation. She removed the Green River Knife from its sheath and began to pry at the lock. It took some time and much scarring of the wood to open the drawer, but open it she did, only to find a small sheaf of papers resting within. Sasa had not learned to read well, so she took no time to look at the hand scribbling on the paper.

Then she heard a muffled woof coming from under the desk. When she looked she saw Wheezer lying on his belly with a small object on the floor between his paws. He smiled happily, but the bottom of the desk prevented his tail from wagging, so that the effort made his bottom jiggle instead. The sight caused Sasa to giggle out loud before she quickly covered her mouth with her hand. Now on her hands and knees, she crawled under the desk with him to examine what he had found. Lying on the floor was a gold button with an engraving in the metal.

"This is very good, Wheezer. I don't know if it is important, but we will take it back to Jackson. I don't understand the picture on this button, but Jackson is smarter than I am," she said.

Before she could rise from under the desk, a noise from the gaping front door startled her. Keeping very quiet, she motioned with her finger to her lips, telling Wheezer to do the same. They watched from under the desk as a pair of shabby boots and brown skinned ankles entered the cabin. The form examined each room, coming to the largest room

137

last, but the visitor only stayed a moment and then was gone. When the visitor was finally outside, Wheezer growled and scurried out from the desk before Sasa could stop him. She banged her head on the bottom of the desk before she could extract herself as well.

As she ran to the front door of the cabin she could hear him barking as his voice faded somewhat, clearly giving chase to something. Then suddenly she heard a scream from the forest and the sound of furious thrashing. Within a moment, Wheezer emerged into the open, trotting toward Sasa with a prize between his teeth. He brought it straight to her, dropped it at her feet and sat, waiting for her to pick the item up.

"Again, Black White Whiskers, you have shown me your courage and worth," she said, holding his prize up to the sunlight streaming in the doorway. "Hm...this piece of cloth looks like you have ripped out the seat of someone's pants," she laughed softly. "I heard him running away. We must go now, quickly, before he brings back whoever sent him here to follow us. We will have to go through the forest beyond the road to go back or we will be found. Do not bark, Wheezer; we must go quietly."

Sasa put the button in her pocket and left the cabin, clutching the papers to her breast. This time Wheezer led the way, helping to find an easy path for Sasa. She sincerely hoped that the things she carried would help them in their search for the truth.

While Sasa and Wheezer were investigating the cabin, Anna was busy trying to find time to snoop. She had gotten up early to help the slaves with breakfast, something she had been doing since the time she had first arrived at her father's cabin. Never had she been more certain that her father was mixed up in something very bad. Oddly, she felt very little sympathy for him. He had made it abundantly clear from the very first day that he was unhappy with her visit, and she had been blaming it on his responsibilities being so great, taking care of all the Cherokee, while she was now certain that he was part of some plan to hurt them instead. And the knowledge galled her. Just to think of the horrible look in Sasa's eyes the night before, when they all had realized her father might have something to do with the death of Sasa's little brother! At that moment, she had wanted to change her name, deny kinship, even leave the cabin, but she had a share of the investigation to complete. Plus, she was now determined to stay until they all could get to the bottom of these crimes and present the guilty for justice to be done, even if it turned out to be Samuel Edwards, her father.

She set the table and brought in the oatmeal and bacon, ready for her father to come in for breakfast, then headed back to the kitchen for the sugar and local honey while Mazy put the coffee pot and cups on the sideboard.

"Oh, Miss Anna, since you been here, I swears the dining room looks downright pretty every morning. Before you come, Masta Edwards, he jus take some coffee and toast an leaves to his office. He don't even bother to set down at dat there table," said Mazy.

"Why, thank you, Mazy, what a nice thing to say. I guess I did not bother to even ask about it, I just assumed he had breakfast at the table," said Anna.

"Well, it's so nice to have a woman's touch, but I jus don't think Masta Edwards even notices one bit. No, suh. Not one bit," Mazy added, as she walked back to the kitchen.

Anna took her seat just as her father came in. She glanced up at him, but the sight of the chill look he had in his eye made her turn her gaze away almost immediately. The last thing she wanted was a confrontation.

"Good morning, Father," she greeted him as he came to the table and seated himself.

Edwards murmured his reply, but so low she could not hear the words. Then he seemed to think of something, and looked intently at her.

"So what are you plannin for today, young lady?" he asked, making it sound like an accusation.

"Oh, not much, Father. I guess I will putter in the kitchen this morning and do some other chores, like checking on the slave quarters of the women..."

"What in tarnation do you think you need to be doin out there? I don't see what business it is of yours," Edwards took a breath long enough for Anna to get a word in.

"Why, Father, you know perfectly well that if someone does not go and check into some of those dwellings from time to time, before long they will have all kinds of bugs and vermin living in there with them, and then they'll spread to the main house. It will not take but just a moment to do. I have the time, so it might as well be me. What are you going to do with your day, Father?"

The question, so bluntly put, caused him to be defensive.

"I don't have to account to you. You just stay out of my doins. Just carry on with your chores and leave me be," he spat out at her.

Anna had to conceal a smile. She had succeeded in getting his mind off of her movements for the day. Now he would avoid the subject. It was no great surprise to her, she thought, as he gulped down his cereal, grabbed his coffee cup and fled to his office. Now Anna could attend to her probe for clues without fear of interruption.

She helped Mazy clear the table, bringing in the last of the dishes. While the servants and Mazy were doing the dishes from water they had pumped and carried in from the well outside, Anna began to look in the cupboards and underneath the counters. She searched all through the kitchen area and in the pantry closet, but found no poison. Running out of options, she struck up a conversation with Mazy.

"Mazy, do we ever have problems with rats in the house?" she asked.

"Well, Miss Anna, we does, sometimes, but we mostly got them kind of vermin out in the stables," replied Mazy.

"Do you keep any poison in the house for rats?"

"No suhree, ma'am. I makes them boys out yonder keep dat stuff in the barns. I don't hold with keepin poison in a kitchen. Looks too much like salt or sugar."

Anna pondered how she could bring up, in a polite way, some of the other questions she needed to ask.

"Mazy, I think I am ready for a cup of tea. Would you like one as well? We can sit here at the kitchen table and sip for a few minutes. My father usually avoids the kitchen anyway," she said, as she smiled sweetly at Mazy.

Mazy was startled. In all her years as a slave, she had never been asked to have tea with the slave owner or their children. She was speechless for a moment, then realized her mouth was gaping open.

"Yes, ma'am. I shor would like dat, Miss Anna. I'll just brew some up now, the kettle is hot on the stove an it won't take but jus a minute," Mazy said as she hurried around the kitchen, excited to be given the opportunity to sit with Anna.

Anna went to the pantry and brought out some shortbread, placing a few on a saucer in the middle of the red and white gingham tablecloth. Mazy brought the tea and cups and they both sat to have their tea.

"Miss Anna, I don't mean nothin by this, ma'am, but I never in my life have ever sat at a table with a white person. But I be grateful. You is such a kind person," Mazy said, sipping her tea.

"I guess you could say I am a different sort of person. I come from the East, in the northern part of the United States, where we do not believe in slavery. There is no reason why I should not have tea with such a loyal servant as you." Anna paused to gather her thoughts. "I have some questions I need your help with as well, Mazy. I don't think I can ask my father. Would you mind talking to me?"

"Miss Anna, I would be happy to answer anythin you want, ma'am, ifin I has the answer," said Mazy.

"One of the questions I have is about a small carved painted frog. Have you ever seen such a thing here about?"

"Yes, ma'am, I has. Those there frogs come from my sister back home in the south. Her man carves them and then Flora paints um. She sends them to me to give out to the chillins here," said Mazy proudly.

"You probably would not know this, but do you know anything about one of the frogs being given to a young Cherokee boy a few months ago?" asked Anna.

Mazy's eyes got huge; her hands began to tremble.

"Miss Anna, I did give the last one of those of mines I had here to a white man dat was with Mr. Edwards. He kinda' scaret me, dat one. I hopes by what is holy dat mans don't come back here. I can tell he is evil jus from the look in his eyes," Mazy shook her head, trying to calm herself.

"I don't understand, Mazy. What would a white man want with one of your carved frogs?"

"Ma'am, all I knows is dat he akes me ifin he could have it one night when he was here. He saw me get it out of a box I kep it in. Then, Miss Anna, I done a very bad thing. Please, Miss Anna, don't tell your papa or he skin me alive he will," said Mazy, tears running down her wide face.

"Calm yourself, Mazy; I have no intention of telling my father anything. I need to know all about that frog, and you will be doing a good deed if you can tell me more, and it would be a good Christian thing to do, Mazy."

"I...I guess so, ma'am. This has weighed on my mind somethin fierce since dat night. Well, what happened was, dat man, he took dat frog and went outside toward the barn with it, an Masta Edwards, he go, too. So I jus could not help myself, ma'am, I could not, for the life of me, figure out why two growed men would want one of my sister's carved frogs. So I sneaked up to the barn. I found a place behind some piled up straw to hide myself, an I watched them. Masta Edwards called dat man Colonel this and Colonel dat. They sits in dat barn room where we keeps the farm tools an poisons.

"I watch through a crack in the boards an I could hear some of what they said. Dat Colonel man, he got some of the poison down from a shelf. I seen him mix some with water and he dipped dat frog in the mixture. I remember cause I thought it was strange he was a wearin gloves. Then, they talked real low like, an I tried to listen, but it was no use a-tall. They talked a long time, then dat Colonel man, he had let dat frog dry, an then he wrapped it up in an old rag an handed it to Masta Edwards. Then he says to the Masta, 'give this to dat Indian boy' an Masta Edwards nodded his head an walked out. I never seen him since dat time, Miss Anna," said Mazy.

Anna sat, holding her breath. She had had no idea she would find out so much evidence so quickly, and it hit her like a ton of bricks. She had reconciled herself with the knowledge that her father was probably guilty of any number of criminal acts, but she was stunned at having the evidence spelled out to her in such clear terms. Now she knew where the poison came from and how the boy had gotten the frog, but not why these men had felt it necessary to kill a five year old Cherokee boy.

Remembering her agreement with Jackson, she had to rush to her room for her shawl to be ready for him to call as he had promised. As she waited on the front porch, many thoughts were swirling in her head. What was Jackson going to do with all of this information? Were Jackson and Sasa, as well as she, in mortal danger here? She would have to be patient for that answer.

Chapter 19

Edwards sat in his office, elbows on his desk and hands covering his face. What was he going to do? All his plans were coming apart at the seams. He knew beyond the shadow of a doubt that Jackson Halley was snooping around the camp. Once again, he had sent Billy to follow the Cherokee girl, but that ignorant slave had come back with the seat of his pants ripped off and now refused to go again, even if threatened with terrible beatings. He seemed to believe that "some beastes is out to take my soul".

Edwards leaned back in his chair and ran a hand through his long greasy hair as perspiration beaded his brow. He knew the shipment of goods would soon come in and that Jackson would certainly see those goods were not what his father had sent. Then what? Plus, Anna was beginning to be a huge problem. How could he do what needed to be done while she was here? Try as he might, and in spite of his bluntness, she just didn't take the hint that he didn't want her here. However, he took solace in the fact that she was just a female. Women did not have the brains to figure much out anyway, and knowing that gave him a measure of safety.

He had not heard from the Colonel for many weeks... and now it looked as if he might be forced to take steps to eliminate Jackson. He knew if he did that, then Jackson's father, Mr. Andrew Halley, would rush down here to investigate, which meant that sooner or later he would be in jeopardy. He hated to not be on hand for this last shipment so that he could collect his share of the take, but it could still all come together, if he planned to get rid of Jackson at the same time as the shipment came in. He would then have to high-tail it to the Rockies, where mountain men still made their living trapping fur for the European fur trade. There was also a heap of money to be made selling whiskey to the plains Indians. He heard tell they would give away every fur they had, their horses and their wives just for a cup of the brew. It could work. Then Anna would have to go back to Boston, at last.

He settled it in his mind, looking at all the angles. Its prospects of new fortunes to be made salved his stress over the present situation. With a clear plan of action, he would leave the Colonel to face the inquisitive eyes of the government. Edwards would not be there to know what happened, and a man could hide real good in the Rockies. With that thought in mind, he began the paper work and reports he did daily... all numbers pulled out of thin air and set on paper. It was a good ruse for him as long as it lasted.

The man still limped after several days of pampering his injured foot, but he was determined to take care of the loose ends that possibly could hang him. There was no railway into Indian Territory, so he would have to travel by horse. Just the thought of putting his foot into a stirrup made him clench his jaw. Fortunately, he had prevailed upon a country doctor to give him a supply of laudanum by claiming he had shot his own foot during a hunting accident; that simpleton of a doctor had been happy to oblige. It would never have occurred to him that he had been a part of that bloody scene at the St. Louis waterfront. His only real problem now was to succeed in getting his foot inside his new boot.

Walking had felt odd, besides being extremely painful, after Andrew Halley took off two of his middle toes with a lucky shot. He had left Andrew to bleed to death, then left the building, never looking back nor staying in the area. *Well, one down and several more to go*, he thought. After he cleaned up the mess in Indian Territory, he would still be able to rape the allotments with impunity. Next time, he would choose his subordinates carefully, plus do a better job of hiding the evidence that had led Andrew to be curious in the first place.

No. After taking care of Sam Edwards and Halley's young pipsqueak of a son, he would be able to convince the War Department to fill the vacancy with someone he himself would recommend. Really, it was child's play, and yet there was always that little chance that something would go awry, something unforeseen. He knew himself to be a resourceful man. Had he not escaped detection after many a close call? In fact, his disguise was so complete he had not even been considered as the culprit, and now it was his mission to make sure the cloak of deception stayed closed.

He traveled down through Missouri, close to the Kansas Territorial border. He would eventually reach Indian Territory, but this time he would not be expected. This time he would be a ghost, wreaking havoc in his wake and leaving as a ghost as well, and no one would know he had been there.

It was difficult to fight through the fog, but he knew there was something left unfinished. What, he was not sure of, but the nagging kept up at him as he struggled through a confusing combination of pain, dreams and terror. Eventually, Andrew opened his eyes for the first time in days. The first thing he noticed was he had difficulty breathing, as though he had just run ten miles and could not catch his breath. Then he noticed the others in the room. He croaked his first words since being shot in the chest.

"Where am I?"

"You are at Dr. Seth Martin's office, in his surgery room," said a young woman just out of sight.

"I can't breathe. Am I dying?" he gasped.

"No, I don't think so," said a male voice coming near. "I think we got to you in time, but you lost a lot of blood and one of your lungs collapsed. It may be some time before it is healed and probably a very long time before you are able to leave here."

"My son...I must warn him," fretted Andrew, becoming agitated.

"Dr. Martin, his blood pressure is rising," warned the young woman.

Dr. Martin stepped over to Andrew's bed. Andrew set his eyes on a fairly young man, with dark hair and horn rimmed glasses. Seth Martin had graduated medical school and immediately took off for the frontier town of St. Louis. He brought his young wife Kathy with him, to brave the unknown but exciting pioneer life ahead of them. There was no lack of patients in this remote place. The town was a rough place where serious injury, gunshot wounds and even death was a common occurrence. He introduced himself to Andrew as he sat in a chair by his bedside and patted Andrew's hand.

"First, you must calm yourself. We will do all we can to help. Obviously, we know who you are from the card you had in your pocket. Your assistant from your office has been by every day to see about you. I imagine he will be here very soon since he usually comes during his noon hour and the time is now 11:45. This time, I will be happy to let him come in if you promise me to keep calm. Any rise in blood pressure is hard on your lungs. The gun shot to your chest was very close to your heart and much tissue was damaged by the bullet on its way in and out the other side."

"The man. The man that shot me, did they catch him?" Andrew croaked.

"No, Mr. Halley, the man got away but we do know that you injured him. We found pieces of two toes left on the floor of the warehouse and a quantity of blood that did not seem to be connected to your injuries. Unfortunately, we were so busy trying to keep you alive while carrying you to my surgery, the trail was lost. It had just gotten dark at the time, plus we have very few law men here in St. Louis. The two we do have were on the other side of town that evening."

"When Mr. Ward, my assistant, comes in, would you please give him some paper, nib and ink? It is imperative that I get a message off today. It may already be too late," said Andrew as he tried to regain his voice.

"You rest for now, Mr. Halley. Your condition is not stable yet. Don't worry, I will admit Mr. Ward, but it will have to be a short visit, mind you," warned Dr. Martin.

Within just a few minutes Andrew's assistant quietly stepped into the sick room where he lay dozing. Mr. Ward was reluctant to wake his employer, but had already been told by the doctor that Mr. Halley had something of import he wanted to dictate. Mr. Ward sat at the writing desk beside the bed, set the paper, pen nib and the ink ready for action and lightly touched Andrew's arm.

He came awake almost instantly. Upon seeing Ward, he smiled and seemed relieved to have the man there.

"Mr. Ward, I have three very important letters to dictate. When they are done, put my seal on the back of them all and take them over to the Arsenal Army Post at 2nd Street and Arsenal Street. Give them directly into the hand of the Post Commander, no other. Please be sure to tell the Commander to open his letter immediately, as the information is of national importance."

"Yes, sir," said Mr. Ward.

Andrew's first letter was to Captain William Belknap, United States Army, Commander, Fort Smith, Arkansas. His next letter was to the Post Commander of the Jefferson Barracks, ten miles south of St. Louis, instructing him to deliver, without delay, the letter to Fort Smith, explaining the life or death situation. He also informed him of the attempt on his life, who the perpetrator was and why he had been attacked, so that it would go on record. Lastly, he dictated a letter to the War Department in Washington City, explaining what he knew so far about the missing allotments, at least about those intended for the Cherokee. He had no idea if similar crimes were being committed against the other tribes who had been guaranteed by a treaty, allotments from the government. He had been so intent on his mission he had raised his head from his pillow, straining his every muscle while dictating.

"Now, Mr. Ward, I must prevail upon you to put wings on your feet. Put the two letters to Army Posts in the Commander's hands even if you have to wait all day and night for him to admit you to his presence. Be sure to tell his aide that this is a matter of national security. Now go, and don't dare come back here until your task is completed. Then you may give the letter to the War Department to the Jefferson Barracks' mail detail to go out with their next packet," Andrew said, as he lay back on his pillow and closed his eyes.

This was all he was able to do. Jackson's life was in danger, not to mention the welfare of thousands of Cherokees. He hoped he had put his requests to the commanders in terms strong enough to get them on the move with no delay. His last thought before drifting off to sleep was: now, there was only prayer as an option and the putting of it into God's hands.

Chapter 20

Jackson prepared to meet Anna at the agreed upon time of ten in the morning. He felt excited, but had no idea why he was looking forward to spending the day with this almost stranger. It had only been just a few days since they met, but he already felt he had known her for some time. With so much hanging over her head, investigating her own father to expose his involvement in a criminal act was a sign of courage he could appreciate. He had never met anyone with so much resolve and tenacity. It was not apparent at first, because she appeared so refined and ladylike. Those were attributes a person would not expect to see in someone who was also bold and courageous. Just the fact that he could not quite figure her out made the prospect of getting to know her better provocative, to say the least.

As he approached the wide veranda stretching around the agency building, he could see Anna waiting anxiously for him. She kept moving from one foot to the other, so he hastened his pace.

"Good morning, Anna. Are you ready for your daily exercise?" he beckoned to her from a few yards away.

When she saw him, she hurried down the stairs, pointedly turned him around and put her arm into his.

"Jackson," she said breathlessly, "I have loads of information for you. It's so important, I almost can't contain myself."

"All right, calm yourself, Anna. We don't want to be noticed by your father in case he is looking out of the agency window. Why don't we walk, no, stroll through the camp? Then when we get to David's lodge, we will step in. I will be able to give you my full attention then," he said, smiling at her.

When they arrived at David's lodge, they found the door flap tied open. They were invited in by Arch, who closed the flap behind them. Once inside, Anna noticed spaces along the bottom of the lodge walls where some of the larger sticks had been removed. Feeling the cool breeze the spaces created she felt thankful, since there was no such ventilation in the agency building with its thick log walls.

David was already sitting on some skins in the place of honor, at the back of the lodge, facing the door with the fire before him. He motioned for Arch to sit down on his left side while Jackson sat down on the other and motioned Anna to sit next to him.

"Anna, we must first smoke the pipe. Back in our homeland, my mother used to prepare the pipe for our family during an important decision making council. She is not here to do this thing. Even though you are a white woman, you are a member of this council to find the truth, so I ask you, would you do us the honor of preparing the pipe for our council if we show you what to do?" said David.

"Oh, I guess I can," Anna said uncertainly, "I am happy to help, but I have not ever done anything like this before."

"It is a great honor to prepare the pipe. Only one who speaks truly can do this. I look in your eyes and I see truth looking back. I will show you how to hold it, and what you must do to assist us. This is a very important meeting for us all, but we must honor the Creator before we begin," David replied.

He pointed to where the pipe was hung on the back wall in a special leather pouch made exclusively for it. He took out the twist of tobacco Jackson had given him as a gift and talked Anna through the packing of the pipe and in what way she should hold the pipe bowl as she handed it to the person of honor, which was him. She felt positively thrilled at being included in this ceremony. While she watched the pipe passed around, each recipient raising it to the four directions as well as towards heaven and earth, she marveled at the fact that the men were not actually inhaling the smoke. So, when the pipe came to her, she did the same, finding the smoke warm and tingly on her tongue. When the tobacco was spent, David knocked the dottle out of the pipe and handed it back to Anna so that she could replace it in its holder on the wall. After sitting down again in her place, she eagerly awaited the discussion to begin.

Jackson was looking at the others, one by one, contemplating how to proceed, when an unexpected scratching came from the door covering. Anna wondered who it might be. David again looked to Anna, but she did not understand why no one was moving to see who it was. With a hint of a smile on his face, Jackson leaned over and explained.

"Anna, even though you do not live here, David has given you the honorary role of Woman of The Lodge. It is customary for the woman to own the lodge and everything in it, and the land as well. As such she would be the one who would decide who could come into the lodge and who could not. Would you mind doing this for our council?" he said, wishing he had more time to fill Anna in.

He studied her face as she considered the request but he soon saw he needn't worry, for Anna was completely fascinated and was considering it an opportunity to learn. She nodded her head once, stood up, smoothing her skirts, and proceeded to pull the covering back.

The man and woman who stood before her were totally unknown to her. She was unsure if they spoke English, so she hesitated to speak first. Likewise, the visitors looked perplexed and shocked at having a white woman greet them at the door of what they knew to be a Cherokee lodge.

"We are Poison Woman and Deer Caller; we are looking for the lodge of David Flint," the woman said as she held her head high and looked down her nose at Anna.

"Yes, of course," she nodded, then looked back at David. Seeing him nod too, she turned back to the visitors. "Please, do come in. David is here."

The two newcomers came in, sat next to Arch in the circle in front of the low burning fire, and said nothing. It puzzled Anna, as she wondered how they knew where to position themselves or why they had not spoken the reason of their coming to see David, but soon she was distracted by quick running steps coming towards the lodge. Before she could rise to greet the visitor, whoever it might be, Wheezer flew under the door covering, slipping around the circle and sitting next to Jackson... it seemed that even the dog knew where to sit. Before a word could be spoken, Sasa quickly entered, following behind Wheezer through the doorway, breathing hard and clutching a bunch of papers. Anna was surprised at the look on her face, which was fear mixed with excitement, but she, too, came in, sat next to Anna and did not speak. Poison Woman raised her hand.

"Deer Caller has asked me to tell you, we are expecting at least one more person for this council," she announced.

It was Anna's turn to lean over to Jackson.

"How in the world did they know there would be a council; who invited them, and why?" she asked.

"Remember, I asked David to check around the camp and question some of the people about what they might have seen. He probably told them to watch for our coming to the lodge, asking them to appear as already invited guests. Only he knows what they have to contribute to our discussion," Jackson answered with a wry grin. He was enjoying sharing these experiences with Anna, since Indian culture and customs were totally unknown to her. He was enjoying the sparkle of curiosity in her eyes and he respected her ability to transform her demeanor to address any given situation. She was proving to be a brave, intelligent young woman unlike any other he had met before.

Another scratch at the door sounded, but this time Poison Woman got up to admit the new guests, not knowing that Anna had been given that honor. Anna was not perturbed, but in fact a little grateful. To Sasa's surprise, Mary Walkingstick stepped in, and with her was a small boy who looked to be five or six years old. Still, after all were seated, no one spoke while Anna continued to be perplexed.

"What are they waiting for?" she asked Jackson, talking behind her hand.

Jackson now smiled, his mouth broad and toothy, accompanied by an almost silent chuckle. "They are waiting for you to do the pipe ceremony again. They can't start until everyone has been welcomed properly and the Creator thanked."

With a grunt, she rose from her place to repeat all that she had done not fifteen minutes before. She was astonished when the pipe made its way over to Poison Woman, who then smoked it with obvious pleasure before passing it on. It was obvious to Anna she had much to learn, but said nothing. Jackson, seeing the confusion in her eyes, leaned over again to explain.

"Poison Woman is a respected elder in the community. She uses herbs to heal the People. She also has knowledge about poisons, and people come to her for advice and counsel. Deer Caller is her brother; he is a Medicine Man. He helps the People with spiritual dances and ceremonies. They are both considered most honored, even more than a warrior. She is very accustomed to the pipe ceremony. If she wants to smoke, then she will smoke. She has no husband to tell her 'no,'" explained Jackson.

Anna silently considered it and decided it was logical, as the pipe made its rounds until finally the tobacco burned itself away. All but Sasa, the small boy and of course, Wheezer, smoked, however, the added people, each first raising the pipe to all the directions for their first puff and then passing it around until the tobacco burned out, taking another thirty minutes.

Finally, the pipe was put away again. Without asking, Poison Woman placed a kettle over the fire to warm as David began to speak.

"For our white guests, we will need to speak in the English," he began. "Jackson asked some of us to find out as much information as we could. Each will speak the truth of what they know, then Jackson will ask his questions. He can figure out what it means. Also, I will be the host of this council since Chief Ross, Chief of the Cherokees, is too far away, many miles to the south, and he has many other problems. The elders we have in this camp are here with us now, and we are honored."

The lodge fell silent, the only light from the low fire in front of the group and the dim light from around the bottom of the lodge where sticks had been removed for ventilation. Then David reached behind himself and pulled out a parfleche made of raw hide, painted with symbols of eagle feathers. Opening the parfleche carefully, he drew out something wrapped in rabbit fur. Anna was holding her breath, her excitement apparent to everyone, but when she looked at the others in the circle she noted that they all looked solemn and respectful, so she willed herself to wait and be patient for what might come next.

David uncovered the item, which appeared to be a stick, decorated with colorful bits of leather and paint. Attached to it was a wild turkey feather. David held it in front of him so that all could see the object.

"For the benefit of our new friend, Anna, I will explain the purpose of the talking feather," he said, as Jackson turned to give her a reassuring smile.

"Our gathering here is a very important occasion. We are here to find out what each of us knows of the truth concerning events that have happened here among us. Each person in the council may only have a piece of the knowledge. We call this gathering a Talking Circle. In the Talking Circle, everyone's voice will be heard and while that person is talking, he or she will not be interrupted...except in this case Jackson may ask questions of the person, for he knows what he is looking for and we do not. To assure that all may say all they want to say, we will use this," David went on, as he held up the feather attached to the stick.

"This is called a Talking Feather. When a person is holding this feather, no others may speak until the feather is passed to somebody else. All in the Talking Circle will have their turn to hold the Talking Feather and speak what is in their heart, but it is important that no negative comment come out of anyone's mouth while another is speaking. This is the way of the Cherokees from the time of our beginning. Jackson, who do you wish to pass the Talking Feather to first?" asked David.

"There is so much information I need that the Talking Feather may be given to some more than once. First, I would like to hear from Sasa," Jackson answered.

Sasa stood up. For just a moment she hesitated, collecting her thoughts, because she knew how important it was to get to the truth. The Talking Feather was passed to her. Everyone watched as Wheezer also got up and stood beside her, as if he also expected to tell about his discoveries. Sasa glanced down at Wheezer as he looked up at her, and they both then faced forward as Sasa began to relate her experiences of the morning's trek to the cabin in the woods. She spoke clearly, relating every step she and Wheezer had taken. The minutes flowed by and Anna wondered what other dangers lurked even now in the camp. A shiver went down her spine as she remembered that sooner or later she would have to face her father and it would be a showdown of an unknown nature; she was already preparing herself for it, but she feared the rage that she felt building inside herself, even now, on behalf of these people who were truly suffering because of her father's crimes.

Chapter 21

The travel was not as slow as a wagon would have been. The Colonel was glad of the horse's ability to traverse the rugged country he had to hurry through. Still wearing the now wrinkled suit pants, a shirt he had bought from a farmer and the coat he had with him when he attacked Andrew Halley, he barely looked like the fine gentlemen he was known as back in civilization, but, at the moment, he did not care about grooming or status. He could transform back into his former glory once his self-given assignment was complete. Then he would have the freedom to do as he pleased with his time and resources.

He was a bit fortunate in that he was able to follow the fairly new Oregon Trail until he reached Independence, Missouri. There was still plenty of game along the streams and valleys, so he never went for very long without fresh meat, but he was not a mountain man and all his experience came from serving in the Georgia militia. Therefore, he would make his kill, carve off a portion of meat that he could consume that day and the next, and be off again after a brief rest, leaving the valuable hide and leftover meat to the scavengers.

He felt fairly safe, armed as he was with his Sharps rifle, a dagger and a brace of pistols. After leaving Independence, however, he was forced into following the new Missouri border south along the Kansas frontier. There were still plenty of Indians in residence: Osage, Kaw, and even Delaware, who would not be so kind to a lone white man traveling through their hunting grounds. He thought about possibly stopping for supplies at Fort Leavenworth, but he did not want to be seen by soldiers of the U.S. Army. No, he would rather arrive in the lands of the Cherokee unnoticed. He was supremely confident in his goal.

Except for the wound to his foot, he felt ready to complete his mission and then to return to Georgia. So far, he had not taken his boot off since the first time he had shoved it on. Each day his ankle and leg swelled tighter into the calf-high leather, but he had no time to stop and worry about it... getting to the camp where he would succeed in removing his hired Agent and Jackson Halley from the ranks of the living had become all important to him. Once he was finished with this tiresome errand, he had any number of directions by which he could leave and affect his escape before anyone could figure it out.

He was coming close; he would soon be a day or two outside of Edwards' Agency and the camp. Each night he slid off his horse to fall to the ground, keeping hold of the reins while he lay there, resting, before he could get the nerve to stand on his damaged foot. The pain, now running up into his hip, had become his constant companion. Each night he camped next to a stream, his thirst unceasing and more insistent than his stomach's call for food. Dragging himself next to his small, smokeless fire, he would lie down, looking up at the huge expanse of the heavens, but only able to see his desire for revenge. Each morning, able to sleep for just a few hours at a time before he was forced to guzzle more water, became an ordeal. He had not experienced such thirst in all his days, but he never stopped to wonder why, so focused on his goal was he. He did notice the foul stench in the air...it seemed to be everywhere, so he ignored the smell and continued.

Without knowing it, he had crossed over into Indian Territory, set aside for the Cherokee. As he kept riding, he saw nothing of note, no movement, no animals and so far, no camp. He also did not see a small group of followers, staying close, but not overtaking him, keeping their distance. Actually, he would have had a hard time seeing them since his eyes had begun to see hazy outlines around objects, but even this he took no note of. Doggedly, he continued, not allowing anything to interfere with the completion of his plan.

Still sequestered in his office, Mr. Edwards poured his third shot of whiskey in an hour. He could feel the noose tighten around his neck, but he could not pinpoint the reason for his trepidation. A faint knock on the door irritated him, forcing him to turn away from his sullen musings.

"What do ya want. I don't want no visitors," he yelled at the closed door.

"Suh? Masta Edwards, suh, it's Billy. You all told me to come back, you know, afta I did what ya asked me to," Billy answered in a loud whisper, his face close to the door. "Does ya want me to come back later, suh?"

Abruptly, the door swung open, hitting the solid log wall behind with a thud. Billy stood startled, suddenly speechless at seeing Mr. Edwards in a totally disheveled state. His dark brown hair looked as if someone had been dragging him by it, his clothes looked wrinkled enough to have been slept in, even though he had put them on fresh that morning, and a bottle of fine whiskey with one tumbler sat on the desk now piled with papers.

Sam Edwards stared at Billy like he was looking at a slimy worm, but he felt even worse inside. He knew he had to find out what Billy learned from following Sasa, so he grabbed Billy by his sweaty linsey woolsey work shirt and dragged him into the room, walking back to his seat behind his desk. Opening the drawer with the special ledger in it, he pulled out instead his new Paterson Colt Percussion Revolver, laying it next to the bottle of whiskey. Billy's eyes about popped out of his head, thinking the gun was meant for him.

"Well, Billy, where in Sam Hill did the brat go, eh?" he asked Billy.

"Well, suh...I can't rightly say what she was a doin."

"For God's sake, just tell me where she went!"

"Uh, she went to an ol cabin south of the camp, suh. It was in deep woods an I followed her real quiet, like you asked me to, suh," Billy replied.

Edwards looked like someone had picked up the gun on the desk and shot him with it, he was so stunned. He got up from his desk, walking slowly around it to stand in front of Billy.

In a choked whisper he asked, "What did she do at that cabin, Billy?"

"It was kinda' spooky, Masta Edwards, suh. I sees her go in but I never sees her go out, so after a long time I went inside. There weren't nothin in there, suh. I went inta all three rooms, suh, an there was nothin but an ol desk. When I came out, somethin grabbed the back of my seat an done ripped a big hole inem. Mazy, she goin to kill me cause she gots to fix em again. I runs all the way home, suh," said Billy, half expecting to be punished because he did not see anything at the cabin to report.

Edwards was actually relieved, but Billy was not too overly relieved since he knew his owner could turn on a nickel and punish him still.

"Go on out, Billy. Go on and tend to your other chores now, ya hear. I got a heap of thinking I've got to do. Now get!" Edwards hollered at Billy as he rushed down the hall, the hole on his backside showing the dark brown crack each time Billy took a step, but Edwards was too consumed with worry to be amused at the sight.

He slammed the door behind him, turned and walked to the window. Gazing out at the shambles where Cherokee families lived, but not seeing them for the pitiable dwellings they were, he stroked his greasy hair back from his forehead. Instead of seeing the people and their plight, he was seeing the steps he felt he must take to extricate himself from possible detection, trying to figure out how he would leave and where he might go, but at the same time wondering if he could somehow fix the problem and still reap all that money he'd gotten used to getting.

He really had no idea who was coming after him; it was something he could feel, like when someone's staring at your back and you can feel their eyes boring through you. However, he was very sure the arrival of Jackson Halley had something to do with the young Cherokee girl going down the southern path to look at the cabin. It was a place where meetings took place in the middle of the night... meetings that meant he would continue to get paid. Even though he knew that nothing except an old desk was at the cabin, he still could not help but feel alarmed. Someone was sniffing around for clues.

Walking to the office door, he swung it wide and called, "Anna...Anna, where is that girl? Mazy, where is Miss Anna?"

Mazy came running from the kitchen and down the hall.

"Masta Edwards, she done gone out for her walk with dat fine gentlemens, Mr. Halley, suh. She should be back soon. You wants me ta tell her, you wants to see her when she gets back to the house, suh?" said Mazy

"No, hang it all, Mazy. Ain't no one around when I need them," said Edwards, crossly. "If and when she does come home, tell her I will see her at dinner. We have important things to discuss. Ya hear?"

"Yes, suh, Masta Edwards, suh," Mazy replied, then walked back to her duties in the kitchen. She knew there would be more to come because she could smell the heavy whiskey smell all over him. It would only get worse from here.

He closed the office door and this time he locked it. Returning to his desk, he sat heavily in his wooden swivel chair. Picking up the Colt revolver he absently spun the cylinder, listening to the soft clicking it made in its rotation. *I have to do something, and soon, too, or that Halley boy will be the death of me,* he thought. Seeming to come to a decision, he began to load the chambers. To load the gun for use, each chamber must first have a measure of gun powder poured in, then a small cotton patch was placed in the hole, and finally a lead ball was placed in next. A lever under the barrel of the gun unhooked from the front and swung down. This allowed a piston-like rod to shove the ball and patch home. He repeated each step for each of the other five holes in the cylinder. Even with the powder and balls loaded, the gun still could not be used until he placed small copper caps over the nipples that the hammer would strike, producing a spark when he pulled the trigger. Once cocked, the gun could shoot just one ball; then the hammer would have to be cocked again and the cylinder would rotate to the next chamber automatically. This was a real innovation over other hand guns available, since up until then, no gun could rotate automatically and be ready for the next shot, much less be able to load six rounds.

He placed the gun on his desk and took a long drink directly from the whiskey bottle, ignoring the tumbler sitting beside it. Yes, he had a plan. It called for sending Anna packing immediately; then he would have use for the gun. In order to escape from Jackson Halley's prying, he would be forced to end his life. In fact, he might not even have to leave the Agency. He could find a way to dispose of the body somewhere and no one would be the wiser. He congratulated himself for a brilliant plan. After all, the Indians were so stupid and weak they would never interfere, and as far as he was aware, all of Jackson's family and friends were over a thousand miles east. He finally began to calm himself, now that he had a course of action.

For two long grueling days, the troop of soldiers picked their way through the dense trees. There was no actual road to Indian Territory directly west of Van Buren, but these were men well accustomed to the terrain. Captain William Belknap, Commander of the as yet uncompleted Fort Smith, was desperately trying to move as swiftly as possible.

His orders were specific: go into Indian Territory and discern if a non-Indian American citizen by the name of Jackson Halley was in need of the U.S. Army's assistance. They were ordered to restore law and order at the Indian Agency nearest to Fort Smith if there was violence, and apprehend certain persons designated in the orders. The orders also stipulated that it might be a matter of life or death, so they would be entering the camp armed for combat, if necessary. Since, by their treaty with the U.S. Government, the Cherokees were to be allowed to govern themselves and administer justice as they saw fit, the troops were under orders to confine their activities to those named.

Getting there quickly was the problem. As long as the Captain had been in the army, he had never seen orders of this kind, because the man named in them was very high in political circles, and wealthy, to boot. His job was not to ask questions, however, but to obey. He only hoped he would get there in time, for he genuinely liked Jackson Halley

Chapter 22

"After the man that followed us left the cabin, Wheezer ran after him. He brought back this," Sasa concluded, as she held out the patch of Billy's pants that the dog had ripped out. "We ran straight back here, but we took a different way back. One of the People told me where we could find you."

David took the Talking Feather from Sasa. "Jackson, my friend, you do not need to hold the Talking Feather to ask your questions. So, feel free to speak to anyone who holds the feather."

As the feather was passed back to Sasa, Jackson turned to her and smiled gently, "Sasa, you are a brave girl. Wheezer is also courageous, as well. Did you find anything in the cabin, any clues at all?"

"I don't know if this will help, but I did find two things. First, I pried open the only drawer that was locked. I found these papers, but I had only just begun to learn to read when we were forced to march, so I decided to not take the time to read them. The second thing I found was a button, a fancy gold one," she answered as she handed over the papers and the button to Jackson's waiting hands.

Jackson took a few moments to look at the papers. A light began to gleam in his eyes as a smirk formed on his mouth.

"You have done very well, Sasa," he said. "You can't know how important these papers are to us. These are copies of invoices for the damaged and rotting goods the Agency bought in place of the good things my father thought were being purchased. This, my friends, is the positive proof of what the Agency has been involved in. We don't really have time to go into it--- let's just say that these papers are probably worth killing for, should the criminals know we have them---but I don't see a connection with the death of Sasa's brother yet," he added, setting down the papers beside him while taking a closer look at the button.

He held the button so a beam of light from the smoke hole would shine on the rich gold, emphasizing the engraving expertly done on the surface. As he rolled it around in the palm of his hand, Anna noticed the color seemed to drain from his suntanned face. His stunned look, coupled with his breath coming in short spurts, alarmed Arch, but before he could react, Jackson spoke again.

"I don't know what to say, Sasa, except that you have supplied us with a very important find. This button is very special. It is true that it costs a lot of money, but that is not what is so special about it. You see," he went on as he looked around the assembled group, "I own a button exactly like it. It is identical. There is only one place this button can come from and I must say it takes a lot of social pull to get one. Or, I should say, a set of them, for these come from a man's red dress coat. The engraving is of a coiled snake ready to strike at its victim, and the words surrounding it are 'DON'T TREAD ON ME.' The snake with the phrase was on a flag used before we gained our independence from the English. It is a very patriotic symbol of the Revolutionary War."

"But Jackson, I do not understand. Why does this button have meaning to you? You said you have a coat just like it. Who gave you the coat?" said a bewildered Sasa.

"These buttons are on coats given only to the members of a men's social club called "The Patriots Club of Boston". I have one of those coats, and so does my father. All the male Halleys have been members of that club since its inception in 1776. What is worse for me is that I cannot imagine any of the men of that club being a party to murder or embezzlement from the U.S. Government. However, this must be the case. What this also means is that we are possibly dealing with not one or two people, but a group of men who have worked out a system of stealing funds from the Cherokee allotments, because these men in Boston do not go traipsing around in Indian Territory, as a rule. So it stands to reason that they operate as a group with possibly one man as the head. He has been here at least once, since we have the evidence here in the button. It does not solve the case, but we are getting very important clues."

"Do you mean, like pieces to a puzzle?" Sasa asked.

"Exactly like that, Sasa. Well put," Jackson replied. "Is there anything more you have to add, Sasa?"

"Yes. When I said we found the button, that was not right. Actually, Wheezer found it and told me it was there," she said.

"Whoof, whoof," Wheezer agreed, wagging his short tail and smiling from ear to ear.

"Ha, ha, ha." Jackson roared with laughter, the entire group joining in. "He agrees with you, Sasa. Indeed he does. Ah, now I must ask you to pass the Talking Feather over to Anna. Anna, would you please relate to me the things you found out in your snooping around inside the house this morning?"

Anna took the Talking Feather as she stood up. She had not thought in terms of having to give something like a speech to people she hardly knew. Just the fact that the evidence she was to deliver would be like a nail on her father's coffin made her shiver while her palms began to perspire, but what choice did she have? She gathered her resolve and spoke boldly of the story that Mazy had related, every part excruciatingly painful to her loving heart. How Mazy had followed Mr. Edwards and the Colonel... whoever he was...going out to the barn, and how they had taken the carved and painted frog from Mazy's hands to turn it into a weapon of death for an innocent five year old boy. The telling of it incensed her all over again, and that made it easier for her to speak, for she knew in her heart of hearts that telling it all was the good and just thing to do.

"Mazy did not know the Colonel's name and she could not say anything about when the frog was given to the boy, but she heard the plan...and the plan was definitely, murder. Only, why two grown men would want to hurt a little boy is totally beyond my comprehension, I must say," she ended with a nod, indicating she was done with her evidence.

"That is horrific," Jackson agreed, then noticed the red creeping up Sasa's throat, as well as how her lips were pressed so tightly together they turned white. She slowly stood with clenched fists, a glaze of rage beginning to veil her eyes, then turned and was already bolting toward the door when Wheezer grabbed hold of her dress with his teeth, tugging hard against the pull of the girl. Anna, who was already standing, jumped into Sasa's path, grasping both her shoulders and shaking her firmly.

"Sasa, you must stay calm. Going after him now would be a mistake. You must allow Jackson to guide us. There is more than my father here to deal with. Please, Sasa, relax and sit down. Calm yourself, I beg you."

Sasa hesitated as if in midair for a few seconds while she thought through Anna's words. Then one tear of frustration slid down her cheek and she collapsed on the floor with a thud, Anna sitting down with her. Anna put her arm around Sasa while she sobbed silently as Wheezer jumped into her lap, licking her face until she almost could not breathe.

"Yes, Wheezer, yes...I will obey Jackson," she said, patting him on the head. Then he made himself comfortable beside her again.

For a moment, Jackson felt a pang of worry concerning his dog, but he quickly pushed the issue away. He would figure out what to do about the attachment between the girl and the dog later, so he turned his attention back to Anna.

"So now we know the weapon used to kill the boy, but not the reason. I fear it must have something to do with the allotments, but I have no clue about how. Anna, things might not be safe at home. If your father were to find out what you know, your life might be in danger," he said with concern written on his face.

"I don't think my father pays the slightest bit of attention to what I do with my day, just as he pays no attention to Mazy and the other slaves he owns. I will only have to be sure that I am home this afternoon long before dinner time. He will expect me to be," she answered.

"You will be home in time. I will be happy to escort you and give any explanations to your father, if need be, but if for any reason you begin to feel uncomfortable, leave immediately and come here. David will be happy to receive you if I am not here. Promise me this," Jackson said firmly.

"Of course, I will," she agreed, trembling, but showing no other sign of fear. "Now, who do I pass this feather to next?"

Poison Woman raised her hand and the feather passed into her grasp as she also stood to speak. The room became exceptionally quiet. To have such an elder of the tribe speak in any council was a great honor, even more so now because of the loss of so many elders while on the march from the East. A medicine woman, who kept the plants and herbs to heal, would never speak in council unless what she needed to say had special meaning to the tribe. Her appearance here only exemplified the solemn duty Poison Woman felt toward the safety and wellbeing of all the People.

"I am Poison Woman, a medicine woman of the People. I am one who is still here after The Trail Where They Cried, and I am old. I heard the call that went out for anyone knowing anything about the boy being with any white man to come forward to relate it. I do not know of that, but I came to this council to help our people who suffer, Jackson. Yes, we suffered from the Long Walk, but this is much worse. Before and during the Long Walk other white men objected to our treatment, as well as to the stealing of our tribal land. They tried to be friends of the Cherokees. These white men protested at meetings of their Congress. Even though it did not change the outcome of what happened to the People, our people knew that our suffering was being witnessed. We knew it would be forever in the memory of the People, and it will not be forgotten, especially among the white man.

"However, since we have come here, we are away from the view of most white men, and we are being made to die a slow and silent death. A dying that has no reason to it. There is almost no more fight left in us. We are alone, with no white men to protest against what is happening far away from the seeing eyes and ears of the government. Therefore, it is important, Jackson, Friend of the Cherokees, for this crime to be brought out to let the sun shine on it, exposing its parts. Our people are dying from the stealing of food, blankets and tools, food pledged to us by the government to keep us alive, blankets to keep us warm in winter, and tools to help us begin to farm the land as we have done for a long time. Something evil is happening here; this murder of Sasa's brother was the act of a desperate man with evil in his heart. We cannot hold our heads up high unless we find the ones who kill us, both slowly and quickly. The men who do these things are a plague among my people. Nothing will go right again if we fail to find them. I am Poison Woman. That is all I have to say."

Poison Woman passed the feather on to Medicine Man. Jackson began to feel the weight of the responsibility he now realized he must bear for all the People. He had initially thought his prime reason for staying to solve the mystery was for the sake of his own father, but now he could see that the People were depending on him to solve the crimes perpetrated against them, and that it was he whom they trusted like one of their own. In an instant he accepted it, and squared his shoulders as Medicine Man began his speech.

Medicine Man stood, solemn, thin and feeble. He took a soiled rag from the pocket of his dirty and ripped pants, which had been given to him by a white man as he had passed a small town on the trail to Indian Territory. It had been an act of kindness in a sea of hate, so he wore the pants daily in honor of that anonymous man. Only Poison Woman knew why he wore those pants until they practically fell off of him. She had mended them until there was no way to fix them again. He took the rag and mopped his brow, blew his nose, took the time to tuck the rag back into his pocket, then, finally began to speak.

"I am Medicine Man. I, as well, do not have information about the boy. I did not see him. I do want to speak of who your adversaries are. All but Anna and Jackson know me and my sister Poison Woman. For you I will say I come on behalf of Sasa and Wheezer," he said. Abruptly, Sasa raised her head with a questioning look at the speaker. "I was ready to go to my ancestors in the other world when she came to me for help with a dog she had found. I turned her away because I wanted nothing to stop me from my dying. Later, she came back with the dog who knew it was not time for me to die. Wheezer saved my life and showed me I still had work to do among my people."

Wheezer yipped and wagged his tail.

"I have said many prayers to the Creator; I have sweat and I have fasted. Some thoughts have come to me. I think there is more than one person that is doing these evil things. I also think we all agree, Mr. Edwards must be one of them, but the other one is someone we do not know. Since my sister and I came to this camp, Edwards has not left the

172

Agency, so it must be that he is told what to do by another. It is someone that only Jackson, Friend of the Cherokees, knows because of the button Sasa found. Not even Arch, his blood brother, knows this other man. My reasoning tells me that Jackson's family are enemies to this person who steals the allotments, and if this bad one was to find you here, Jackson, investigating, he would want to see you die, so you must be careful. If you are to help the People, you must be wary; if you are to help Sasa and Anna, you must be ready for him. I fear he is coming, and he has killed before. I am Medicine Man. That is all I have to say," said Medicine Man, locking gazes with Jackson.

"I hear your words and I will heed your warnings. I, Jackson, am grateful for your wisdom. I believe you are right. We, all of us, need to be aware of any new face in our midst, especially if that person is white. If this person is responsible for starving the People, he would not stop at killing any of you," Jackson said to the Medicine Man as well as to the group.

Jackson had to stop speaking and for a moment he closed his eyes, because it finally hit him that the person who was in the cabin, and the person who was in contact with Edwards, was a club member and most assuredly white, as well as wealthy. There might be nothing this person would not do to keep his perfidy a secret. The fact sobered him. Then it came to him: the thought that his father was possibly in danger as well. He sat with his eyes closed for so long, the group wondered if he was in a trance.

When he opened his eyes again, everyone could see a new gleam in them. A mixture of fear and determination to see this through to the end, but knowing the outcome might be bitter. Across the circle from him sat Mary Walkingstick with her arm around the small boy she had brought with her. He had almost forgotten about him because he tended to edge himself behind her, hiding his face, but peeking out to look at the group from time to time. From all appearances, he looked like any other small Cherokee boy: dark straight hair, round cheeks, full lips and large dark eyes, but his seemingly full face belied the true nature of his health. The boy was actually skinny to the point of malnutrition, and since he wore only a long shirt, the swelling of his knees and the curve of his lower legs were visible along with scabby patches here and there on his skin.

Mary patted him on the shoulder, asking him to answer Jackson's questions.

"I will need to tell you his words in the English for he only speaks the language of the People," Mary cautioned, glaring as if she dared anyone to object.

The feather was passed to the boy, who appeared flabbergasted and overwhelmed by the trust being placed on him for the first time in his young life. Seeing David nod to him in approval, the boy stood straighter, his chin firmed, and his grasp on the feather became reverent.

"I am Usti Ga La Gi Na," he began in Cherokee, as Mary translated, almost in unison with his words. "I am Little Buck. I was the friend of the boy who no longer is with us, Sasa's brother. We played together after we all arrived here, many times. One day my friend said he wanted to find food for his family. I said there was no food and he said he thought Mr. Edwards had food and maybe he would give this food to us if we asked him for his help. I did not want to go with him, but I could not stop him from going, so I followed him when he went up to the Agency lodge. He knocked on the door, but no one came, so we went around to the back of the lodge to see if Mr. Edwards was there working in the barns.

"I stayed right behind him, but when he found Mr. Edwards we saw he was with another white man. Mr. Edwards did not see me, but I could see him. This other man was handing the green paper the white men say is money to

Mr. Edwards, and saying some words. I did not know the words; they were in the English and my friend did not understand what the words meant, either. When the other man yelled at him, we ran away. We were very afraid we had done something we would be punished for, so we did not tell anyone about the white man yelling."

Little Buck stopped abruptly; the look of fear, like the frantic fear you see in the eyes of a deer before he is killed, filled the boy's face. Jackson hastened to put him at ease.

"You are not in trouble, my friend," he said in Cherokee. "You have done well in telling us this thing. Please be at ease; you did nothing wrong. May I ask you a question, Little Buck? Did you and your friend talk about these white men later?"

Little Buck's fear melted away as he faced Jackson's encouraging smile. Eagerly, he became a willing participant in the council.

"Yes, Jackson, I do remember another time. It was some days after that day when we ran. I saw my friend walking away from the Agency with a bundle. I asked him if he would like to go look for frogs in one of the streams nearby. He told me no, that he had the most special frog in all the world, and that now his family would have food, a good place to build their lodge, and everything they ever needed. He even said that his father would get well. I asked him how these things could come to be, but he stopped talking about it. He said it was a great secret he could never tell me about, then he went home." Proudly, he stood as tall as his small frame allowed and said, "I am Little Buck. That is all I have to say." He quickly looked at Mary for assurance he had conducted himself with honor in the council. She nodded her approval, but he did not change his solemn expression. His eyes, though, shone with pure pride.

Jackson turned to look at Arch, who had sat through the entire council without uttering a word. Arch had always

175

been a friend who smiled a lot, enjoyed learning new things and claimed he was blessed to be able to be part owner in the mule breeding business with Jackson. However, he now had a strange look on his face. Jackson motioned the boy to give Arch the talking feather, but he slowly shook his head, declining the offer and then fixing his gaze straight in front of him without a sound. Jackson had never seen him so grim, but he knew better than to discuss it now. It would be an embarrassment to Arch to ask him, in the council, why he refused to participate.

"David, is this all the information the group has to tell the council?" asked Jackson.

The feather was passed to David, and, like the others, he stood to reply to Jackson's query. He had no problems forming his words, because of the missionary school he had attended. David had done well, so well he could have pursued placement in a university, if he could have gained admittance, but the forced removal to Indian Territory had brought his bright future to an end. Still, he was proud of what he had learned, and faced Jackson as an equal.

"I only have heard of vague sightings of the boy with an object covered in rags. No one seems to have paid much attention. Everyone we spoke to had been more concerned with making it through another day, or about who might die next in their own lodges. Some say they remembered seeing the boy with a white man, which gave them a reason to wonder, especially because the boy was with a white man many of the tribe do not trust; since he was in no immediate danger, however, and they saw him smiling, they thought no more about it, and then quickly forgot about the occurrence."

Just as David finished speaking, the sound of some sort of commotion taking place outside made them all wonder what was happening. Then the person who was calling out, as if lost, finally came close enough for them to understand her words.

"Miss Anna, are you here? Miss Anna, oh lordy ifn I don't find you soon, we both be in trouble, missy. Miss Anna, please be here."

Anna and Jackson turned to each other, Anna holding her breath with eyes gaping wide. He nodded to her and immediately she jumped to her feet and raised her long skirt off the ground while running for the lodge opening, spurting out in the open just in time to see Mazy, still hollering at the top of her lungs, running around crazily about fifty yards further farther into the camp. Running after her, she had to raise her voice in order to get Mazy to come out of her frightened haze long enough to understand that the person she sought was right behind her.

"Mazy! Mazy, dear, I am right here. Goodness, stop that screeching. Father could hear you all the way to the Agency," Anna said, as she finally caught up with her.

"Oh, Miss Anna, praise the Lord I done found you. Miss Anna, we in terrible trouble. Your father, he's a stompin and a poundin on his desk, he say he wants you home this instant," cried Mazy, holding on to Anna as she looked around the camp in complete bewilderment. "I's sorry, Miss Anna. I figured there would be hell to pay ifn I didn't go a lookin for you. Miss Anna, I is awful scardt this time. He is actin like a man possessed. When he was a yellin, goin from room to room a hollering out for ya, he say he is goin to put you out an sends you back this very night! He ain't ever acted like dat, even drinkin like he done this day.

"He ain't had nothin to eat ceptin dat ole whiskey of his. He evens got dat gun of his out. It's loaded and alayin on his desk. Miss Anna, I come to get ya, not to bring you home, ma'am. No suhree. I think you should high-tail it somewheres else Miss..."

"Anna, what is going on? Are you in danger?" asked Jackson.

Jackson had been not far behind Anna, listening to Mazy's account of the state of mind Anna's father was in. Something extreme must be bothering Edwards for him to make plans for her departure at the spur of the moment like this.

"I am not sure, Jackson. Mazy is certain that I am, however, and I must confess that I don't know my father that well, so I really don't know if he would hurt his own daughter or not. But Jackson, I have no intention of, as Mazy says, 'high-tailing it' out of trouble. There is more at stake here than my personal safety, and I intend to see it through. We promised Sasa, did we not? Mazy, come with us to the lodge of a friend, and we will decide what to do next," Anna replied, already leading the way.

Mazy followed in silence, but was trembling all over. She had never been in an Indian lodge, and even though she had been in Indian Territory for months, she had never ventured into the camp. Not that she hadn't seen their pitiful state, but what could she have done for them? Her own situation had been rocky at best. Her own children had been sold right before her eyes; her husband had disappeared one night, after a terrible beating by Mr. Edwards, years before, when they lived down south. She had thought he had run away, but as the years went by she had begun to doubt his even being alive, for she felt sure he would have gotten a message to her some way. Now, by warning Miss Anna of her father's plans to pack her away, she had put herself in some danger as well, as there was nothing keeping him from legally killing his own slaves. So, with no plans for a way to keep out of the trouble she had placed herself in, she would have to trust in Anna and in her new found friend. She followed Anna to the council lodge and, when invited, she stepped into a world she could have only imagined.

It was true that some of the Cherokee families owned slaves. These had trudged and suffered along with their owners on the long trail. The Cherokee had tried desperately to fit into their neighbors' world, back in their homelands of Georgia, Tennessee and South Carolina, and some had felt the best way to do that was to also own slaves. But that had not changed the minds of the white settlers and land owners. For them it was an oddity to see a race they felt was barely human owning slaves, who they thought were animals. Mazy had only been owned by whites, so this experience was new and interesting.

Now the group settled down again, except for Wheezer. Sasa looked around the lodge and did not see him. She motioned to Jackson to alert him that Wheezer was gone. They both rose at once to go outside, but upon opening the door flap, they found him sitting with his back to the lodge, obviously on guard. Wheezer turned his head and saw his two best friends standing in the entrance, but made no move to come into the lodge. Jackson realized what was now Wheezer's self-given job.

"Thank you, Wheezer. I see you are on guard. You are the best dog ever," he said as he turned to go into the lodge, but Sasa touched his arm with questions in her eyes.

"Oh, everything is all right. I think with Mazy coming and her being upset, Wheezer feels that the group needs someone to protect us while we talk this out. He will either yip to let us know someone is here to see us or growl if an enemy approaches. Even though he is very smart, it is something that is bred into Jack Russells, and he does it very well," Jackson told her, which seemed to be explanation enough for Sasa, for she entered the lodge with no further worry.

Now the group would have to decide what to do next. They had very little time, since Anna and Mazy were now both missing from the house and they knew what Edwards was planning to do. Showing up for dinner now would be a gross mistake. Jackson knew that the showdown

179

would have to be tonight and that the confrontation could be deadly.

Chapter 23

The few days that it took for the Colonel to get close to the temporary camp where he might position himself within striking distance of the one person he was seeking to destroy, seemed an impossibly long time to him. Now, he was just outside the camp and it was late afternoon. So close, but as yet he had not seen Jackson in the camp. He would be patient, and the copse of trees he was hiding in made it very difficult to see him, even if close by.

He could no longer feel anything from his hip down to the foot on the side where he'd been shot by Andrew Halley, in his last desperate attempt to stop him from destroying his son before he himself died. He was sure that once his errand was finished, he would be able to limp to some country doctor and set things straight. His overwhelming desire for water had drastically diminished, and now he hardly noticed if he had eaten or taken sufficient liquid in for the day.

His goal was all encompassing, and he seemed not to notice the followers who kept pace with him each day. Not wanting to be seen just yet, they stayed behind cover and their leader kept them in line as they traveled several hundred yards behind the Colonel. No, they would wait for just the right time. Some in the group were getting anxious, wanting to attack, to take what they could, with no remorse, and then make a run for it. They were openly challenging the leader, but a well-placed rebuke was always enough to put them in their places, and so, on they followed. However, the leader knew the right time would be coming soon. Then he would take charge and the entire group would benefit, as they always had. Being a close knit group, each knew he could count on the other members to do their jobs. They would take all there was to take, then disappear back into the wilderness, looking for their next target. This was their life, a harsh one, maybe, but it kept them alive, which could be a tricky thing to do here in this hard country. Yes, it would be soon.

Edwards paced the floor with renewed desperation. He could feel the tension in the air. His daughter had not come back from the camp, his house slave, Mazy, was gone-- no one knew where--- and he could feel a great sense of foreboding settling down on him like a heavy wet blanket. He had thought his plan would work, but it all depended on Anna being shipped out of this camp this very night, and even that decision was not going as planned. He could not say why he was feeling so anxious, but the tension was so heavy around him it felt as though he could reach out and touch it.

He glanced back at his gun. Could be he would have to make use of it before the night was out. Jackson Halley had said he wanted to go over some of the bills of lading and there was no better time than when he brought Anna back home. However, he could not show Jackson anything that would not incriminate him. If it had been anyone else, he could have talked his way out of it, but, being part of the Halley family, Jackson would know what was supposed to have been delivered and what actually was delivered. His next step would be to report it to Halley's Financial and then on to the War Department.

His chance would have to be tonight. Either he must escape or he must kill Jackson Halley. Either way, he had to get rid of Anna, who was so full of righteous indignation she would never be able to keep it a secret, nor would she agree to it in the first place. The plan was just not working out because of not knowing where either Anna or Jackson were at this very moment. Taking care of the slave, Mazy, was no problem. He owned her, so he could dispose of her in any way he saw fit. There was no law against killing your own slaves. Even Billy was of no use to him now. But, what if he were forced to dispose of his own daughter? Could he do it? He might not have a choice, and for that he felt sorry. No one had asked her to come, anyhow, so it was her fault. Now, all he could do was wait and watch.

The little lodge where the council had taken place was quiet, but all the participants were still there. In silence, they considered what part they must all play in this dreadful night. Finally, Jackson woke from his reverie.

"I am sorry to you all, but our hand has been forced. Neither Anna nor Mazy can go home without my coming with them. That will mean a showdown with Edwards. So here is what I want you all to do. I would like Poison Woman and Medicine Man to please go back to your lodge; nothing will be said of your help so that you will be safe from revenge should it occur. Also, Mary Walkingstick, would you please take Usti Ga La Gi Na home? I am sure his parents would not want him involved in something this dangerous. We thank you very much for all of your help. Now the only way to find out the rest will be to get it from Edwards himself. Your names won't be mentioned. Peace go with you," said Jackson.

After those named had left the lodge, Jackson turned to Arch.

"My brother, you have been silent the whole day. Can you tell me now what is in your heart? Is there some wisdom that I may find in your words before we must leave?"

Arch looked directly into Jackson's eyes and slowly nodded. With a swish of his arm he indicated he would like to speak with Jackson outside. Jackson excused himself as he went out to stand beside Wheezer, so that Jackson could hear what Arch needed to say. They stood together in the late afternoon sunset, neither talking. Jackson knew he had to be patient. Cherokees did not do things in a hasty manner. If something was serious, they would think long and hard before expressing what was in their heart. Then Arch turned and grasped Jackson's shoulder firmly.

"Jackson, my blood brother. I owe you so much I can never repay all that you have done. But now, you may not want to have us in business with you, you may not want to be blood brothers with Archibald Flint or the entire clan the Flints belong to, the Wolf Clan," said Arch.

"I don't understand, Arch. There is nothing that can come between us. We are two ends of the same stick. You must tell me what the matter is. I cannot help you if you do not say the words," replied Jackson.

"My heart is breaking, Jackson," Arch answered. "There has been talk and much turmoil in all of the camps and lodges of the Cherokees in Indian Territory. Our problem in this camp is but a small part of it. It is true that some whites are stealing our allotments from us. They think we are ignorant heathens, but we are just as civilized as they are. The biggest problems are coming from the inside. It is like the snake who eats a weasel and for a while is content, until he finds that he is being eaten from the inside out and there is no defense against himself.

"That is what is happening with the Cherokees. There is much hatred now among the Old Settlers and the new Trail Where They Cried people. The smaller group, the Old Settlers, set up their own government when they came here, some years ago, but now that the Chief of all the Cherokees is here, he brings the same government that was established by our people back in Georgia. It is a government patterned off of the United States government and it is good. That is only one of the arguments.

"A worse one is the hatred towards the New Echota Treaty signers who forced all the tribe on that terrible march. Supporters of Chief John Ross, who did not sign the treaty and tried to tell the government the treaty had not been signed by the Chief, have vowed vengeance for the

184

over four thousand dead on the trail, not to mention the ones who have died here in the camps. The few old ones we have left have said that death is at the end of the road our nation is now on. It is not enough that the whites forced us to move and we lost so many on the way; we now have to worry if we will have civil war among the Cherokee.

"Jackson, I know that this night is important to your quest, but you must be careful now. If the camp finds out what is really happening here with the food allotments, there may be an all-out blood bath, and when people are that crazed, they don't look to see who they are striking out at. Something is going to happen soon, so we must get this over and done with, then make our way back to Van Buren as quickly as we can," he concluded, lowering his head a bit to signal he was done speaking.

"Arch, I had no idea that all this was happening. It is sad to think that the tribe could destroy itself at a time when they really need to pull together to overcome this awful blow. Our duty lies here, right now, with these people. If we don't at least stop Edwards and whoever has hired him, then how can we hope to ferret out the rest of the stealing from all of the great tribes? No, it has to start here with us," Jackson replied.

Arch considered for a moment, then said, "Yes, you are right."

"It would be very dangerous for you to be present when we confront Edwards tonight," Jackson went on. "If something goes wrong, he could put you into jail and claim you attacked a white man. Sasa is insisting she must be present tonight. I want her to stay away, but how can I deny her the chance to confront the possible murderer of her brother? I will have to keep a sharp eye on her and try to protect Anna at the same time. However, I do have something I need you to do."

"Speak it and it will be done," said Arch.

"Go to David's lodge; pack our things. Have them packed on the mules and ready to leave just in case we have to make a run for our lives," said Jackson.

"I will have it all ready," Arch guaranteed.

Jackson returned to the waiting group, still in David's lodge. As he entered, Anna ran to him, concern in her eyes.

"Jackson, the way Mazy talks, I think my father is quite out of his mind. He is liable to do anything, hurt anybody. I wouldn't doubt he would hurt me if it came to that. I can't bear the thought that someone might die because of me," she said, looking straight up into Jackson's caring eyes. Jackson cupped his hands about Anna's face.

"Anna, it really is not your fault. This thing your father has done was begun a long time before you came to stay with him. He would have had to be planning this for at least a couple of years. He had no idea it would be found out so quickly. We have the proof of that, but what we don't yet know are the details about the boy's murder, and exactly whom that button belongs to. Your father may be a cornered animal, but that is not going to stop us from finding out the truth.

"I can't back away now, Anna. This must be done, no matter the consequences. How can you or I sleep at night knowing what your father and others are continuing to do to the Cherokees? They really are my brothers, don't you see?"

Anna saw the determination in his eyes as she looked up, so close she almost forgot the deep anxiety that plagued her. Her heart beat a little faster from the touch of his hands around her face. Then, the moment faded as they both realized they were being watched. Sasa stood not too very far away from the couple. Pleasure showed plainly on her face. Wheezer stood beside her, wagging his tail. Anna, suddenly self-conscious, quickly looked down at the dusty floor of the lodge. Jackson, too, dropped his hands and began to pace the short distance inside.

Why, I do declare, commented Mazy to herself after watching the exchange between them. *What a strange place for a romance to begin,* she thought. Especially when none of them were sure of the outcome this day would lay bare.

Chapter 24

Jackson finally stopped his pacing. He glanced outside the door, pushing the flap to the side. The Indian Territory sun was just setting.

"Well, it is definitely past dinnertime now. Edwards must know you won't be coming. I think it is time we started over. Mazy, I know this will sound backwards, but you will need to come with Anna. If you are with his daughter, then Edwards can't say you are a runaway slave and have you shot. David and Arch are tending to getting our gear together, so that leaves the four of us, plus Wheezer. There is some safety in numbers, but if he pulls a gun, I want you women to take cover and let me handle it. Promise me this," said Jackson.

The three all nodded their agreement. There was no way to know if Wheezer understood, but he was used to following his own desires anyway. Jack Russells were singularly self-willed, as some owners of them soon found out after puppy-hood. Jackson had quit trying to control him a long time ago.

The Indian Agency cabin was not very far away, so the group did not hasten their pace. Each had their own expectations and anxieties plaguing their thoughts, but they had already passed the point of no return. Whatever was going to happen this night could not be stopped now.

Jackson made sure his gun was loaded and ready. He was an expert shot, and tonight it might mean the difference between life or death. Sasa also had her new Green River knife ready in its sheath at her hip, just underneath the tail of her shirt. Even though she had not had it long, she was getting fairly accurate with her throw. Jackson hoped she would not be in harm's way enough to have to use it.

As they approached the agency compound, Jackson noticed that only the front office was lit by an oil lamp.

188

Going through the front door might prove a problem. Edwards could just start shooting without bothering to answer the door.

"Mazy," Jackson said, signaling her to come closer, "is there a better way into the house that will give us some measure of protection? It looks like he is in the front office."

"Yes, suh, they is. Ifin we go around to the back door, we can come in through the kitchen. Masta Edwards, he never goes in or out dat door. It likely he won't even hear us," Mazy answered.

Jackson nodded, then signaled with a wave of his hand the direction he would be going, and motioned for them to keep their heads down as well. Anna crept right behind him, her eyes wide and nervous. Mazy and Sasa kept together, with Wheezer bringing up the rear. Wheezer also looked tense, his ears standing up with their tips flipped over, listening for every sound.

The sun was almost gone now; darkness reduced the shadows and the only way the group stayed together was by the sound of their own breathing. Sasa noticed something and moved forward to report it to Jackson.

"Jackson, there is something different tonight. I do not hear the crickets or any night sounds. That usually means danger, when the creatures stop talking," she told him.

Jackson just gave her a quick nod. He had no idea what it might mean. The person he looked for was in the cabin, and as far as he knew he had no enemies in the surrounding woods, so he dismissed that thought from his mind to concentrate on the task ahead.

They all slipped into the kitchen and closed the back door, then Anna took the lead and motioned to Jackson that she had to be the first to knock on Edwards' door. Jackson knew it was the most logical thing to do, but he feared for her safety, so he stayed close at hand. Anna crept to the door, then softly knocked.

189

"Father, are you in? I need to talk with you," she said in a quivering voice.

First there was no sound from the inner room, then, suddenly Edwards threw the door open. The group was startled, and with the bright light shining in their eyes it took a second for them to realize he had his gun drawn on them. Edwards stood before them unshaven, crumpled and bleary eyed from drink, the gun slightly shaking in his hand.

"Ah, you finally decided to grace me with your presence. Well, ain't we a cozy little foursome, and what an array we have here. We got my own dear daughter, who might as well be a perfect stranger to me. I can see you have decided to be a traitor, along with that nigger, Mazy. Don't think she won't pay, daughter of mine. And looky here, we got Sasa. That brat of a brother of yorn is the cause of all my problems. You and your damn Cherokee kind. Last but not least, Andrew Halley's pipsqueak of a son, Jackson. You thought you got one over on me, didn't ya. Ha! Well it's me that's got you now; what does ya think of that, mister?" Edwards said as he glared at them with ripe hate on his face.

Sasa quickly looked behind her and discovered Wheezer gone, but she was too frightened now to worry about it. Edwards was motioning them to enter the office.

"Now, Jackson, hand over that there gun, place it on the desk, and no fancy stuff, neither. Fine, fine. I been thinkin on this for some time, but this is workin out just fine for me. It's so nice to have you all together at the same time. That a way I can get rid of you right quick like. Oh, Anna honey, don't look so damned surprised. You was just too strong willed for your own good. From the first day you showed up you didn't seem to know your own place. Well, I never wanted you here... in fact, I never wanted you, period. It was your Ma that wanted children, not me, so it's not like I'll be losing anything, is it?" crooned Edwards.

190

"Why don't you let Sasa go home, Edwards? She hasn't done you any harm," said Jackson.

"No!" yelled Sasa. "I won't go. Not until he tells me about my brother."

"So you want to know about the injun boy, huh? Well, I think I can oblige you on that score. Hey, did you know I never even knew his name? Well, it don't matter none, cause I took care of his meddling right quick."

"What do you mean by 'his meddling'?" asked Jackson.

"I don't mind telling ya now. You won't be able to tell anybody after tonight anyways. I suspect you already know that I been gettin some of my own share of all that money the government is a throwin away on these here injuns. It weren't hard a-tall, no, sir. But one day, that little brother of yorn was a snooping around here and happened to see me a gettin paid my portion of the loot due to me. My, let's say, benefactor was here and your brother saw him give me that money. In fact, it was his idea what to do about a keepin the boy quiet. Pretty ingenious, I must say so myself," Edwards explained.

"You stupid man. He had no idea what you were doing. He was probably more interested in seeing real money. He was too young to know why you were getting paid!" screamed Sasa.

"Well, better safe than sorry, I always say," Edwards replied, not showing any remorse for a life taken unnecessarily.

Jackson had no idea how they were going to get out of this jam, but he knew he had to keep Edwards talking. Mazy was clinging to Anna, who was looking at her father with new found hatred , and Sasa was standing bravely on her own, defiant and resolute. The more information he had, the better, so he said, "What did he tell you to do?"

191

"You know, I think that man knows more ways of killin then I ever thought of. He noticed that carved frog of Mazy's. He up and asked her for it. We took it back to the shed and he soaked that blamed thing in rat poison for a few minutes. He let it dry some before he said it was ready, then I gave it to the boy. That kid shoulda died from just playin with that painted frog, but it seemed he hid it away and only got it out once in a while. When the boy didn't die right off..." He paused, chuckling. "This will knock you over with a feather, it will, I went and told that boy the frog was a Wishin Frog. He could have all the wishes he wanted ifin he licked it once for every wish, but I told him he had to keep it a secret or the wishes wouldn't come true. I imagine he told you about the frog anyhow," said Edwards

"No," said Sasa, "He never told me. I knew nothing about it."

The color drained from Edwards' face. "You mean to tell me, that boy never said anything about that frog to you?"

"No, he never told his sister. It looks like you gave yourself away, Edwards," said Jackson.

Edwards grabbed for his whiskey and took a long swallow, still holding the shaky gun on the group.

"Don't matter none anyhow," said Edwards, "You was already here to investigate me anyway."

Jackson mouth turned to a wide grin in spite of the fix they were in. "There, you are wrong again, Edwards. I came here to look for my dog. He got lost in the forest and it just so happened that Sasa saved him. I had never met Sasa before this and I had no other reason to come here. The rest was all in your own mind, Edwards."

Once the realization that he had caused his own demise became clear, Edwards' face began to harden and he looked at the group with a desire for revenge written plainly on it.

"All right, so I did this to myself. I can fix it all right now, and I intend to do just that. Everybody, turn around and march out that front door across the hall. We are goin for a little stroll in the moonlight. Anna, grab the oil lamp on my desk; I'll need the light to do what I gotta do."

Jackson had no opportunity to try to overpower Edwards yet. He was hoping for just one moment when he was less on his guard. One thing he was sure of was that Edwards could not shoot them all at once. When he shot that Colt, he would have to cock it again before he could get another shot off, and in the drunken state he was in, it would not be a very fast move. It might be his only chance to get them all out of this mess.

Edwards made them trudge out beyond the camp for about a quarter of a mile. Mazy was whimpering, clinging on to Anna's side. Jackson put his arm around Sasa's shoulder as they walked.

"Wheezer is gone," she whispered to him. "I don't know where he went."

"Don't worry," Jackson answered. "He is probably keeping track of us. Try to stay calm, Sasa, we may not have much of a chance to make it out of this."

"I am not worried, Jackson. The Creator has seen Mr. Edwards' evil. He will be punished, I know it," she said. "Do you hear, Jackson? Still no night sounds. No frogs, no crickets, no owls. Something is wrong."

Again, Jackson felt no reason to worry about it, his mind being taken up with trying to extract himself and his friends from the fate of death looming ahead of them. After all, how can you reason with a crazy man? There was no doubt that Edwards was mad. Anything might cause him to pull that trigger. When and if he did, Jackson needed to react instantaneously.

Their trek stopped abruptly and Edwards motioned with the gun for them to move deeper into the trees.

Jackson knew the time for action was coming, but he still saw no way to intervene without the risk of someone being hurt in the process. He needed to buy time.

"Sasa told me you came by her lodge," he said. "Were you looking for the frog you gave to her brother?"

Edwards' eyes began to focus. Jackson had hit on a loose end Edwards had forgotten about.

"Now that you mention it, yes. I suppose you are going to tell me it was buried with the boy," said Edwards.

"No, in fact, I have seen it. Did it not look like a frog that had already jumped and had its legs stretched out behind him? I think it was a bluish green with orange, yellow and red swirls, dots and lines. I know where it is," said Jackson.

"Where is it, Jackson? You better tell me, pronto, before I fill your gut with some very costly lead," said Edwards, trying to bluff his way into finding the location of the frog.

"Well, let's see. I pushed it into a hole in one of the trees close to Sasa's lodge. You should have no problem finding it. Of course, if there was someone I told about it, you know, to keep it for my father when he comes for inspection... well, when we don't come back from this meeting he might just think it would be a perfect time to remove it for safe keeping. Just in case," said Jackson in a very reasonable voice.

Sasa peered into Jackson's eyes. She knew he was taking a risk by telling a complete lie to try and save them all. She knew darn well Jackson had not had time to do any of that. As far as she knew, the frog was still lying on the floor of David's lodge, where they had left it after the council meeting.

"Oh, now, I see what you are up to. Your a thinkin I might just not shoot all of youins ifin I think I could get my hands on that frog. I think you're lying about ever seein it.

Don't think that will save your skins," replied Edwards, sweat breaking out on his face as desperation filled his eyes.

"No, I'm not lying. Otherwise, how would I know what color and shape the frog was made in? Sasa never got to see it until she found it, then showed it to me. So, I thought a little protection would be in order. If you hurt any of us, including Mazy, the next time you see that poisonous frog you will be at your trial for murder. On the other hand, if you just got on your horse and rode off into the sunset, meaning west, you might have a good chance of keeping your skin."

Edwards had started to pace while Jackson was talking. This was a tough spot. Even if he killed all of them, the evidence could still be used against him. He knew he had no hope of ever finding that frog. He felt the whole camp was working against him now. He even briefly thought about the immediate consequences if he killed the whole group. He was still in Indian Territory, and the Cherokees would hunt him down. He'd be dead before he could reach the Kansas border. As the options available to him dwindled, he began to feel hopeless. He slowly sat down on a boulder and wept, but kept holding the gun on the group.

"My whole life has been one blunder after another. The cards are stacked against me. I don't know why I should have to suffer the punishment that is really due to the mastermind of this whole operation. He is the one that put the poison on the frog, he is the one who told me to give it to the boy, and he is also the one that was in an all fired hurry for the poison to work and told me to get the boy to lick it. Why should I have to bear it all?" he cried, as anger mingled with his words, saliva spitting out of his mouth as he whined.

"I think I know something that would go a long way with the authorities. You might only get charged with stealing. It might not be so bad," said Jackson.

195

The others of the foursome looked at each other nervously. Could it be that Jackson would be successful in getting them out of this fix they were in? They all seemed to know to keep their mouths shut while he worked his magic.

"What? What could I do that would help me now?"

"If you told me who your boss is, I could make sure *he* gets charged with the murder, not you. That way, you might not have to serve much of a sentence. Besides, the authorities and the Ward Department really want the leader, the one who put this all together. That would be a good thing to do if saving your skin is what you are aiming at," reasoned Jackson.

"Really? I... I don't think I have ever killed a kid in my life, not even when I was in the Army. Yes, I think you might have somethin there," said Edwards, brightening to this new possibility. "Even your father might be grateful to me for rootin him out for you. I might even be a hero in some people's eyes. I could come out of this smellin like a rose," mused Edwards.

"Sure, I think you might be right, Edwards. The government will want the head guy anyway. So, who is your boss? Where does he live?"

Edwards stood up with a new resolution on his face, hopeful, like a drowning man reaching for the hand that would pull him to safety.

"His name is..." but Edwards could not finish because of the loud report of a gun coming from behind the group. The ball smacked Edwards between the eyes, then he dropped to the ground.

The group was too stunned to register any feelings just yet. The foursome turned as one in the direction of the trees behind them. The darkness was complete within the trees as they tried to peer through the night. Anna raised the lamp, but they could see nothing until a figure limped forward. Sasa was the only person in the group who had

196

never seen this man before. Her puzzled expression went unnoticed, though. Jackson, Anna and Mazy had all seen this man, albeit at different times and circumstances, but they recognized him just the same.

Anna knew the man as the one she had met in the dead of night to exchange messages with for her father. Mazy knew him as the man who had taken the painted frog from her hands to use as a weapon against an unsuspecting little boy. However, Jackson knew him best, as the pompous ass who reveled in the misfortunes of the Cherokee, Colonel Dumont Jeffries. His astonishment was complete.

"Why, Jackson, my boy, how interesting to come across you here in the backwoods of Indian Territory. I believe our last meeting was a bit strained, don't you agree? Well, no matter. I think we can rectify that tonight," the Colonel said as he limped closer in the glare of the lamp.

"Oh! You are surprised to see me here. Yes, I'm sure you are, suh. I must tell you, though, our meeting has not been by accident, no, indeed not. You see, I have traveled all the way from St. Louis, just to see you, my boy. No, no, don't say anything now. I have a few things I wish to say first," he said as a slow creepy grin enveloped his grimy and travel worn face.

Jackson was alert at once, for there was something odd in the Colonel's manner. Then all sorts of questions started popping up into his mind at alarming speed, questions he felt he maybe had the answers for after all. Such as, why would Colonel Jeffries kill Edwards? Easy; to get rid of a liability and his business partner. Why would he come on horseback all the way from St. Louis, saying he came to see him? He supposed he had found out where he was and had decided to eliminate him so he could keep his secret 'golden goose', bringing in the money at the expense of the Cherokees. The thought of St. Louis, however, brought Jackson up short. He knew his father had made his St. Louis office his home base for a while until the company was out of danger. Then a question came to him that he could not answer, and the question gave him a sense of dread. Why was the Colonel in St. Louis in the first place? He was not the type of man who liked to be out of society and the comforts it could bring, and St. Louis was a frontier town... raw, practically ungoverned and offering very few, if any, creature comforts. He followed that train of thought only for a few seconds, until Sasa interrupted it.

"So, you are the white man who killed my little brother," she seethed, her fists clenched as she stood with her feet apart, ready to launch herself at him. "You are a dog and lower than dirt. The Creator will not allow you to go unpunished. You are an evil man."

Sasa was partially shielded from the Colonel's view by Jackson's tall frame. She successfully had reached under her shirt, resting her hand on the hilt of her Green River knife, getting ready to take the Colonel's life. She remained calm, waiting for the right moment for a clear throw.

"Shut up, you filthy Indian," said the Colonel. "Edwards should have gotten rid of you long ago instead of worrying about that stupid frog, but don't worry; I am here to clean the mess up."

Anna, with Mazy still clinging to her side, inched over close enough to whisper to Jackson.

"Do you smell that? I am about to retch. It smells as if something is dead," she said with wrinkled nose and a deep frown.

"I don't know what it is, Anna. He does not seem to notice it," said Jackson.

The smell was indeed ripe and it was not going away. Then Sasa pointed toward the Colonel's boots but said nothing. The Colonel was too busy gloating to see their exchange. Jackson looked where Sasa had pointed and saw a very curious thing: a long stream of something green and slimy was oozing up, bubbling, then running down the Colonel's knee high boot. Flies were alighting on it, but the Colonel seemed totally oblivious to its existence. Then Jackson looked closer at the Colonel's face and found that the hollows he thought were just the light and shadow playing across his face were actually deep dark crevasses in his cheeks and under his eyes. His skin had a gray sallow tone to it and his eyes were wild, flitting here and there, but not really seeing the details of what was before him, since he had not even noticed Sasa pointing to his boot.

Jackson snapped back to the Colonel as he was saying...

"I saw your father in St. Louis and, might I say, I did not leave him well. No, not well at all, suh. In fact, Jackson, your dear father is, oh, how shall I say it...dead. Yes, and I had the satisfaction of delivering the fatal shot. What do you say to that, my boy?" the Colonel said as he swayed from side to side, coughing between every few words.

Jackson was struck dumb. The possibilities ran through his mind as if he could logically render null and void what this swaying derelict of a man was saying. He listened intently to the Colonel as he continued.

"What! Nothing to say? Don't you believe me? I assure you, suh, I shot him in the chest at close range while I looked straight into his unbelieving eyes. Too bad, my boy, that he did not have any parting words for you. Oh, well, it really does not matter anyway, since you and the rest of your motley friends here will all be dead very soon now. I traveled here to kill you, Jackson my boy, but I just had to see your face when I delivered the sad news of your father's demise. And I made sure he knew, before he died, that I was on my way to end your life. An appropriate parting gift, don't you think?"

Jackson could not think about his father now. He had his friends to protect. As the Colonel continued to goad him, he edged in front of Anna, hoping to protect her with his own body. Anna began to do the same with Sasa, but she refused to budge. Sasa was totally consumed with her hatred for this man, the inventor of her brother's bizarre death. It seemed she was not worried about her own safety; her only goal now was to give back the same as he had given. Grasping her Green River knife concealed at her side, she took a step forward, but was stopped by an unearthly snarling growl coming from behind her. She stood still, not knowing for sure what to do next.

Jackson also heard the menacing guttural growl and soon caught sight of Wheezer, crouching down, practically slinking on his belly. Every hair on his back was standing at attention, his eyes seemed to glow in the dark, reflecting the dim light of the lamp Anna carried, and his lips were pulled completely back from all of his sharp canines, making them look much bigger. Absolutely focused on his goal, Wheezer continued to creep forward, only a few inches with each move, and finally the Colonel took notice of him.

"What in the Sam Hill is that? He...he looks rabid," he said, as he began to back up slowly.

Even though the Colonel had the gun, ready to shoot, in his hand, he seemed to forget he was holding it. The sight of the fierce dog so unnerved him that he began to stumble over his own feet. Wheezer continued to advance and the Colonel continued to stumble back one step at a time.

"Do something Jackson, kill it...kill it. The creature looks possessed...I can't stand it, where did it come from, Jackson, my boy...do something," he screeched.

Jackson, however, was too busy being mesmerized by the most unusual sight he had ever seen, which had appeared directly behind the Colonel. Understanding dawned in his mind and he looked down at his dog with a slight smile, but made no attempt to stop him from advancing.

"Jackson, I...I take it all back. I swear I never hurt your father. Now, kill that creature, Jackson. Jackson!...I," the Colonel cried.

At that same moment, he stumbled one last time. As Wheezer swept forward the Colonel fell back into a mass of fur and teeth, tearing at his clothes and flesh. Jackson quickly caught Wheezer by the scruff of his neck to keep him out of the melee while Anna and Sasa stood stock still, watching the Colonel being torn limb from limb by a pack of hungry wolves. The wolves had followed him for many miles, lured by the smell of the rotting flesh of his leg, which had so infected his body with gangrene that he would not have lived long, anyhow. Anna had mixed feelings, but seeing her father killed in front of her caused her to have no sorrow for the man who had enticed and entrapped him into his game of greed and embezzlement. Sasa was not seeing the blur of blood and flesh as the pack of about ten or eleven gray wolves satisfied their long held-back hunger. She was seeing her brother as he once was. She felt the closure she needed to end the mourning over a great injustice.

Mazy had turned her face away, placing her hands over her ears and muttering a prayer to "Sweet Jesus" and "God Almighty", but the others neither turned away nor did they block out the sounds of a man being devoured alive. Finally, Jackson nudged the girls, turning them back toward the Agency building, still holding Wheezer, who wriggled every which way trying to get loose to attack the predators.

On that walk back to the camp, with the sounds of the terrible, grisly feast still echoing behind him, Jackson's mind was a clutter of questions. He would have to ride back to his place in Van Buren as quickly as possible so he could check on his father. There was so much to do before he could leave, though, but first he hoped there was still a drink or two left in Edwards' office, for his nerves needed bracing. So they walked on, four abreast, down the path back to the camp. It occurred to Jackson that he had not needed to do anything, really, as if the hand of God had arranged for the wages to be paid to both the men who most assuredly would have killed all of them in cold blood. His relief in that fact was enormous.

Wheezer also felt fulfilled. He did not know the ins and outs, but he did know that the threat to his loved ones was over. When the group had approached the agency on their way to see Edwards, he had been able to smell the rotting flesh of the Colonel's leg in the air and he had also noticed the silencing of the night noises which meant that someone or something was out in the woods, waiting. He could also smell the wolves. It was the wolves that he needed to protect Jackson and Sasa from, so he investigated where the scents were emanating from and waited up wind of the pack until the humans emerged out of the agency building. He had known that the man holding his friends at gunpoint was also a predator, so his growl, so fierce and bold, was meant for the man and the wolves. Now his job was done, and done well. He could revert back to the loving companion, adored by both Jackson and Sasa.

Sasa, on the other hand, was feeling a bit empty. When she had the puzzle to work out, she did not have to be reminded that she was alone. Now that the killers were dead, she knew Jackson would go home and take his dog with him, and that fact gave her great sadness. She walked in silence.

Anna also was feeling alone. She had come to love being around the Cherokee people. She wanted to learn more about their life and customs, but without her father here, she did not have a reason to remain. At the same time, there was Jackson, whom she was just beginning to have feelings for. Knowing his father had recently died, he probably would not want her around while he privately mourned him. She felt she would be intruding on him and his family. So there was nothing to do but to go back to Boston and take up the life of a society miss again. The prospect looked gloomy indeed.

Lastly, Mazy was totally unsure of what would happen to her now. Probably, she would be sold at the slave market and have to get used to a new master who might be good or bad. That was the life of a slave, but she would be sorry to be torn from Anna, whom she had come to care for.

The few weeks they all had spent here in this forced destination and home of the Cherokee people had changed all their lives and opened as well as closed doors. They all had cause to celebrate over their victory, but at the same time, they hated losing the closeness they had come to depend on here in Indian Territory. It would be a bitter pill to take.

Chapter 25

Sasa and Wheezer sat in her lodge with no fire burning. Jackson had told her to go to bed. He still had many things to do before he could stop and get a couple hours of sleep, he had said, and she might as well take Wheezer with her. It had been a very long day indeed. Now, after all that had happened, it was hard to realize how fast it all came together. In one long day, her anger over the injustice of her brother's murder had been quenched with the cold drenching of death. If there was anything that strengthened her faith in the Creator, it was this day's events. She felt that the likelihood of all the small bits of information the group had gathered, known by just the right persons and then acted upon, coalescing into the solid proof of murder and embezzlement, then concluding so succinctly with finality, was beyond measure. Only the Great One, the Creator, could have made it happen this way, without any of them getting hurt and without any of them having blood on their own hands.

Now her future lay before her, but what was it? All she could see ahead were endless days of trying to survive before winter. Then there was a great possibility that she might not make it through her first winter in Indian Territory. It was true that many of her camp neighbors would help her along, but there was still the problem with getting the promised goods from the allotments to be able to survive. Jackson had said this was not the end of that problem. He said it was only the tip of a great mountain of thievery and it might take years to root out the wrongdoers. However, her needs were much more immediate. The prospect of Jackson, Anna, Arch and Wheezer going home was more than she could stand to think of, so she sat in the darkened lodge, stroking Wheezer's head and waiting for the dawn, still hours away.

Anna felt refreshed after a quick cool wipe down with a moistened cloth from a basin of water laced with a few drops of lavender essence. She took more time than usual to change into a clean dress. She took her glistening pale hair down from its pins, brushed it until it shone and allowed it to fall over her shoulders. Choosing to wear a simple pastel green morning dress with salmon trim, she swept out of her room to meet Jackson in the parlor where Mazy was keeping him company.

"You look lovely, Anna," he greeted her. "I am sorry that I am not able to make myself more presentable at the moment, for I did not bring those kinds of accouterments with me on this trip. While I am relieved that we are safe, I don't know whether to believe Colonel Jeffries about the death of my father, or not. It would seem the Colonel did receive the wound to his foot, but I am just not ready for what might await me back home. So, please forgive my solemn mood; I hope he was lying.

"At any rate, Mazy has been wonderful and has cooked us a bite to eat while we talk. We don't need to eat in the dining room...here is much more comfortable," he went on.

"Oh Jackson, I am so very sorry," she replied. "You must be so anxious, but keep in mind what seemed to be the Colonel's nature. He enjoyed making you squirm. For now, though, let us concentrate on the task at hand so that you can be completely ready for your journey tomorrow.

"I, too, am glad to stay in this room. The dining room holds some unpleasant memories just now. Thank you, Mazy, for taking care of us after this horrendous day. You must be ready to collapse. I asked Jackson to make sure you stayed so that we might talk before you went to bed. There is much to discuss." Anna voice was calm and soothing in the quiet room.

Mazy looked as if she were about to say something, when a hard knock on the Agency door shattered the quiet. Mazy went to answer it, returning with a tall man in a United States Army uniform. Jackson recognized him at once.

"Captain Belknap, you look like you've been riding hard," he said.

"Indeed I have, Jackson. I have been sent on an errand of great importance, first and foremost, to check on your safety. It seems there is a gentleman gone rogue heading here to do you harm," the Captain replied.

Jackson could not help the tiny grin that crept onto his face for the narrow escape he had experienced, but it was also tinged with sadness for the news that he feared the Captain would deliver to him next.

"I am happy to inform you, Captain, that the man you speak of, a certain Colonel Jeffries, did arrive here. However, he met his own demise before he could harm anyone of us. Ah, except for Mr. Edwards, whom the Colonel killed upon first arriving here at the Agency. If it had not been for my dog Wheezer---oh, of course, you know him as Jack---well, if it hadn't been for him, we would all be corpses at this very moment. I will be happy to relate exactly what happened, but first you might want to tell your men to travel due north on the path through the woods. There, about a half mile past this camp, you may find some remnants of the Colonel. However, if they don't leave soon, your men are likely to not find much left at all."

The Captain's stern posture visibly relaxed as he removed his hat after he noticed a lady was in the room. Now, his curiosity was piqued, but he took a few moments to give the instructions to his men before he returned to the little group in the parlor.

"I am so sorry that you were put in such danger, Jackson. Your father sent us a letter...,"

"My father? He's not dead? Jeffries said he had shot him in the chest at short range," said an excited Jackson.

"He did, indeed, but through sheer guts and determination Andrew Halley pulled through. A lesser man would surely have died from that hole the Colonel put in him. Even before he knew if he would live or die, he dispatched a letter to Fort Smith, advising me of the plan of the Colonel to come to this Agency in order to destroy you. Your father gave almost as good as he got, though." The Captain paused as Jackson's eyebrows shot up in puzzlement. "He shot the Colonel in the foot, blew two toes clean off. I know that because the report came to me from the Army outpost near there. However, even if he was wounded in the foot as bad as that, the lawmen lost his trail after he crossed a stream, I suppose heading here. Tell me, what happened to him? I will need a complete briefing on what happened here. Your father will be relieved in the utmost once he is sure of your survival," said the Captain.

"Well, Captain, pull up a chair and help yourself to the refreshments. I suppose you brought several of your company. Mazy, would you mind asking one of the other kitchen girls to get the men from the Army some food and drink, especially the ones the Captain sent off to find the remains of the Colonel? Then return here, please, as there are matters that only you can relate. Later, we will have more things to discuss, just the three of us," Jackson said.

Throughout the late evening, into the morning hours, the story was told and explained down to finite detail. The Captain was nonplussed over the fact that it had turned out with such an odd turn of events. After he retired to his tent, which had been set up out in the compound, Anna, Jackson and Mazy discussed many things, finally coming to a decision which allowed them to remove to separate rooms for sleep. Deciding to stay in the house with them, since there was no one to see to the safety of the women, Jackson sent word to

Arch that all was well, and that he should be ready to leave in the morning.

The three had been so exhausted they overslept. All were accustomed to getting up at or before dawn, but the extreme emotions of the previous day, plus the late night discussion, caused them to sleep on until they were suddenly brought out of bed by the beating of drums, bells and Cherokee song.

Anna hurriedly dressed. When she came into the parlor, Jackson and Mazy were just arriving as well.

"What is going on?" Anna asked, her eyes wide and worried.

Jackson had long been accustomed to the Cherokee dances, chants and drums.

"It's the Cherokee," he explained, as he looked out the front window. "Apparently, they are having a celebration. Come, this will be a sight you will never forget in all your life."

And indeed, it was a sight, for once out of the Agency building, Anna could see a people transformed. She was astonished to see the very people who, just the day before, had been broken, poor, sad and depressed, now wearing the best of whatever they possessed. Some families had been able to preserve elaborate regalia and dresses made of white doe skin or dark dresses with cowrie shells sewn in a neat design. Some of the young girls had tin jingles sewn all over their dresses that made a happy sound when they walked or danced. Many had moccasins, beaded or quilled with bright designs. Throughout the crowd Anna could see feathers of various shades decorating staffs. Many women danced with shawls or capes, some of them holding feathered dance fans in their hands. The men wore brightly colored turbans on their heads, or their hair was cut in a mohawk. Some had vivid colors of paint on their faces, and even those who had arrived in Indian Territory with nothing at all save for rags, danced happily.

The sound was also extremely exhilarating. Several men sat around a very large drum, all with a beater in their hand, beating out a specific rhythm in unison, all singing a song in Cherokee while two semi-circles of dancers danced joyously around in the circle set up just outside the Agency building. Young, old, women, men, all had smiles on their faces. Anna noticed the beat seemed to go through her body, becoming part of it, like a beating heart.

When Jackson, Anna and Mazy emerged from the building and came down the steps, the drums fell silent as Medicine Man and Poison Woman then led another group over to stand beside them; Sasa, Wheezer, Arch and David Flint were all in that group. Poison Woman stood by her brother as he made a speech, silently giving him her full support. He looked like a man reborn, younger and with hope.

The captain and his men respectfully stood off to the side, not interfering, but knowing all the same what this was all about.

Finally, after all was quiet, Medicine Man spoke.

"Jackson, Friend Of The Cherokee, we wish to honor you and all of your friends. You have given us hope for our future. You have brought justice to Sasa for the loss of her little brother. You have exposed the bad deeds of that Agency man..." He avoided naming Edwards because he could not speak the name of the dead, "and you have made it possible for us to make it alive through this winter. The captain of Fort Smith has said he will help to provide what the Agency man did not. For all this we are grateful.

"We are also proud of our young Sasa. She was fearless and bold. She would have made a good warrior. We are happy that the daughter of the Agency man did not kill her own flesh and blood. That would have been a very bad thing in this camp.

"There is one among you whom we have great affection for, one who helped in every way he could. One who brought you, Jackson, Friend Of The Cherokee, to us, and so we believe he was sent to help us by the Creator. That one is Wheezer. He will forever be known to us as Wheezer, Cherokee Warrior Dog. Any human who raises a hand to harm Wheezer, makes an enemy of the Cherokee Nation."

Wheezer sat at attention, looking straight forward as if he knew what was being said about him. He did not look to the left or the right, holding his head up proudly as he sat between Sasa and Jackson.

"This dance is in your honor, all of you who have helped the Cherokee. We now pronounce you all blood brothers and sisters of our tribe. We know you must leave us, but we hope you will stay a while yet and enjoy the dance, then go in peace. That is all I have to say."

Now it was Jackson's turn to speak. He had to, because if he did not it would be an insult. He squared his shoulders.

"We are all very glad that no more harm has come to the Cherokee this day," he began. "We are honored by this dance and we are happy to be your brothers and sisters. Believe me when I say, Wheezer is also proud to be of service to the Cherokee.

"There is one thing that I must ask the tribe before we leave. Sasa is alone now. It is true that you all will help to take care of her, but she will be past the age when she can go to school by the time they get one set up here. Anna and I would like the honor of taking Sasa to Van Buren, only a short ride away, to live at my ranch, where she will be taught in the ways of the white man, but not forgetting her Cherokee ways. Then, she will be able to be of better help to her people. I have not asked Sasa to do this thing. First, I would like to have permission from this camp. Arch Flint is also bringing back with us David, his brother, since the rest of his family are living at the ranch, so Sasa will not lack contact with her own Cherokee blood. Will the tribe honor us with its permission?" said Jackson, not glancing at Sasa yet.

"I speak for this camp when I say, yes. Sasa may go if she wishes it. We can think of no better friend for her to be with. When she comes home, she will be ready to help her people learn what we must know to protect our way of life in the future. She may go in peace. I, Medicine Man, have said it."

Now, Sasa looked up at Jackson with visible tears in her eyes. She had been dreading the moment when she would have to say goodbye to Wheezer. Being parted from him was like tearing her heart out of her own body. She would not have to do this now. Gladness filled her heart and she nodded her head in the affirmative, while the drums and the dancing resumed.

They stayed at the camp for another night so that Sasa could collect her things and say her farewells to her friends. She took Wheezer into many lodges where he was given bits of food, petted and blessed. Wheezer was satisfied. He seemed to know that Sasa was coming with him. Now he would have both of his most favorite people to love.

Anna, too, had been asked to come to Van Buren and Fort Smith. The captain said that he would arrange for her to stay at a very reputable boarding house in Fort Smith. Jackson would pay for her keep for as long as she desired it. He secretly hoped she would never have to leave.

Mazy actually now belonged to Anna. She had inherited all of her father's property, some of which she gave out to the families at the camp; the rest she packed so that the Captain and his men could help bring it back for her. Since she did not believe in slavery, she promised to give Mazy her freedom. Then, if Mazy desired a job, she could be Anna's companion and lady's maid, with an appropriate salary. Anna, for her part, promised to teach her to read and write.

As a gesture of kindness, Anna issued all of her father's slaves their freedom papers. They could now choose to stay on in Indian Territory or go with the group back to Arkansas. The Captain assigned three of his men to maintain the Agency until a new Agent could be sent to take over, but Jackson confiscated all of the books and papers so that his father would be able to sort out how much damage had been done to his investment and how much money had been stolen, as well as how much replacement goods the Cherokee were owed. Jackson would also make a report to the United States War Department in hopes that a better system could be found to administer the allotments to the native peoples.

As the group set out along Lee Creek, heading back toward Van Buren, Sasa hung back a moment with Wheezer by her side. She knelt down next to him.

"Wheezer, I am going to come back one day. I am going to help my people. Now that you are honored by my people, maybe you can help them, too," she said, watching Wheezer's face.

In response, Wheezer turned to gaze at Sasa, then issued his own form of affirmation and agreement... he gave her a big wet kiss. Then Sasa rose and they walked side by side toward the future. Together.

The End

Enjoy a preview of Wheezer's next exciting adventure, *Wheezer and the Shy Coyote.*

Preface

It was a hot, breezy, but humid afternoon the day Kathy visited the Old Fort Museum in Fort Smith, Arkansas. Why did they always have to take these kinds of trips in the hot summer months? Already tired of hearing about old this and old that, the past was long dead, and she was more interested in the here and now. She barely heard the guide as they walked along the path that lead them past the oldest site of the earlier fort built on the land they called, Belle Point. The Arkansas River lazily flowed past them. Just looking at it made her feel sleepy. Kathy wanted nothing better than to head back to their motel room, luckily just a few blocks away on Garrison.

Ira was all eyes and ears. It had been that way ever since he found out that he was Cherokee Indian. In fact, not just a little, but enough that he qualified to get his citizenship card from the tribe. So, it was natural that he would want to know as much as he could find out about the area. She would give him that, but how long does someone have to look at the old river before they saw enough? Ira turned to see Kathy waiting on the walkway. He had crept closer to the edge of the river bank, and was examining where the river had taken a chunk out of the side of the shore. He motioned for her to join him, and she reluctantly acquiesced. As she got closer, she was able to hear the guide continue her rehearsed spiel.

"The river banks have changed many times over the years, but less so since the dams were put in which have regulated the flow somewhat. We still get high water sometimes which eats away at the sandy bank, but then deposits it somewhere else further down," said the guide.

Kathy got closer to look, a little worried about the side of the bank collapsing under them. Just before she looked away, a glint of sunlight played on something along

213

the shore. She saw it in the corner of her eye, and she quickly looked back.

"What is that?" she asked the attendant, pointing to the object.

"Oh, probably some trash from upstream. We sometimes have to go through and clean the banks from all the garbage that gets swept up here."

Kathy looked a little closer.

"I don't think it's trash. It's half buried in the bank," said Kathy.

Curiosity was one of the things that got Kathy into trouble. Once something intrigued her, nothing would stop her from checking it out.

"It looks as though it has a handle on it. I am going to reach over the bank and pull it out," said Kathy.

"I'm afraid I can't allow you to do that, miss. Our insurance does not cover exploration on our grounds. You could be hurt, or you could fall in," said the guide, all the while, Kathy was down on her hands and knees moving closer to her target, taking no heed to the guide's warnings.

"Don't waste your breath," said Ira. "She's pretty bull headed. Always has been, at least for the last forty years of marriage."

Ira chuckled at the guide's consternation.

"Almost there, ugh. . . ugh," said Kathy as she tugged on the handle of what looked like some kind of old crockery. "Got it!"

Kathy crawled back up the bank and presented her prize to the guide.

"What do you think it is?" asked Ira.

The guide looked it over first, then Kathy took it from the guide's hands.

"It's a jug of some sort; it even has a cork in the top. Ira, can you pull this cork out with that corkscrew you have on that fishing tool you keep in your pocket?" said Kathy, boredom and lethargy utterly gone from her mind.

"Sure Honey, got it right here," said Ira, as he pulled out the screw from the combination knife, corkscrew, file, bottle opener, screw driver and pliers tools in one.

POP!! The cork came free with a good bit of tugging. Without getting any closer to the mouth of the jug, they could smell the aroma, which was enough to burn the little hairs out of their noses.

"What the?" said Ira, holding it out as far as his arm would reach.

"I know what this is," said the guide. "This is an old jug of Indian whiskey! What a find. And imagine, it was right here under the dirt the whole time."

"What do you mean by Indian whiskey?" asked Kathy.

"Well, back in the early 1840's, there was a big struggle here at the fort and the town. They called it the Whiskey Wars. Selling whiskey to the Indians was strictly against the law, but the townsfolk made and traded it to the Indians faster than anyone could keep them from it. Yes, as I recall, there was a lot of violence connected with it as well. Yes, a lot of history right here in this old jug. I better get this to the curator at the museum. They may want to look for more. Who knows, this may have been an old stash hidden right here just waiting to be picked up. Heaven knows why it wasn't. . .

Chapter 1

She sniffed the air picking up the tangy odor of fresh meat, but she saw no animal in sight. She rarely came this close to the settlement of the two-leggeds, and she crouched close to the ground with anxiety. Every guard hair of the fur on her back was standing up, but she was not sure what the danger was or where. Her belly growled savagely; it was sometimes difficult to carry a litter of pups when snow still clung to the tall brown grass in the open meadows.

She had always been an excellent hunter, but she had stayed home in the den, waiting for her coyote mate to come back with food. It was taking too long for him to return and she was ravenous with hunger, so she slipped out of the den, her belly hanging low, almost ready for the spring when she would produce her litter in the fine, warm den the two had prepared.

Again, the wafting odor slipped past her nose, and the saliva began to form on her tongue, collect around her canines and then drip from her mouth. The need to feed was the most important thing, nothing else mattered, and it began to override the feeling of danger that had cautioned her before. Now, she crept forward, not seeing anything ahead, only the smell to lead her on, and then there it was, just lying in the snow, a fresh piece of succulent red meat. The closer she came to it, the more enticing it became. One last look around in all directions caused her to relax somewhat, and she took one more step to place her paw on the slab of meat so she might rip a chunk off and gulp it down right away. Later, she could drag it away to a secluded place to feed at leisure, but her burning need was upon her then and nothing could stop her.

Snap!! She jumped, but her body did not obey. Somehow, she was caught; something held her paw, squeezing it, biting into her fur and flesh, blood beginning to drip on the bright white of the snow. No matter how hard she tugged, or bit at the hard, solid thing that held her close to the ground, she could not get away. She yipped and howled, tugged and jumped to no avail, and finally she slumped next to the thing that tormented her. Slowly she began to lick her leg where it was being held tight, but it did not staunch the flow of the dripping blood. Her paw had become numb now, and she began to tremble with cold and fear.

Then, far across the meadow she saw movement. A tiny dark speck coming closer, but she did not have to see it clearly to know what the movement was. Just the way it moved she could tell it was a two-legged coming straight to her. She tried again and again to achieve release, but it would not budge even the slightest bit. As the figure approached, she saw it carried a dark stick across its arm, walking right up to her, bold and sure.

"Ah, I see I caught ya. Ya won't be stealing any of my sheep now, will ya?" the two-legged said as it looked down on the poor beast. But she did not have any idea what it was saying, or what the noises meant.

"A good clean catch. You would have never gotten away, the teeth have split the bone of the leg, but thankfully I won't need your legs when I skin ya. I can sell your pelt and what a nice pelt it is to. In fact, I have not seen one so nice, mostly white. And I see I caught you just in time too. You're carrying a load of pups in ya, and I don't need any more trouble. Yes, a fine day of trapping this has been," the two-legged said.

As she watched, crouched down baring her canines at him, frantic to get loose for all she was worth, the two-legged brought the dark stick up to his eye, "click" and the world went black.

He watched the big house quietly, not moving a

muscle, nor flicking an ear. His yellow piercing eyes watched; his nose watched; yes, and even his ears watched. The small figure on the lawn held something in her hands while she seemed to stare intently at it. The coyote had no idea what this human was doing, but it interested him just the same. He came to this place every afternoon now for weeks. Sometimes he would stay a short while, or sometimes it would be half a day. Then he would slink out of sight, back to his den, his empty den.

The coyote and his mate had occupied that small hole in the hard ground. There is where they raised their pups, several litters of them. She had always been there, then she was gone. At first, he looked everywhere for her. He checked every hole in the ground, every pasture where they used to wait for sick buffalo calves to stumble by, every stream where they used to play at the water's edge, and even in places he knew she would never go. Like the increasing number of human dwellings springing up here and there, especially beside the big river, but he knew if she had gone too close to those dwellings, the two-leggeds would have killed her the moment they spotted her in the tall grass. He mourned for her, ached for her warm fur against his in the night. He missed playing with the pups while he and his mate taught them how to hunt.

She had been a splendid mate. He appreciated her beautiful silver tipped cream fur, unusual for a coyote. His was a mixture of tan and gold with white under his jaw, his fur was tipped in black. He always knew she was special, and, as coyotes always do, they had mated for life. Now his days were aimless wanderings. Trying to hunt, but finding all the places he went reminded him of her, at least until the day he happened by the large white house where the girl lived. He had accidentally gotten much closer to the human's dwelling place than he normally would have. The girl human had been outside, sitting on ropes tied to a thick branch of a large tree, swinging back and forth, on and on. Today she had her friend with her, a dog. He could tell they were friends, just by the body language of the dog. They played in the yard as the dog yapped a shrill bark, begging for the chase to begin. He could read those movements, like a language among all canines. The dog had not noticed him, he was still too far away, but his eyesight was keener than even a dog, as long as he stayed quiet and hidden, like now.

There were other things that he could read in the body language the dog displayed. Every day he learned something new about the dog and his friend. He learned that the dog trusted the human completely, and also that he was her protector. The dog would, most likely, fight to the death to protect the girl. He remembered he would have done the same for his mate, had he known she was in danger. And by the girl's movements, he could see that she had a deep feeling for the dog. He wondered what it would be like to have a human for a friend, but it was almost too much to consider. The plain fact was, humans killed coyotes, and that was that. The coyote was not sure exactly how the humans killed his kind, but it was usually accompanied by a loud bang. Sometimes something would hit the ground hard beside him, and it made him run all that much faster. He had seen other coyotes killed in that manner, so he always kept his distance from human kind. Until the day, he saw the girl.

There was something about her that drew him to this spot to watch every day. He should have felt fear, but fear was totally absent from his mind. Instead, he felt a longing. Watching her play with the dog puzzled him greatly. He understood play; his mate and pups would romp and play with him while the sun still shone, then when it did not, the hunting lessons began. There was something different in the play between the girl and the dog which kept the coyote pondering, day after day. Was it possible that this human did not kill coyotes?

Looking at the gray overcast sky, smelling the breeze he could tell water would soon fall on his head, so he crept on his belly away from the house and the girl, then trotted away to his lonely den. He would be back tomorrow to carry on the vigil, for what reason he did not yet understand.

Wheezer paused momentarily, gazing out at the fields beyond. The coyote had been there again. Wheezer noticed him many days while he was out with Sasa, playing chase in the yard. The coyote puzzled him. He did not feel threatened by this wild animal that came almost on a daily basis to sit in the grass and watch, just watch. Wheezer was, of course, curious, but something told him, it was not the time to make an introduction. There was something sad in the way the coyote held himself. However, Wheezer had not known very many coyotes, so it was difficult to tell for sure. Wheezer hoped he would come in and play, but the coyote never came any closer, never gave him a chance to make his acquaintance. Wheezer turned to chase Sasa around the tree once more. She would tire out before he did, because he could play this game for a long time.

Sasa finally sat down on the porch of her new home in Van Buren, Arkansas, out of breath. Her glossy blue-black hair clung to her cheeks and neck, which glistened in the late afternoon sun. She patted her soft cheeks dry with the hem of her calico skirt, then fanned herself with her hand.

"Whew, Wheezer, I can't run any more. I just can't," said an out-of-breath Sasa.

Wheezer flew around the tree with the swing two more times before he noticed Sasa was not chasing him anymore. He ran, full tilt for Sasa sitting on the stairs, coming to a screeching halt, planted his elbows on the ground with his bottom high in the air and his short tail wagging at such a pace, it was a blur to try to look at it.

"Come on Wheezer, you win," said Sasa.

"Arf! Arf! Grrrrrrrrrr," replied Wheezer.

Wheezer was not ready to take "no" for an answer, so he ran up the couple of steps to Sasa, grabbing hold of the tie that laced her apron, and gave it a firm tug. Without much effort, it fell from her waist.

"Shame on you, Wheezer. That is mine. You don't have to wear aprons, or even clothes, but if you did, I would not pull your things off of you," complained Sasa.

Wheezer's answer was to turn in circles so quickly it was amazing that he could stay upright.

"Oh alright," said Sasa with a grin as she got back up to give chase for one more time around the yard, gaily laughing while Wheezer smiled from ear to ear, running and romping with delight, always able to stay ahead of her easily.

This was a far cry from what her life had been such a short time ago. She and her Cherokee family were part of the thousands that walked all the way from their homeland in the east to Indian Territory the year before in 1839. The Cherokee people named this forced removal from their homeland, Nunahi duna Dlo Hilu-i or 'The Trail Where They Cried'. She had arrived there with her parents and little brother Usti Yansa; his name meant Little Buffalo. He died not long after their arrival, but she still felt the hurt and pain of it.

Life is so different now, she thought. She was extremely happy with the new things she was learning from Miss Anna, and she could truly want for nothing, living here in Jackson Halley's large house, but it was decidedly different from her life with the Cherokee. Jackson said she could go and visit any time she liked, it was all up to her. She made the choice, no one forced her when Jackson offered to make her his ward and educate her so she could later help her tribe. But nothing was the same here. No groups of children playing stick ball in the grass; no old grandmother to teach her the old stories of her people. When all was said and done, there were good things and bad to each choice. She chose the one that would help her people the most, plus there was Wheezer. She could not ever leave Wheezer. She owed him her life, and he was the one who found the painted toy frog, the one that was used to murder her little brother after it was painted with rat poison. That little Jack Russell Terrier had won her heart, and she would always be loyal to him.

Wheezer had belonged to Jackson before Sasa rescued him out of the forest east of their camp. Jackson had had a fire at his ranch with an explosion of stored gun powder. At that time, Wheezer's name had been Jack, but she named him Wheezer after she found him at death's door from a snake bite. Jackson had as much right to Wheezer, and she even more so. She could never take Wheezer from Jackson, and she would never leave Wheezer, so the decision was already made. She would stay and learn. Every morning she had classes with Miss Anna, which was an exquisite joy to her, but there were things that were troubling her.

Sasa finally slowed to a sluggish walk and sat down again on the steps of the house. Wheezer seemed to know this was the end of the chase game for today, and dutifully sat down beside her.

"Ah, Wheezer, I am worried. Did you know that when I go to Anna's house across the river and behind Fort Smith for my lessons, I am yelled at by the people on the ferry? They call me names I don't understand, and they say a Cherokee should not be allowed to come to that side of the river and walk through the town like I owned it," Sasa told Wheezer.

Wheezer pricked up his ears, listening with intent. As Sasa poured out her worries, Wheezer placed a gentle paw on her knee.

"I know you worry, but I have to learn all I can about the white man's world. Jackson says, someday it will be particularly important for my people. I am worried though, because the men from the fort look at me like they can look right through me. Some holler for me to come over to them and talk, but somehow I do not think that is what they want. And the town's people will not talk to me. They refuse to let me come in their store unless Jackson or Anna is with me. Then they are forced to allow me in because they don't want to lose Jackson as a customer. He is one of the few people around here with money to spend. And that is only because of his mule breeding. Fort Smith pays him extremely well for his mules, but I don't think they like me or the Cherokee that are in business with Jackson to be over here.

"Jackson says they can't do anything about it. It is his land, and I am legally his ward."

Wheezer took his paw off her knee and cocked his head the other way, like he was asking a question.

"Oh, a ward is like being adopted, uh...like I am Jackson's family," said Sasa as she patted Wheezer on the head and looked directly into his amber-brown eyes. Then he smiled.

Sasa knew there could even be worse things happen if she did not learn the ways of the white people and use that knowledge to protect them from evil, greedy whites, bent on destroying them.

She leaned her head back against the tall white pillar that held up the tall portico. She absently smoothed down the wrinkles in the skirt of her tan and white calico cotton dress, while Wheezer crept up to lay his head on her lap. She placed her hand gently on his mostly white fur and stroked rhythmically while she thought.

Last year she had been in dire straits. It was hard to believe that she had survived that horrible forced march from her home in the East. She did not want to remember the cruelty she experienced each day of that miserable journey, but it was something the mind refused to put away.

It seemed a terrible nightmare when she thought of the day the soldiers came to her family's log cabin. She had been helping her mother set the table for the evening meal. Her father had not come home yet, and they were hurrying to have it ready for him when he came back from his fields. Her family farmed not a small plot of land in New Echota, now part of Georgia. Sasa had not gotten to go to the missionary school there because she was needed at home. Father said that Usti Yansa (Little Buffalo), her little brother, would be the first to go and learn both the white man's letters, and also the fairly new Cherokee written language. It was important to her father that at least one of his children be educated as Chief John Ross had been. That is why he spent many hours in the fields, education cost money.

Just as her father came through the door, she could hear horses coming quickly up the road to the cabin.

"By order of the U.S. Government, you must vacate your home now," someone yelled at the house.

Father turned, with surprise written over his face, as the white soldiers stormed into the house. They pushed us out of the front door by the point of their short knives on the ends of their guns.

"Where are we going? At least let us take our coats or a blanket and some food," Mother cried.

"No, leave it all where it is. Nothing belongs to you, now get or I'll shoot!" replied the soldier on the horse.

"Sir, these are just children. Please let us take what we can for them," Sasa's mother pleaded.

The soldier on the horse hesitated a moment, "You have one minute, and only one. Grab only something to cover yourselves, nothing more."

Mother scrambled to the cupboard where she kept the quilts she had made through the years. In all, they were able to take one blanket for each, plus mother made sure all had socks which she swiftly stuffed between the stack of quilts. Then, out they marched, leaving the pot over the fire to burn, leaving every item they owned, some passed down from the ancestors of Sasa's family, never to be seen again. Later, Sasa heard from a neighbor who was taken a few hours later, that their house had been emptied, all put in a pile in the front yard and set ablaze, or was carried away by the soldiers. That was when she knew, down in her gut, she would never see that home again.

That trip took months. Every day, people died, every day someone began to be sick, and you could almost count the days to their end. First day, shivers. Second day, deep cough. Third day, breathing difficult. Fourth day, allowed to ride on the wagon, and on the fifth day, dead. Some days there were so many dead, the soldiers refused to wait for them to be buried. She saw mothers carrying their dead babies, refusing to just leave them by the roadside. Most of those mothers died, as well.

Every day was filled with dread. The soldiers that were there to guide them and who were supposed to help them, turned out to be evil men, some of them thought nothing of killing an Indian. On one of the coldest days of the march, she had been walking with a woman and her three children. The oldest girl, who was a couple of years younger than Sasa, was helping her mother carry the baby while the mother helped her young son along the trail. He was just a toddler and he was a chubby boy, so it made it difficult to carry him, mile after mile, and his little legs could just not keep up with the group. The soldier nearest them came by on his horse, and hit them with his crop, but it only made the boy cry and stumble to the ground. Sasa wished she could wipe out the memory of the next thing that happened, but she knew it would be there until the day she died.

The soldier must have gotten too irritated, and tired of pushing that family along as the toddler could not go as fast as the soldier wanted them to go. After riding by slowly on his horse, staring meanly at the little boy, he passed them, and for a little while, she heard nothing. Then, the sound of a fast moving horse coming up behind alerted them a soldier was coming, but there was no time to react. As the soldier trotted by, he leaned down and grabbed the boy's chubby arm, swung him like a rag doll, and bashed his head against a tree. The sound his skull made when it crushed was a sickening watery thud. After the mother saw what the soldier had done, she took her new baby and buried it under her clothes so that the soldier could not grab at it. But, it ended badly for that family anyway. The woman and both of her other children died of sickness, or heartache as far as Sasa could tell, not too many days after that day.

Sasa never understood why she lived. Why she made it to Indian Territory and lived when her parents and little brother were dead. But then she remembered that she almost did not make it.

After they arrived in Indian Territory, the man that murdered her little brother had been looting the food allotments along with many men from the east. She was blessed to have Jackson Halley to take care of her. That first winter in Indian Territory, over one thousand Cherokee died of starvation. Even though they solved who was looting the allotments, men who were now dead, the looting continued to happen throughout Indian Territory. Sasa realized she could have been one of those poor starving people who died last winter if it had not been for Jackson and Wheezer. So, she must show her appreciation for the gift of life from the Creator, and do what she can, to be a good Cherokee and help her people.

While she rested on the porch step, Wheezer sat up quickly, directly in front of her, a smile plastered over his intelligent face with his short, stubby tail wagging furiously. Then, from inside the house, Sasa heard the cook holler, "Supper's on the table, come an' get it!"

"We better hurry, Wheezer. If we are late, she will put our plate away, and then make us eat it for breakfast, cold," said Sasa, as she scurried into the house through the red oak doors, with Wheezer at her heels.

Wheezer thought it made no difference if the food was hot or cold, he liked it either way. Masey always had a bowl of food ready for him when she called for supper. You didn't have to tell him twice to come eat.

"I am coming, Masey," said Sasa, as she ran to the pantry behind the kitchen to wash her hands. As she dried her hands on the linen cloth hanging beside the square zinc tub where they washed the vegetables, she could hear the voices of Jackson and Arch coming from the dining room. She briefly checked her appearance in the small mirror that hung on the wall beside the doorway, then smoothed her crumpled apron before going into the dining room.

As she entered the room, she quietly walked across the blue and blood red Turkey rug on the hardwood floor. Taking her seat at the handmade maple table and chairs, just as Anna had taught her, she kept her arms from resting on the table. She had said it was not mannerly for a lady to place her arms on the dining table, even though men might do it with impunity. There was still so much to learn, but Sasa was determined.

"Yonaguska is dead. It happened last year in April, and we are just now hearing about it," said Jackson Halley. "Some of the headmen and chiefs heard about it this last winter, but I am sure they did not think to tell us. We are not exactly on the path to Fort Smith from their homes and camps. He died in April 1839, just after the last group arrived in Indian Territory." Sasa and Arch stared in astonishment.

"How, how did we get word?" Arch murmured quietly. His somber eyes looking off into the distance through the dining room window, while Sasa looked stricken to tears.

"It was related in a letter and order for fifteen more mules to be broken as mounts, which I received yesterday from the commander at the Fort. Ah, Sasa I am truly sorry. This information will not bode well for the Cherokee."

Sasa slowly slipped her napkin from the table, absently unfolded the linen, not saying anything. She knew how this news could hurt her people. Yonaguska was a powerful Chief among the Cherokee; indeed he was a legend. He had seen many wars with the whites and had always been a steadfast spiritual leader for his people and found peaceable ways to resist the onslaught of the white.

He had said the whiskey, rum and spirituous liquor was making the Creator angry with the People for weakening themselves with the "Black Drink", and that the People must not drink it anymore. His whole village had to agree to give it up. He had his son, a white man adopted as a boy, Will Thomas, write out the pledge, and had all of his people of the town of Qualla make their marks as agreement. All the Cherokee knew what that pledge said, "The undersigned Cherokee, belonging to the town of Qualla, agree to abandon the use of spirituous liquors." As the story went, liquor and drunkenness were almost unheard of in Qualla before the forced removal to the west. Sasa wondered why the Creator allowed blow and blow to hit her people. Had he abandoned them? Now that Yonaguska was dead, who was there to remind the people of what the spirituous liquor could do to the Cherokee Nation? She was startled out of her reverie.

"It is as if all restraint has been lifted from the People," said Arch, his temper showing by the darkening of his already tan face. "Once we were under one Chief Of All and our great men of vision like Yonaguska who reminded us of our spiritual duty. We strove to put away our uncivilized ways, but now we seem to be in complete chaos. Our young men will trade anything they lay their hands on, just for a cupful of very bad whiskey," he growled, balling up his fists and banging on the table top, making the silverware rattle.

"Arch, I don't know what we can do about it when the town's merchants and soldiers take part in selling it right under the nose of Stuart," said Jackson. Irritation etched deep in the lines of his forehead, but compassion dwelt there, as well. He wanted to help, but this problem seems gargantuan compared to others that faced Indian Territory.

"But, Jackson, our young men are so depressed; they look for anything that will relieve their despair. Sure, we caught a small part of those who stole the allotments of food and supplies from the Cherokee last year, but it has not stopped it completely, not by a long shot. There has been no progress within the Cherokee Nation after the murders of those members of the Treaty Party, the headmen who signed away our land in the east. And the fight over who shall govern the Cherokee Nation is all consuming. There are too many factions wanting their own way. And while they dither the weeks and months away, the whites, little by little, turn our young men into drunken wrecks, and our agents steal our allotment right from under the nose of government," said Arch. He knew that his best friend and business partner wanted nothing more than to help the Cherokee. Jackson had proved it over many years of association.

Sasa did not speak, she just listened, absorbing the words and arranging the problems in her mind like a jigsaw puzzle. In fact, that is what she did with any large problem that came her way. She never panicked, but always stopped to pull the various pieces of knowledge and clues together until she had a clear picture of the problem before she tried to find the solution. But, this was more than just a problem. This hit her personally, for she was working to learn all that she could, so she might save her people in some small way.

Her large round eyes were lowered, but evidence of extreme thought could be seen by the flicking of her dark, long lashes against her brown cheeks. Would she be too late?

Wheezer slunk under the table to sit at Sasa's feet. He could feel the tension in the room and knew something was making his humans unhappy. He slicked all his hairs down against his body, tucked what little tail he had under and drooped his normally pricked up ears down. He placed a paw on her knee, and she gently patted it. Then he lay down at her feet, and proceeded to lick Sasa's ankles. This was his way of bringing comfort and support to her and she understood it. There was nothing Wheezer would not do for Sasa, and the feeling was duplicated in her. *I may need you my friend, if the time comes,* she thought. *We must find a way to be of help to the People.*

Jackson Halley sat in the library of his home listening to Sasa and Wheezer play in the yard. He had tied his sandy brown hair, simply gathering it to the nape of his neck, but he had unconsciously run his fingers through it while in thought and now several loose strands fell across his chiseled tanned cheek bones. His blue-gray eyes were partially hooded by his heavy lids as he rested his chin in the palm of his hand with his elbow firmly on his desk amid his business correspondence.

He had essentially taken the girl as part of his family, his ward, and an immense responsibility it was, too. He had not actually thought it out when the necessity had been thrust upon him last year over in Indian Territory. That was when he had met Anna Edwards, the daughter of the Indian Agent in the interim camp for the Cherokee removed from the East. He had been drawn in to investigating what was happening to the food stuffs that were to be provided to the new arrivals. What he found was a web of conspiracy, and then death. The man Anna had not known well as her father, turned out to be a most corrupt criminal, capable of killing children. Anna had turned out to be the polar opposite of her father. In fact, she had helped in the investigation and confrontation of the terrible deeds her father was guilty of.

But, Jackson thought, *not only was she true and just, where her father was base and corrupt, Anna turned out to be someone I could love, make a home for, and have a family with. But, how can I ask her to marry a mule breeder? She is used to the finer things, fine society, glittering balls and society teas. My life is here now, and I can't go back, nor do I want that life again. I have Sasa to think about, and the city is no place for her. Not until she is comfortable with the way to behave among that type of society. If I were to take her now, Sasa would be ridiculed as a savage, and then she might never want to learn white ways to help her people. That means that if I take a wife, it will have to be someone who can make a life here with me. Anna seems like she wants to be with me, but I am just so unsure. Oh! Why can't I just ask her? Why do I clam up when she is around?*

Arch, or Archibald Flint, Jackson's best friend and a full-blood Cherokee, had told him numerous times that he was being too timid. Arch was never one for many words, but when he did talk, he usually was right.

Arch had taken a pretty significant step when he came out to Van Buren with Jackson, before the removal of his people to Indian Territory. Jackson's father, Andrew Halley, had invested heavily in many Cherokee businesses for many years. Jackson worked with his father and was destined to take over Halley's Financial, headquartered in Boston, now in St. Louis, when the furor to grab the ancestral lands from the helpless Cherokee became a frenzy. Halley's almost went under. To take the burden of Jackson's salary from his father, Jackson took his savings and moved west with Arch and Arch's family to partner in a mule breeding business in Van

Buren. It was already bearing fruit. With the Army just across the Arkansas River at Fort Smith, Jackson's mules were always needed, not to mention what the Army would need in the future.

Author's Note

The characters in *Wheezer And The Painted* Frog are not all fictional. Captain Belknap, commander of Fort Smith, was the real commander in 1839, however, I used him fictionally. The camp in Indian Territory where the story takes place is fictional, although I used what information I could glean from history to aid me in my depiction of it.

The Jack Russell Terrier, Wheezer, is a real dog and I based his actions in the book on his actual abilities and temperament. He is my dog, but I should say I am his person.

Jack Russell Terriers have a long and interesting history. The breed is named after Rev. John Russell who lived in the 1820's. He was an avid foxhunter and was always interested in breeding a dog to aid in the retrieval of the fox after it disappeared into its hole, what foxhunters call 'going to ground' and also to 'bolt' their quarry, or drive it from its den to begin the chase. One of the problems with terriers of that day was that once they followed their prey down to the den, they were wont to kill the fox instead of forcing out for the hunt.

Rev. Russell created a breed that was mostly white, with tan or black-and-tan patches. They were small, from 14 to 16 inches and had strong chests also 14 to 16 inches in their circumference. The breed is unusually smart and know what is expected of them when they are alone with their quarry, without instruction from the hunter.

It is unclear at what point the breed became known as 'Jack Russell Terriers' and today there are actually two strains of the breed with similar temperament but different body dimensions. One is called the English Jack Russell or 'puddin' and is shorter of leg, more compact and a good choice for going into fox holes. The other has become known as the Parson Jack Russell, also referred to as the American

Jack Russell by some. These have longer legs, a sleeker body and longer neck. Both have v-shaped ears that fold forward, alert intelligent eyes and boundless energy.

It does not matter which you choose, the English or the Parson Jack Russell. Both will keep you hopping. Their favorite game is the chase, they can't get enough of it. They will happily go after anything that moves, including your vacuum cleaner. They refuse to be left out of any activity and fully expect you to play at all times of the day or night.

Jacks do not know their own size so they see no problem in picking up a branch many times too big for them or trying to take a large bone of a dog that is much bigger. They are always on guard for anything they feel belongs to them and that includes you. Barking is a trait that is bred into them and if they are in a hole or stuck somewhere, they will bark until someone comes to pull them out. They make a point to get everyone out of bed if they feel it is time to start the day.

Having a Jack in the house is like having a six-year old child. They are easily the smartest dog breed, but beware. Jack Russells will not tolerate abuse, so hitting them for punishment is not an option. If you want a dog that obeys your every command, do not get a Jack Russell Terrier, but if you want a dog that is always fun, always happy to be with you, always learning new things to get in to, and a dog that will find endless ways to make you smile, then a Jack Russell Terrier is for you.

About the Author:

Kitty Sutton was born Kathleen Kelley to a Cherokee/Irish family. Both sides of her family were from performing families in Kansas City, Missouri and Kitty was trained from an early age in dance, vocal, art and musical instruments. Her father was a Naval band leader. During the Great Depression, her mother helped to support her family by tap dancing in the speakeasys even though she was just a child; she was very tall for her age but made up like an adult. Kitty had music and art on all sides of her family which ultimately helped to feed her imaginative mind and desire to succeed.

Kitty married a wonderful Cherokee artist from Oklahoma, in fact the very area that she writes about in her Wheezer series of novels. After raising her family, Kitty came to Branson, Missouri and performed in her own one woman show there for twelve years. To honor her father, she performed under the name Kitty Kelley. She has three music albums and several original songs to her credit and is best known for her comical, feel good song called It Ain't Over Till The Fat Lady Sings. Kitty has been writing for many years and in 2011 we accepted her manuscript of an historical Native American murder mystery. First in a series of stories featuring Wheezer, a Jack Russell Terrier and his Cherokee friend, Sasa, it is called, *Wheezer And The Painted Frog*. Kitty lives in the southwestern corner of Missouri near Branson with her husband of 40 years and her three Jack Russell Terriers, one of which is the real and wonderful Wheezer.

235

More From Inknbeans Press

If you enjoyed this book, please visit Inknbeans.com and discover our other fine authors.

Made in the USA
San Bernardino, CA
29 August 2017